Liars and Rascals

Liars and Rascals

Mennonite Short Stories

edited by
Hildi Froese Tiessen

University of Waterloo Press

Liars and Rascals: Mennonite Short Stories

Copyright © 1989 |Hildi Froese Tiessen

ISBN 0-88898-080-9

University of Waterloo Press
Dana Porter Library
University of Waterloo
Waterloo, Ontario, Canada
N2L 3G1

Designed by Dave Bartholomew, Graphic Services, University of Waterloo

Printed and bound at Graphic Services, University of Waterloo

Canadian Cataloguing in Publication Data

Main entry under title:

Liars and rascals

ISBN 0-88898-080-9

1. Short stories, Canadian (English).*   2. Canadian
fiction (English) – Mennonite authors.*
3. Canadian fiction (English) – 20th century.*
I. Tiessen, Hildi Froese.

PS8321.L52 1989   C813'.01'0892287   C87-095192-X
PR9197.33.M46L52 1989

Liars and Rascals: Mennonite Short Stories was produced with the financial assistance of the Multiculturalism Program of the Department of the Secretary of State of Canada.

A Sand Hills Book

Permissions

Acknowledgements

This volume is invested with the time and energy of many people, to whom thanks are due. For each of their parts in the production of *Liars and Rascals* I would like to thank the authors, first of all, and Charlotte Cox, Sheila Moore, Peter Erb, Maureen Ralph, Christine Moser, Caroleah Yetman, Lori Ann Bumstead, Theron Kramer, Louis Costa, Arlene Timmins, Wendy Whitecloud, Hart Bezner, Carl Langford, Bruce Uttley, Marg MacMillan, Rosemary Smith, Ann Snider, Paul Tiessen, Dave Bartholomew, and Gloria Smith.

Thanks too, always, to Matthew and Christopher.

Table of Contents

Introduction

The curious title of this collection, *Liars and Rascals,* along with the compelling portrait on the book's cover, will, perhaps, rightly suggest to the reader something of the sometimes harsh, but more often gentle sense of mischief that propels character and action in so many of these wonderfully evocative stories. But it is less the characters who people these narratives than the writers themselves who are the mischief-makers here, who confront their readers with new ways of configuring what is true and in so doing, subvert the familiar, comfortable assumptions that sustain convention.

Given the Canadian Mennonites' lack of receptivity to the arts during the first half of this century and beyond, one would not have thought that this community would have spawned and nurtured one of the most vigorous minority literary cultures enriching the Canadian mainstream in the 1970s and 80s. Something of the self-possessed Mennonite world out of which these powerful, contemporary stories have emerged is revealed gently, ironically, in two biographical sketches featuring the writers Jacob H. Janzen and Rudy Wiebe, pre-eminent "liars and rascals" among the Mennonites, their people.

Jacob H. Janzen, already known among Mennonites as a writer of drama and fiction when he emigrated from Russia to Canada in 1924, had played a prominent role in giving shape to the promising Mennonite literary culture that had emerged in the German-speaking Russian Mennonite colonies in the late eighteen-hundreds. He had seen this same literary culture snuffed out in its infancy during the chaotic first decades of this century.

The Mennonites in his new, Canadian homeland, Janzen later lamented (in his essay on "The Literature of the Russo-Canadian Mennonites," published in *Mennonite Life* in 1946) revealed themselves to be a reluctant audience of the arts, seemingly lacking, in particular, a nuanced understanding of the nature and value of literary culture:

when I came to Canada and in my broken English tried to make plain to a Mennonite bishop that I was a "novelist" (that being the translation for "Schriftsteller" in my dictionary), he was much surprised. He then tried to make plain to me that "novelists" were fiction writers and that fiction was a lie. I surely would not want to represent myself to him as a professional liar.

With typical good humour and aplomb, Janzen added:

I admitted to myself, but not aloud to him, that I was just that kind of "liar" which had caused him such a shock.

Janzen, along with novelist and dramatist Arnold Dyck, was to campaign vigorously during the 1920s, 30s, and 40s, for the acceptance and development of indigenous arts among the Mennonites of Canada. Both of them perceived one of their most important roles to be the nurturing of the Mennonite audience which had, after all, Janzen argued, developed by 1935 a favourable enough response to interesting narratives about non-Mennonites—whether they recorded the lives of the saints or the adventures of pioneers and Indians on the American frontier. But this same audience remained decidedly unreceptive to indigenous fiction, as Janzen observed:

Mennonitism was regarded in certain respects as a "terra sancta" on which the jugglery of belle-lettres dared not appear. That Mennonites would write in this genre [fiction] was simply sin. After all, [Mennonites themselves] could not treat Mennonitism that way.

The attitude towards fiction that prompted Janzen's remarks in 1946 remained to a large degree unchanged until the 1960s and beyond—that is, until long after many Canadian Mennonites had established themselves as urban professionals mainly in the cities of the Canadian Prairies. This antipathy (at best) or (at worst) antagonism towards indigenous fiction in particular was revealed most forcefully in 1962, when Rudy Wiebe's first novel, *Peace Shall Destroy Many*, was published by McClelland and Stewart. Unlike Arnold Dyck's predominantly nostalgic treatment of Russian-Mennonite life in *Lost in the Steppe* (privately printed in German in Winnipeg some fifteen years before), Wiebe's novel represented the first critical, contemporary view of Mennonite life on the Canadian prairies; moreover, it was published in English and drew its audience from across the country.

The unprecedented furore that followed the publication of a

novel in which Wiebe opened a private people's private affairs to public scrutiny resulted in the author's leaving his editorial post with a Mennonite magazine in Winnipeg and seeking sanctuary, at least temporarily, in the U.S.A. He did return to the Canadian West four years later, to take up a post teaching creative writing at the University of Alberta. It was from there that one day in the early 1970s he took an excursion to the Mennonite Museum in Steinbach, Manitoba, where I remember his being introduced to a museum employee. Upon hearing the author's name, Wiebe's new acquaintance, a gentle man whose recollections, it seemed, intuitively distilled the sensibilities of his people, exclaimed (in Low German), "Not the rascal"! Indeed it was; but Wiebe, nonplussed by the all-too-familiar insinuation, shrugged and conjectured aloud that the man must be thinking of someone else.

A world in which authors of fiction (indigenous fiction in particular) are regarded as liars and rascals is familiar enough to all the writers whose stories make up this volume. Although some have long ago abandoned the beliefs and conventions of their forebears, all write out of the Mennonite ethos in which they were nurtured, an ethos which dictated that embellishment of object or word was sin. What was true was objective and clear and one-dimensional. The play of the imagination was frivolous and worldly; at worst, it was an expression of the cardinal sin of pride.

The works of short fiction gathered here fall easily enough into the volume's three divisions (discovery, outsiders, coming of age); yet they could as readily have been ordered otherwise, to reflect some of the other planes on which these richly-textured stories overlap and intersect. Like great stories everywhere, they speak of love and regret, self-discovery and betrayal, community and isolation.

Some of these works are published here for the second (or third) time; a few have never appeared in print before. Together in one volume, they can play off each other in the reader's mind: augment and illumine each other's characters, enlarge and challenge each other's themes, propositions and obsessions.

For a people whose suspicion of the writer of fiction has been a given for hundreds of years, the Mennonites have produced an exceptional generation of contemporary storytellers—and, through them, a national audience and an indigenous, minority-culture audience for whom these liars and rascals have become the bearers of what is true, even as they objectify and subvert the old culture in the process of discovering the new.   – H.F.T.

I. Discovery

Rudy Wiebe

Chinook Christmas

The winter I turned nine was our first in southern Alberta, and the white scars of irrigation ditches circling lower and lower into the long, shallow hollow of our town uneven across the Canadian Pacific Railway seemed to me then like the trenches of some besieging army: the grey wrinkled snow driven there off the tilted fields, long, long welts carved in parallels below the square top of Big Chief Mountain sixty miles west where the implacable General of the Winds stood forever roaring at his troops: Advance! Relentless wind whining, roaring in one's head all fall, the trees bent so low east that one day I straightened up on the pedals of my bicycle and discovered I could stand motionless, balanced, the wind's weight a wall, a power that held me shivering uneasily facing into it.

But then I was nudged, pushed, clubbed and I let the wind wheel me round like always and I spread my arms akimbo, my jacket held wide at the waist and went no hands sailing along the gravel street, through three ridged stop corners on the fly to Jakie's house and leaned into his yard like a racing sloop, all canvas spread, and met him wobbling forward on his bike beside the little irrigation ditch that was filling their cistern for winter so I knocked him into that grey water and then he knocked me into it too.

"Let's ride to the main ditch," he said, trying to blink through the mud in his eyes.

"Sure," I said. "We'll get it anyways, we might as well get it good."

He was three years older than I and that summer we had become uneasy friends with the town's whole length of one-way wind between us because we were second cousins (twice removed at that, my father said, but for Canadian Mennonites that means a lot sometimes) and because of Anni and mostly because neither of us had any other friends. My sister Anni always knew what she wanted.

"We have to have a Christmas tree," she said. "How'll we ever find one here, nothing but sugarbeet fields and ditches?"

She was fourteen and the spring before when we left our bush homestead up north so my father could work on an irrigation dairy and Mama and Anni and I could thin beets, she had already been kissed there once or twice under a full moon, and she still thought that a good deal better than getting sunburned between endless beet rows, wrinkling up, hunched over like every other poor woman and child she saw stoop-shouldered in every field. Up north she and I always ploughed our Christmas tree out of the muskeg, our dog bounding high through soft cushions of snow, the air so motionless between the muskeg spruce—flounced, layered and blazing white with brown and green edges.

"There's a tree on old Heidebrecht's front lawn," I said. "It's real pretty."

"Oh sure," and Anni sang, "Chop, chop, hoora-a-a-il, Christmas in ja-a-a-il, how can we fa-a-a-il, they will throw out our heads in a pa-a-a-il."

"Anyways," I told her, "a Christmas tree isn't even Christian, it's heathen." Old Ema Racht—"Always Right," (but in low German it rhymes, Ema Racht Heidebrecht)—had the biggest Mennonite house in town; he had finally sold his farm to one of his sons for an unbelievable price—that was what he was mostly right at, buying low and selling very high—and now he drove a black Buick to church twice every Sunday with his ancient daughter as stiff and erect as himself beside him; he always roared the motor until a cloud of bluish smoke was visible through the rear window before he slowly let out the clutch and began to move, shoving in the clutch a little as soon as the car threatened to go too quickly but never taking his foot off the gas. All summer his lawn, shaded by giant cottonwoods and blue-coned spruce, was bright green like a frog's belly.

"A Christmas tree's heathen? Who said, smarty head?" Anni twirled around me.

"In Sunday school, Mr. Rempel," I said. He was tall with broad shoulders and had "adorable," Anni had once confessed, curly blond hair.

That stopped her; for two seconds. But I saw immediately it was astonishment at my still holding that outdated opinion that was spreading like a cat's tongue licking over her face. She laughed aloud. "He's no fun," she said irrelevantly. "In fact, he's kinda dumb."

"How do you know?" I hit her with all I had: "You've never even *talked* to him."

"He's a curly blond," over her shoulder, going into the kitchen. I never had enough for Anni, of anything.

The Christmas kitchen was a whole pasture of smells gone crazy in spring, not only from two kinds of cookies, oatmeal with one chocolate chip topping each and pale almost brownly-bluish shapes of ammonia creatures Mama had let me stamp out of thick dough, but also cinnamon rolls with their bottoms up exuding sweet brown syrup and dimpled raisins like twirled targets to aim an uncontrollable finger at—"Mama, Eric's poking the rolls!"—and tiny square pyrushkis with their tops folded up into peaked and quartered little tents of ridged golden crust that oozed juices, red strawberry and royal purple saskatoon and pale creamy apple, how for the love of Christmas and stomach could anyone keep their hands—"Eric!"

And outside was chinook. The night before, a small bow of light had grown along the western horizon under the ceiling of clouds hammered down overhead like solid rafters; at the end of the day, the monolith of Big Chief Mountain sat for a moment against blue and an orange streak like a knife-tip about to slit open the rest of the horizon, a faint smell of crushed irrigated clover in summer slipping through to wander over the glazed drifts. And also a touch of warmth, very nearly a flare of mad possibility in the cold; today it blazed into actuality, my head huge as if its plates were unhinged for I could breathe that clover without sniffing after it, all the air burned with it, the drifts already wrinkling down into sodden sponges and the air swimming limpid like creek water on a May morning. Chinook! It fondled my bare head. Our chickens sang behind their windows. I opened the door and their acrid avian mist was swallowed whole, disappeared into the morning brilliance of chinook; our white-faced cow lifted her head above the dry alfalfa of her manger, her ears gesturing gently as they did whenever she was moved to ponderous, liquid-eyed bovine contentment. Go on Boss, you bulgy hay-chewer, your warm flanks to butt my head against, your long soft teats swishing hot milk between my rhythmic fingers, go on you globed warm femaleness, and breathe all that spring, that momentary maddening spring the day before Christmas.

"There are still some trees left, Mrs. Orleski on her lot," I said to Anni, shifting the basket of *zweibach* to my other arm. She carried two pails of layered pastry for Tante Tien and though they were heavier, they were actually easier to carry because she could walk balanced. The basket in the basket of my bike would have been best, but the chinook had only licked the gravel street dry in blotches and left the rest wet, running everywhere under the snow-levelled ditches. It was everywhere slurp and slide and temptation to not catch your balance before you tucked your head and rolled soft and squitchy and were all over coated with three-times gumbo like your laden boots.

"She told us, a tree costs at least a dollar," Anni said.

"Yeah, the miserblist one, we'd never—"

"That's no word, 'miserblist'."

"Miser-erbilist?"

"Miser-erb*a*list, rhymes with 'herb-*a*list'." Anni sang, skipping a puddle too nonchalantly perhaps and slipping beautifully but sliding herself into balance so that nothing but her left pail-bottom came up small gravel and heavy, heavy gumbo. We wiped it off with snow, left the food in Tante Tien's barren kitchen with her small horde of children rolling their small barbarian eyes at the steamy warmth of things and ran out before the small barbarian fingers could—"Eric and I have to get back because Mama needs us and Father is coming home right after supper and the. . . ." Anni had hauled me out with her long arm and swinging muddy pail and there was Jakie leaning against the cottonwood in the front yard, looking absolutely Chicago gangster to the very bend of his leg and cap pulled tight over his eyes.

"If you want a tree so bad," he said, "why don't you take it?"

Anni actually stopped and looked at him. Chinooks touch

everyone differently: all he needed was a short machine gun.

"There's never nobody there at night," he said.

It was very hard to read Anni's expression, and Jakie must have made the same mistake I made because he continued, still looking at his fingernails which were very long and smooth with nice moons at their base, "Anyways, who'd miss one shitty little tree?"

"I presume," Anni said, and her tone warned me instantly, "I presume that if there is *never nobody* there, there must *always* be *somebody*, and I presume further that not even an habitual criminal would be so idiotic as to steal under such conditions, leave alone someone honest at Christmas when a chinook is blowing."

Her statement would have been stronger without either Christmas or chinook, and I think Anni felt so too because we hadn't left Jakie more than half a block behind, still leaning against the tree and studying the perfect moons of his fingernails, when she inexplicably commented, "He won't even get as far as his stupid dad, he'll just end up in jail."

"What's the matter with Oncle Willm?" I asked. To tell the truth, I liked Oncle Willm. He was certainly the strongest man in town, not much taller than me but so broad he walked sideways through any door and he could place his thick arms under half a beef and hoist it around and up onto a hook in one immense motion without breathing hard or slipping on the sawdust under his butcher's chopping block. Unlike any other Mennonite grown-up, he cracked jokes with me and so did Mrs. Cartwright who sold the meat for him. Mrs. Cartwright was always dressed so perfectly, her face as careful as a picture, and when she leaned over the counter, laughing, I always wanted to laugh with her like every man who bought meat there though I never saw a woman who did, her lips and teeth so red and white and marvellously, smoothly exact. She laughed like no woman I had ever seen, deeply, powerfully, her entire vivid body pushing itself out at me and moving with it until I felt tight and awkward, somehow—inexplicably then—ashamed.

"He's *not* our uncle, thank Jehoshaphat," Anni snapped, and then seeing me goggle-eyed, said quickly, "There's Mr. Ireland, let's catch a ride!"

Mr. Ireland's dray with its unmatched greys was moving

toward the train station but it seemed that in any case Anni had intended not to go directly home but rather "downtown" as we called it—our town had three parallel streets south of the tracks and three north with avenues at right angles numbered 100 at the centre, and higher and lower on either side in anticipation of more or less measureless and endless expansion—so we hopped aboard and bounced along dangling our legs off the tailgate. The horses trotted while Mr. Ireland sang, the biggest grey plopping out hot, steamy buns, and Mr. Ireland interrupted himself to mutter, "Enough time for that, Jock, get on with you!", slapping the mountainous rear gently with a flat rein, and they appeared behind the wagon under us in perfect single-file pattern like a queue of smooth-headed children, steaming slightly as they sank out of sight in the gumbo. The chinook blustered violently through trees and over a roof and suddenly Mr. Ireland roared with it as we passed the Japanese Buddhist church that was swallowing a snake of small brown children,

"Oh, he shot her through the window,
And the bullet's in her yet!"

and the dray sighed silently across Main Street at 101 Avenue on its flat balloon tires salvaged from World War II fighter planes. A huge black truck with its grain box standing tight full of Hutterites, beards and polka-dotted kerchiefs facing into the wind, rolled past and squitched all of a grey pothole at us, but missed.

"Do men have yets too?" I asked Anni.

"Yets?"

"He sang, 'the bullet's in her yet'."

Anni laughed. "No," she spluttered, "only women. And you have to shoot them through their windows to hit their yets!"

But then, still laughing, she knocked one of our pails off and we had to jump anyways because we were passing the high front of the largest grocery and hardware store, Doerksen Bros. Props., and that's where Mrs. Orleski had her Christmas trees leaning against the wall. Mrs. Orleski usually sold Lethbridge *Heralds* at the corner for a nickel, perhaps two or three a day since Hermie Kudreck had the town sewed up with home delivery—Hermie owned a CCM three-speed by the time he was ten,

a Harley Davidson at fifteen, and an Olds convertible at nineteen, all starting from *Herald* saturation of our town—but when
Doerksen Brothers started playing Christmas carols on the
gramophone at the back of their store, she shifted to the vacant
lot: one day it was white, bare, the next heavy green, thick with
needled aroma like the mountains where Mrs. Orleski said her
son worked deep in the Crowsnest Mines. I could not imagine
that then, crows' nests were bundles of sticks notched high in
poplars and a coal mine was. . . . When her son came home for
one day at Christmas you could see the coal engrained in his
skin like topsoil in the drifts of a three-day prairie blizzard. His
shoulders had a hockey player's powerful slope and were only a
little narrower than Oncle Willm's and he liked to show his
favourite muscle, a bulge when he bent his elbow that heaved up
and clenched itself rock-hard and not even Whipper Billy
Watson the heavyweight wrestling champion of the world could
muster that; he knew, for he had once challenged Watson and
that dead-white mound of muscle from Toronto had backed off:
nothing but the usual stuff in his arm.

"Jolly old St. Nicholas, lean your ear this way. . ."
murmured the wall of the store. If Doerksen Brothers, Anni said,
leaned any farther they would fall over.

"You kits still lookin'?" Mrs. Orleski pulled her hands from
between her three summer coats and whatever else she wore
underneath, sweaters and skirts and every kind of unmention-
able. "Sell, lotsa sell this year, see," and she gestured around
with her arms wide, a little stump of a fireplug turning as if
about to break into dance. There were only three trees left, three
scrunchy trees in a trampled scatter of spruce-tips and sodden
snow; abruptly she wheeled and her nostrils flared into the
chinook, opening hugely like gills in fast water, "Here, here!
They leave it, the leetle branch, they leave it lotsa. . ." and she
was stooping, gathering with the swift inevitable hands of workers, "Sometimes stump, have it too much branch. . ." and she
thrust them at me, offering in the wimpling eddy of the sun-and-
wind-warmed wall a stinging memory of motionless feathered
muskeg, our black dog plunging head and tail through the crys-
talline velvet sinking of it, the indented spoors of rabbits and a
slither of weasels: Mrs. Orleski's two stubby arms filled with
spruce boughs like a proffered squirrel nest stuffed fat and full

and warm for the winter, "You take it, is good, hang it some places, Mama happy so. . . ." Offering the wistful windy madness a gift.

"I'm sorry," Anni said, and I stared at her in horror. "We still have no money."

"Wha? I no take it, your money. . . give for nutting, you, take!"

And I took and ran. Anni behind me argued, the very bend of her body declaring you cannot accept a gift from someone as poor as yourself and certainly not from anyone richer and so you refuse to accept anything from anyone, ever; and finally thanked the old lady, almost angrily as if forced and following me with her long legs scissoring through the last sunshine past the principal's yellow and green house and across the schoolyard. The little Japanese houses stood one by one along the south side of the street, their double windows with their pale never-opened blinds dreaming even in the long winter like unfathomable Buddhas. "It's Christmas, and anyway it cleans up her lot." But any word of mine just set Anni's teeth more visibly into her bottom lip, her head lower into the branches as if she would chew needles. Both her pails were stuck full, my basket was too small for all my armful but I didn't drop a twig all the way home and I slid neither flat nor flying in the mud either.

Old Ema Racht passed us, alone like a procession in his smoking Buick. In the rich darkness of the car his whiskers flared from the sides of his face like white flames reaching for the side windows as he drove without headlights, his arms braced rigid before him and his eyes peering ahead as if to illumine the fluid road with their glare. The chinook seeped spruce through my head; had I known about such things then I would have known I was at least drunk when I heaved up my branches, waved, shouted, "Froe Wiehnachte!" and his head turned round to us trudging the shoulder of the road, heavily around like a spray of cannon wheeling and he saw me, his eyes briefly the driven ends of spikes, and the huge polished flank of the car lurched toward me as at a recognition before his head trundled back and cocked forward again on his long neck over the steering wheel and his stiff arms kept his shoulders rammed back against the seat and his beaked nose defied that lunatic wind, dared it to squirm him into the gumbo ditch, he would *not* turn

that wheel, he would *not* raise either his right foot from the gas
or his left foot from the clutch and so he roared away into the
warm settling dusk of Christmas Eve, finally merging far ahead
of us into the misty dinosaur legs of the bare cottonwoods
surrounding his immense yard: an antideluvian monster roaring
in futile and foehnish anthem the cacophonous wonders of the
Christ-child season. Gifts upon gifts, the smell of gas and clutch-
plate snipped at our nostrils through the green of spruce till we
saw the rectangular windows of our house stunned golden
everyone with the vanished sun reflecting from the laden, burn-
ing bellies of the clouds, and the mud squishing under our feet
and the prick of spruce on our cold wrists and fingers. I looked
at Anni. Her hair streamed flat under wind, the cloven flames of
window and sky glistened, blazed in her eyes.

"Don't say a word," she said.

And I did that. Even when I saw our father was already
home because the dairy pick-up was parked beside our door, I
said nothing. But once inside, oh, talk! Our house was packed
tight with smells like nuts in a Christmas cake and we hung our
branches singing everywhere until its two rooms seemed flung
all over with a green and poignant spray. Then we stepped into
the fresh darkness and the purring, dialed cab of the truck
wafted us to church, a wide building where the men sat in two
broad aisles on the right and the women in two aisles on the left
and we children crammed in front directly under the benign (for
tonight) faces of the ministers leaning over the pulpit and the
choir curved around behind them, we sang those Christmas
songs our people had brought from half a world away, so out of
place now in the treeless, flat irrigation prairies but not at all out
of spirit:

> *Leise rieselt der Schnee*
> *Still und starr ruht der See;*
> *Weihnachtlich glaenzet der Wald,*
> *Freue dich, Christkind kommt bald!*

the high beautiful voices of the women, the deep heavy voices of
the men, and the bright thread of my father's tenor between
them where he sat behind me among rich farmers and store-
keepers and workers and teachers and unemployed labourers.
Two ministers spoke, very short and mostly stories, and there

were several long prayers and the choir sang, several children's groups sang, and then we all sang again,

> *Nun ist sie erschienen,*
> *die himmlische Sonne. . .*

and

> *O Fest aller heiligen Feste,*
> *O Weihnacht, du lieblicher Schein. . .*

and then young men came in with big boxes and gave every child a small brown bag which we were not allowed to open in church but we could so easily feel whether we had an orange or an apple and there was at least one chocolate bar and almost a whole handful of peanuts and either six or seven candies, and then we sang

> *Stille Nacht, heilige Nacht*
> *Alles schlaeft, einsam wacht*
> *Nur das traute, hochheilige Paar,*
> *Das im Stalle zur Bethlehem war*
> *Bei dem himmlischen Kind,*
> *Bei dem himmlischen Kind.*

And then without talking or running around we all went quickly and quietly home. No clouds now, the sky was brilliant, clear black with crystals of stars frozen over us, the air silent as a curtain: tomorrow would be very cold. And on our front step was a small wooden box. I bumped against it as I jumped for the door trying to get in fast to see whether I had an O Henry or a Sweet Marie in my bag.

The board squeaked up—what was that? Those are oranges, my father said, Japanese oranges. They can be eaten. Roundly moist in their pale wrappers, they unzipped themselves under his finger-nail symmetrically with a strange, sharp sweetness like regular little oriental shelves opening. Who could have left them for us? Such a vividly useless gift, all you could do was eat it. So we did: Anni and I each ate nine.

Then my father read, as he always did, from "And there went out a decree from Caesar Augustus. . ." all the way to where the shepherds returned to their flocks glorifying and praising God, and then we each said a very short prayer with the house so quiet now I could hear the coal shift as it burned in the stove and Anni and I placed our plates—like always the very biggest we could find—on the kitchen table under the spruce branches all ready for the gifts we knew we would get from the "Nate Klous"— always useful gifts like toothbrushes or socks or a shirt at most—and then we climbed up the narrow stairs to our two small rooms with a final, tenth, Japanese shelving itself lingeringly into our mouths.

"Who was it?" Anni asked, breathing orange in the darkness.

I said, "Who knows?" But I did. I knew it as certainly as a child knows everything at Christmas. As certainly as the hard clear sanity of the north wind's song beginning at the window, and in my ear, our little house I believe swaying gently like a cradle, very, very gently.

David Waltner-Toews

A Sunny Day In Canada

Fourscore and ten years have I lived, as the ancients would have said. They loved euphemisms. I am ancient and my bones ache. Rachel, my wife, is one year less. If life were a fair sport, I should be winning. But if life is a game, it is a rich man's game, like golf. The higher you score, the less likely you are to win. Blessed are the poor in years.

It is a sunny day in Canada! We have been having all kinds of weather this spring, but today it is sunny. This afternoon, I have been asked to speak at Isaac Reimer's funeral. We were said to be good friends, especially these last few years here in the nursing home. Shall I tell them how he never remembered me from day to day? How every morning he greeted me as if for the first time? Shall I tell how that good man, who never touched tobacco in his life, bummed cigarettes from the orderly? Shall I tell them how he died a year ago, when his mind left, and not just last week, when he greeted me for the last time just before he went to the hospital? I take that back, for Rachel's sake.

"By the light of the gold, and silvery moon,/and that right soon." So says Rachel, who once wrote poetry, and now lives in it. I think the couplet must be significant, she says it so often. Is there a sense of urgency there? Something will happen "right soon." Gold and silver—intimations of heaven. The moon—"For now we see through a glass darkly, but then, face to face." In the full light, as on this sunny morning.

"Winston tastes good, like a cigarette should," she continues, giggling, and then, in explanation to any who might not know her and who might therefore misinterpret her meaning, she adds, "And I don't even smoke." What is her meaning? That the world is attractive, despite all its sinfulness? At this end of the journey. Or is it a subtle condemnation of me, who devoted my life to ungrateful college students, leaving her at home to raise a family and watch television? Now she has her revenge! Feeding me commercials like pablum, in this two-bed, inescapably pastel pink room. Nursery, nursing home—the choice of names is no accident.

But Rachel is sweet, five feet four, a frail wisp of a woman with clear blue eyes and white, white hair. In her blue-flowered flannel nightgown she floats, jerkily, like a paper doll suspended by a string. She steadies herself against the bed, against a chair, and then against the wall on her way to the bathroom. Some things her body remembers, thank God. She has two good bowel movements every day, and never an accident. But her lightness, that is what I love. One morning, she will lift up through the window like a kite, up, up, growing smaller and smaller into the blue prairie sky. I shall be holding the string. When she arrives up there, she will give a little tug, and I too will be pulled loose. I shall float up after her, unstuck from earth.

Let me tell you about my body. My body is a skeleton wrapped in parchment. The orderly discovers this archeological artifact every morning, tucked into a cave of white sheets and woollen blankets: bald as a plucked chicken, the legs bent up towards the chest, twisted around each other. Doctor Toews says the body is reverting to foetal posture, which just shows how far removed from the womb he is. The legs are locked into that awkward and painful position as if held by steel springs. The orderly—Johnny, is that his name? a Thiessen boy anyway—must pry the springs apart when he performs the morning wash ritual on these bones.

"Oh, that itches. Blackheads I guess, eh?" The old body speaks in simple sentences. We progress, in this place, from long sentences to short phrases to a few key words and finally to silence and eternal peace. The staff helps us in this unlearning of language, this progression which is the reverse of childhood. By now, most of us here speak in simple sentences. The old body knows it is not blackheads; it is the dry, papery skin. The orderly takes a squeeze bottle of white lotion from the bedside table, squirts it into his hands, and massages my back. Once, before he knew better, he squirted the cold lotion directly onto the parchment. It felt like an icicle perforating me.

What will I say at the funeral? That in the morning, when we are washed, the orderly lets us wash our own privates? That the aide who prepares Rachel for the day waits until Johnny Thiessen is done with me? Is it so that the aide will not see me, or so that I will not see Rachel? Last night, she came into my bed. She just lay next to me with her hands on my body, with my hands on her body. Not a word: for three hours, we had eternal peace. As suddenly as she arrived, she left, in the middle of the night, by the light of the gold and silvery moon.

 "God damn it, that hurts!" Was that meant for me? No. That was George Wilmer. He is not a Mennonite and I don't know how he got into a Mennonite nursing home. You can tell he is not a Mennonite because he curses in English. Mennonites only curse in Low German.

I am fully clothed now, in a clean white sportshirt and green slacks, black socks and brown leather shoes. I have had a good bowel movement. I am sitting in my wheelchair, in the hallway. I am waiting to be taken to breakfast, over an hour from now. They have gotten the easy people ready first. Now they are starting to work on the hard ones, like George. While I am waiting, I must think of something for the funeral. I could tell the story of Lazarus. No. Isaac Reimer was an old man. He died. God rest his soul. Johnny Thiessen has parked me just outside George Wilmer's door. Lord preserve me.

"Hey, hey you—Johnny. Do you know I'm getting out this weekend? I'll get my truck on Saturday. Got a couple of big loads to haul all lined up. Lots of money in that, you know. A man can get rich nowadays driving a truck. And then on Sunday, Betty and I are going up to the lake. Betty said she would." George Wilmer does not talk, he growls with gravel in his throat. He is not aging gracefully. His body had a stroke on the left side, his big fat quivering body. He does not admit to inhabiting that body. He lives in another body, young and muscular. A body that will go with Betty, the chubby blonde aide, to the lake this weekend. When Johnny heaves the hefty, half-paralysed body into the wheelchair, George helps as little as possible. It's not his body. Why should he?

George is pushed into the hall and parked just ahead of me, next to Annie Kroeker's door. Annie Kroeker is a room full of people.

"Where's Betty?" says George, gripping the arm of his wheelchair tightly in his one good hand. No one answers. He beats his fist down on the steel chair arm. "Damn it, where's Betty!" he shouts.

Johnny's black-topped, tousled head pokes out of a room across the hall. "I think it's her day off," he says, before disappearing into the room again.

"Day off?!"

"Well, good morning to you too." Now Annie has heard. She has a guest. "Day off," the man said, just like, "Good day." Annie does not wait for an explanation of this unusual greeting. She continues. "It's so nice of you to come. Oh, you've brought a pie. Blueberry! I love blueberry pie. And how are the children? Get out! Get out of my house! Oh, it's you, is it? So nice to meet you."

"Oh shut up!" George yells into her room.

"Get out, and take your children with you, the beasts!"

"You crazy old woman!"

"And here's your pie!"

George settles into his chair like a flour sack and leans his face into his hand.

We have two meals at this nursing home, one at ten-thirty and one at three-thirty. We also have snacks, at one o'clock and six. Between meals we wait for meals. We watch television. On Sunday morning, there is a church service in the chapel. A different minister speaks each week. Last week, a young people's group from the pentecostal church came. They sang and clapped their hands and praised God for his glory. We had farmer's sausage for dinner, and Rachel spilled the whole plate into her lap.

"It's just that time of the month," I explained to the aide. Rachel beamed at me. Sometimes she understands things very well.

The aide guides Rachel into the hall and sets her on a chair beside me. She is dressed in a forest-green cotton dress with white lace trim at the neck and ankles, and pink slippers. The green of her dress is the same green as my slacks. We are a pair. Our daughter Sally made these clothes for us. Pete and Sally are so thoughtful.

18

Dear Pete and Sally,
      It is a sunny day here in Canada. We have been having all kinds of weather but our health is good. Thank you for the dress and slacks, and more especially for the socks and underwear, which got here just in time. Wishing you good health and God's love. Just now we are waiting for breakfast,
love,
Father

"Good morning," I say to Rachel. I swing my claw over to her chair and dangle it over the glossy wooden armrest. She strokes it. To her, it is a thin white cat.

"By the light of the gold, and silvery moon," she says.

Sometimes I am very lonely. Pete and Sally are a comfort, but they live far away, in Minneapolis, and can seldom visit. Two of the other children live right here in Winnipeg, but they don't come. When they do come, they sit and fidget, and don't know what to say.

"Hey, hey you I need a shave!" George grabs Johnny as the orderly hurries past, untucking the white shirt from the white trousers and revealing a white undershirt. Johnny stops, removes the hand from his shirt, and sets it back in George's lap.

"In a few minutes," he says, hurrying down the hall, tucking his shirt back in.

Annie welcomes George to her home again. He curses her, his shady jowls quivering, waving his fist.

Isaac Reimer where are you? Have I forgotten you so soon? One week ago you went to the hospital. Now they say you have gone to be with your Maker. I hope his Maker gives him a new liver. They say it was liver trouble. Isaac was a small, quiet man who always had a cheerful "Good morning!" for everyone. He was a good minister in his time, and spoke with quiet authority even when bumming a cigarette. His niece brought him donuts which he shared with all of us. We shall miss him. I do miss him, this morning. Isaac Reimer was almost blind, so all mornings were the same to him; he chose them all to be sunny, even when it rained. I wonder how he died, if there was pain. They never tell us those things, as if we were children and needed to be protected.

Albert Fenske shuffles by in his housecoat and slippers. His soft grey hair is not yet combed. Three weeks ago he came here after a mild stroke. Now he is slowly recovering, but still forgets many things. He is only seventy years old.

"Breakfast time!" he announces to us.

"Oh, you have brought a pie. I love blueberry pie," answers Annie's hard, thin voice.

"It's too early for breakfast yet," I say to Rachel. "They're never this early. The time is very important to these nursing home people. 'Time is money,' says the administrator."

Rachel pats my hand and sighs. "Well, I don't know about that," she says.

When we are all out in the hallway, the aides and orderlies go back to our rooms. They change the sheets and make the beds. This is so that, after breakfast, some of us may go to our rooms to lie down. The staff knows, eating breakfast in this place is quite a strain: cold porridge and prune juice, toast and coffee.

I clamp my hand around the glass and jerkily guide it towards my face. It is like operating a crane. Or like one of those machines they have at the Red River Exhibition. You put in a quarter. This activates a mechanical arm with a toothed, hinged bucket at its extremity. You guide the bucket-claw towards the prize you want—anything: cheap watches, pocket knives, compasses, cigarette lighters, silver dollars, key chains, prune juice, a spoonful of Sunny Boy Cereal. The prize must be picked up and carried over to a hole. You drop it into the hole and lo, you are guaranteed a good bowel movement today! Of course, I would never admit to playing those machines; it was a form of gambling, a worldly, unthrifty activity not to be indulged in. But when you are in high school, it is important to find out what exactly it is you are not indulging in.

At the breakfast table, it is possible to separate the gamblers from the pious. In this nursing home, the evidence of piety is overwhelming. Our parents and ministers would be pleased. Everywhere, the mechanical arms are failing, prizes are lost: the spoonfuls of porridge never quite navigate the distance to the hole. At the very lips the cereal slips and splatters on my white bib. The prune juice is spilled when reaching for the coffee, the coffee spilled when reaching for the juice. Poor Rachel, who is even less mechanically inclined than I, fares even worse. We leave behind a disaster area, eat our toast, and return to our rooms to await the next meal. I am unfair; the aides and orderlies do help us sometimes, but who wants to be fed like a baby?

"Has anyone seen Mr. Fenske?" The nurse is standing primly beside the table. She has a worried furrow in her brow.

The orderlies and aides look around the room. He is not here.

"I thought he was in the other dining room," says the Thiessen boy. The nurse is shaking her head from side to side and he imitates her. "Oh oh," he says. Then she nods her head up and down. Again, he imitates her.

"Got away from us, did he? Well I guess we'd better notify the police."

In order to speak at the funeral this afternoon, I shall be allowed to leave the home. Reverend Sawatsky will come to get us. I have asked that Rachel be allowed to come as well. After the service, I will ask Reverend Sawatsky to let us sit out under the trees somewhere. Rachel will bring her shawl: I must remember that. It will be cool. Outside there will be birds singing, hidden in the bright and dark layers of leaves. Children will be throwing a red, white, and blue hollow rubber ball to one another. They will be young children, and a wild toss will be thrown into my lap. I will catch it like a bride's bouquet, and the Lord will grant us childhood again. I think I know what I will say at the funeral.

I am rolled into the television lounge, facing the blank grey square of glass set in dark brown wood. Rachel is taken by the arm and guided to a chair beside me. The television will not be turned on until this afternoon, but the physical object is a good focus for thinking. George is rolled in next to me on the other side from Rachel; he has been shaved and exudes a fragrance of Old Spice Lime. He stares at the television and growls.

"I'm going out with Betty this afternoon. She's coming to get me, you know, and we're going to the lake." He runs his quaking right hand up over the few threads of brown hair landscaping the fringes of his polished head.

A pretty, young aide has just brought in one of the grey little ladies whom I do not know. "Aw, do you really think so?" says the aide, patting George's skull.

"It's true, damn it! It's true!" His whole body tenses as if he is pushing a boulder away from him. He turns to me with a sudden grin. "By God we're going to have a good time. I'll show my wife, that no good whore. She sleeps with the manager of this place, you know."

"I hope the baby is all right," says Rachel, thoughtfully.

George sinks back, his hand covering his eyes.

Johnny comes to take me to my bubble bath. Three times every week I am set in a tub where the water swirls and bubbles warmly all around me. Dr. Toews says it is to limber up my legs. Johnny pries at the springs and massages the bone. "Oh, my poor old aching body," I say when he does that. I love to just sit there. This body I live in just wants to be left alone. The bath is a good place for thinking.

When you are teaching church history, you must know all about the world. I tell my students that to understand themselves, they must understand the world. For man was not meant to be alone. God saw that it was not good for man to be alone. People are not complete by themselves, and therefore cannot be understood by themselves. That is why we have the church.

"He took one of the big tricycles? Downtown? A oneway street!" Johnny is just outside the door. He is coming in to lift me out of the bath and dry off my body. He will cover it with clothes and set it in a wheelchair.

"So, they found Mr. Fenske, did they?" I say, making conversation.

"Yup, they sure did," says Johnny.

I am rolled into the lounge. There are six or seven people here now. Rachel is still here, smiling sweetly, twisting a white handkerchief between her fingers.

"Mr. Wilmer, your wife is here to see you," announces an aide behind me. Mrs. Wilmer waddles in. She must weigh three hundred pounds and wheezes with every step. George smiles boyishly up at her.

"Hello, dear," he says.

She grips his wheelchair and sucks and blows and heaves the two of them down the hall towards his room. "Having a nice day?" she gasps.

Rachel holds the handkerchief up over her face, just below her eyes. She is making eyes at me. When Johnny comes back into the lounge I ask him to take us back to our room. We'd like to rest a little. I have a funeral to go to this afternoon. Isaac

Reimer's funeral. One morning Isaac walked right out the front door and into the street. He walked firmly and quickly, as if he knew where he was going. He was almost run over by a truck. Johnny drives me back to the room first. He will make a second trip to walk Rachel. By making two trips it is easier to fill the time.

"Consider the lilies of the field," I will say at the funeral. "They neither sow nor reap; yet I tell you, not even Solomon in all his splendour was arrayed like one of these." Isaac Reimer was like one of these. Today he truly is a lily of the field. His body will be in the earth like a root, and his soul clothed in immortality. If I could just understand this: the mystery of the human body, its beginnings and its endings, then I think I could understand the whole world. I am tucked between the cool clean sheets in my underwear. Johnny has gone to fetch Rachel.

"Nurse, nurse, come quickly!" I can hear him calling from the other end of the hall. "It's Mrs. Wiebe. Better call an ambulance. And Dr. Toews." What has happened? What is wrong with Rachel? Dear Jesus, what is the matter? Footsteps are clattering in the hall. How I wish I could walk now! To run to her! Dear God give me strength. I nudge my feet over the edge of the bed. If I can just hook them on the bed frame, I can use them as a lever. Take the sheet in this claw and pull it away from the body. Press the feet against the cold steel. Heave. I only lift up a few inches. My arms try to help. Once more, Lord help me, heave. I swing my body up, dizzily, but cannot stop at the peak. Like a ferris wheel seat my head soars up and over and pulls my body down toward the floor. I am fleeing into darkness, into light. I am disappearing from myself. In the distance, I can hear a siren.

When I awake, I am tucked into bed and the nurse is standing over me.

"I take it then, that I am not in heaven?"

The nurse smiles and shakes her pert, white-capped head. "Just a few broken bones," she said. "Nothing that can't be fixed."

I know better. I remember, suddenly. "Rachel. Where is Rachel? How his she?"

The nurse lays a gentle hand on my arm. "Rachel had a slight accident," she says. "She is in the hospital."

"How long?"

"For a few days, maybe. Maybe longer."

"What kind of accident?"

"I can't tell you."

"You can't?"

"Doctor's orders."

"She's my wife."

"But Doctor Toews said explicitly."

"Are you married?"

She looks away from my eyes and fingers the blanket. "Yes."

"If something happened to your husband, would you want to know?"

"Doctor Toews is afraid for your heart."

"This isn't helping."

She is gripping the blanket tightly in her fist. Her dark brown eyes shift around the room.

"Listen, if my wife is dying, then I may have a heart attack and die, and we will die together. Or I may not have a heart attack. I may have a heart attack if you don't tell me anything because I may imagine she is dying."

She loosens the grip on the blanket.

"She had a stroke," she says, looking back into my eyes. "But please don't tell Dr. Toews I told you."

Then she leaves. George Wilmer had a stroke. A stroke can leave you paralysed. Does it always leave you bitter? What would it feel like, if half my body were paralysed? I close my eyes and try to imagine: not much different than it feels now. I am very tired. I go to sleep.

At one o'clock we have a snack of cookies and milk or juice. I am propped up on the pillows in my bed and Johnny brings me my tray. Everything seems to be happening so fast, time accelerating like a motorcycle I am riding. Dr. Toews is sitting on Rachel's bed, his hands folding and unfolding.

"I don't know how to tell you this," he says.

I am careening along a narrow road along a cliff, spectacular new mountains rising up around me, sinking away from me in ever-changing new formations, so that the road constantly, unpredictably changes course. I must concentrate. Dear God help me. I must see everything, feel, hear, sense everything.

Totally. My life depends on it. I am roaring into a bright light.

"Crackers! God damn crackers! Diabetes, hell. It's a plot. Everyone else gets cookies. I'll sue the manager. He sleeps with my wife, the s.o.b."

Doctor Toews is sitting on the bed. On Rachel's bed. George Wilmer, across the hall, is unhappy with his snack. I push my tray table away. Doctor Toews stands up.

"I'm afraid your wife," says the doctor, sandwiching my hand like a bone between the thick fleshy slices of his hand, "I'm afraid she's not with us any more."

I want to make a joke of it, to look around the room and say, "No, I guess she isn't." I am too tired. I want to sleep now. I have been asked to speak at Isaac Reimer's funeral this afternoon. What shall I tell them? The doctor is hurrying on.

"I've phoned Reverend Sawatsky," he says, "and tried to contact your children. Sally and Peter will be flying up this afternoon."

I pull the skin down over my eyes like window blinds, so the world cannot see me. The pillow is soft, brought from home.

Dear Peter and Sally,
It is a sunny day in Canada. We are having all kinds of weather. Thank you for the dress and slacks and underwear. They came just in time.
love

Dear, dear Rachel, my lovely kite, I am coming

Sandra Birdsell

Niagara Falls

In January, Henry J. Zacharias had his first stroke.

It was late afternoon, around four o'clock, when Elizabeth began the eleven-mile drive from the hospital in Reinfeld to their farm, a trip she would make over and over. "I keep a close watch on that heart of mine," Johnny Cash sang as she travelled down the long stretch of road that connected the town with the highway. She switched off the radio. Music didn't seem right at a time like this. She drove cautiously, holding onto the wheel too tightly, fearing an accident. It was at times like these, when your nerves were stretched too tight, that things went wrong. She passed by the feed mill and slowed down as she approached Ellis's Greenhouses. Should she stop and let him know about Henry, that she wouldn't be able to come in for the seeding? No. He would wonder how she could even think about such things.

The thump of tires against the pavement felt rhythmic and sure, but the point at which she aimed seemed fixed and unreachable as the horizon which sometimes in winter disappeared so that she couldn't tell, where was sky, where was land? She was vaguely aware of a cluster of brown trees in the middle of a field, huddled together in a bank of snow like old women at a funeral, long shadows, their skirts blotting out the wash of pastel sky-colours reflected all about in the hard snow. Minutes later (how many, five, fifteen?) she passed by her lane, past the buildings all yellow with green trim that distinguished Henry J. Zacharias's farm from the others; from Henry P. Zacharias (no relation), who was called Hank by his neighbours and whose farm was twice the size of theirs and stretched all the way to Roland.

Realizing her error, she braked quickly, felt the wheels skid on ice. She held her breath to contain her rising panic, steering into the skid instinctively, thinking, already I have gotten myself into trouble, felt the vehicle swing out of the slide, pass centre and fishtail sharply. Today she couldn't go off the road, not today because then Hank P. would have to come with his tractor to pull her out and (one thing for certain) she didn't want to have to ask him for anything, but the wheels caught at buried gravel and the car steadied. She breathed a prayer of relief. She backed the car slowly toward the lane. The driveway had disappeared. She searched through the windshield for some sign of it, a track that would guide her safely into the yard, but the combination of waning light and fresh snow had erased all traces of it. The house itself appeared abandoned, the windows dark mirrors reflecting the setting sun. She was cut off from her house. She got out of the car and walked down the lane. The fluffy snow, ankle-deep, bit at her bare skin. She hadn't stopped to put boots on this morning when she saw Henry fall. She'd run from the house not thinking, just oh God, oh God. One minute he was walking, strong, and the next, like a bird crashing into the window, he faltered, his arms flailing, looking for something to hold on to, and he was down, a brilliant red plaid heap in the snow. Fresh snow covered the spot near the mailbox where he'd fallen. She walked back to the car and followed her footprints into the lane, passed them by, and then braver, drove by faith into the circle of her yard.

She waited in the car until she'd stopped shaking and then went into the house. She stamped snow from her feet and walked across the kitchen, her steps sluggish, as though she waded through water, to the calendar which hung beside the telephone. "Arrive Niagara Falls, 8 am," she'd written on it that morning. Only a week away from their first vacation, an anniversary present from their only son, John, and his wife, Sharon. She picked up the pencil and wrote, "Henry goes to the hospital." Her spidery, odd-shaped letters ran off the square into the next date. Henry was there in Reinfeld in the hospital and she was here, at the farm. The floor cracked suddenly as though someone just entered the room. Phone John's place, she told herself, see if they're back from the city yet. But she didn't pick up the receiver. She knew too much. She'd seen the doctor thump hard with the heel of his palm against Henry's breast-bone to try to rouse him. She knew his illness would take up many squares on the calendar. Inside his head, a large field had been marked off. She'd stood beside his bed and watched him fall deeper into sleep. Where are you? she'd asked him silently, and then, where am I? Was she the one who had fallen asleep today?

"I'll give the money for the train tickets back to John," she'd told Henry at the hospital. She meant to say, don't you worry now. She was surprised when he responded. He moved his hand across the blanket towards her own.

"Seed," he said. "John should be spending money for seed, not trips." His voice came from a great distance. And she thought again, it is a dream. I'll open my eyes and be in my room upstairs.

She held his curled fingers lightly between her large hands. "I'll tell him you said so." Their son wasn't a farmer. He owned a large implement dealership in Reinfeld. Henry was confused, or was he saying, tell John to look after things?

"John spends entirely too much money," Henry said, and Elizabeth thought that maybe his illness wasn't so bad after all, if he could still think to speak out against John. But several hours later, Henry grew too weak to talk and he sank into sleep.

Elizabeth turned from the telephone. The bad news would keep for a while. She read the words she'd written on the calendar. She picked up the pencil which dangled from its string and in tiny, controlled letters she wrote, "All day it snowed." She would train herself to live alone.

She switched on the stove and filled the kettle with water. The mantle clock in the dining room chimed the hour. She went into the room and turned on the light as though that would lessen the effect of the clock's counting. All around the walls on varnished shelves was her collection of china plates. She didn't like china, but it was what other women did. John and Sharon were delighted. They never knew what to buy for her and so they bought a plate from each place they visited. She had a plate with a picture of the Niagara Falls on it. When she'd seen John's slides of the falls, they made her feel like the bonging of the clock made her feel, off balance and clutching the air about her. "Horseshoe Falls," the plate was inscribed, "160 feet high, 2,950 feet wide, 500,000 tons of water a minute," which to her was the same as saying, "every second a baby is born." It was unfathomable.

But it wasn't these plates she'd come searching for, but for something older, something that came from a different time. She found it on the shelf in the china cupboard, the porcelain cup and saucer that had come from Russia. Her mother had brought it with her and had written down that she was to have it when she married. She felt its smoothness against the thick callouses of her palms and took the cup into the kitchen. She filled it with hot water and sat down at the table and pressed its fluted edge to her lips. She looked out the window. The moon had risen and beneath it stretched the winter-blue curve of Henry's fields. Before she'd begun to work in the greenhouses, she'd preferred winter. She'd never been able to face the stark bleakness of Henry's fields without feeling numbed by the ugliness. She hated how she'd battled daily the wind that swept in under windowsills, covering everything with gritty black silt. Her headaches used to come with those high winds. She preferred the depression that the immense stillness of winter carried because in winter, it was clean. She massaged her chest where an odd ache had begun to form and thought about who she should telephone. She should really try to get hold of John just in case he had come home from the city a day earlier than expected and heard about his father. And then she realized that if that happened, he would call her. She didn't have the energy to call John and face the questions he would ask, not letting her finish saying what she'd formed in her mind. Should she call Mika? No, her sister seemed to enjoy hearing bad news and would grab hold of the information and make it seem worse than it really was. Irma. Irma worked in the greenhouses with her. Better to call Irma because Irma understood. She was married to a cranky, bitter man who had lost his legs. And she, eyelids heavy with the thought of it, was married to Henry who today had entered his own place. She had lost his mind.

Elizabeth opened her eyes, realized it was morning and was amazed that she'd slept so soundly. The first thing she saw was Henry's boots on the carpet across the room, beside his bed, and she remembered a week ago, Henry walking three miles to Hank P.'s place. To keep him talking in the barn long enough until the polls closed to prevent Hank P., who was Liberal, from casting his vote. What did you talk about for such a long time? she'd asked, her heart doing its familiar flip flop each time he'd come back from talking with Hank P. We talked about God, and what He means to me, Henry said.

Everything is lawful, Henry often said, but not everything is good and so they were one of few left in the farming area around Reinfeld who didn't have the tell-tale television antenna on top of their roof. Occasionally, she drove into town and watched Ed Sullivan at Irma's place. She had never been able to match Henry's goodness, she thought, as her eyes met his Bible lying on the table beside his bed. She went into what used to be John's bedroom, her sewing room, and stood looking for a moment at the dress pattern spread across the worktable, pieces cut in half lengthwise so that she could add tissue, enlarge the pattern to fit. Yes, that's how it is, she told herself, eating and drinking and never thinking that tomorrow it could all end. She felt guilty immediately. I'm beginning to sound more and more like Mika, she chastened herself, it's a stroke, he could come out of it yet. Above her worktable, the window where she'd been standing when it had happened. She dressed and went down-stairs and erased the vacation plans from the calendar. She didn't allow herself to ask how she felt about this. What had happened had happened. It wasn't Henry's fault that she would never get to see the falls. She had nothing to complain about when it came to Henry. She often said to Irma with a clear heart that she had no complaints at all.

Except for the farm, Irma reminded her when she'd said, Henry is all right, I have no complaints. Henry was seventy-two, she forty-seven. Most men his age had already built their retire-ment houses in Reinfeld, erected fake windmills in their back yards, wishing wells in the front yards, constructed sturdy fences and died. But neither one of them had wanted that. Henry secretly hoped that John would still take up the farm and she, when Mr. Ellis had confided in her his intention to sell, that they would sell the farm and buy the greenhouses. And so when Irma reminded her, "except for the farm," the frustration and despera-tion of past years was as fresh and tart as an unripe apple. The farm wasn't hers to sell. Do, don't ask, Irma said once. Just tell. Irma's husband had no legs, she didn't need to ask for anything, she thought, as she plaited her long auburn hair. She watched herself do this, saw her awkward fingers fumbling with the tiny pins, her face, rounder; she'd been gaining weight. The mirror told her what she still didn't feel completely: you are here, real, alive, and Henry is the one asleep.

Before she telephoned John, she called the hospital and asked, how is he? The same, the nurse said. He spent a quiet night. Henry was too quiet. His falling was like a feather resting among feathers. She telephoned John and gave him the news and arranged to meet him at the hospital. When she hung up some of the tension that had gathered in her shoulder blades fled. She picked up the pencil and wrote, "My first day alone" and beneath that, "Phone Mr. Ellis soon."

In mid-February, as Elizabeth turned off from the highway onto the road that led to Reinfeld, the sun sparkled on crusty snow and on rooftops and she thought Reinfeld looked like a Christmas card picture of Bethlehem shining with the blue tinge of a pointing star, making it special, set apart, unlike the other towns that hugged the American border. The highway didn't pass through Reinfeld's centre, splitting it in two. It wasn't necessary to string gaudy lights above the street or to have a sign that said, "Welcome to Reinfeld." Its borders were symmetrical, the streets, predictable, and the sameness in the decoration of the houses made her feel that nothing would ever change. She drove towards the hospital thinking that despite everything, she was content.

She walked into Henry's room. He looked at her, blinked several times and said, "Chicks. Have you ordered the chicks yet?"

"What?" Elizabeth asked, startled. Her own dream-like state had diminished and she had reconciled herself to his, that it was permanent. His place had become real. The walls were green. His cubicle had a tall, narrow window that looked out over the town of Reinfeld. A brass radiator beneath it. Beside his bed, a wooden one-drawer chest, painted brown. Above it, a mirror. Henry, in a wheelchair, staring down at the curled fingers in his lap, a towel tied beneath his arms to hold him upright. Henry's white legs, thinner, dangling uselessly as the attendant lifted him in and out of bed. Because she was strong and healthy, Henry's place seemed confined. But she knew the effort it took for him just to breathe and so she knew that for him, it was the right size. But now, his voice a whisper, but his voice, saying to her, "Chicks, have you ordered the chicks yet?"

She'd called Mr. Ellis and had gone back to work transplanting tomatoes and her life had become routine. She was confident enough to try variations to the old pattern, sleeping in past seven o'clock, staying up later at night, continuing the nightly ritual of drinking hot water from the porcelain cup that had come from Russia.

"He spoke to me," Elizabeth said to the nurse. She'd run from the room, grabbed hold of the first person she came upon.

"Oh, he speaks often," the nurse said. "Especially during the night. He talks about an accident. We feel that he hears things."

"Things, what things?" Accident and chicks. Her face grew flushed.

"Oh, the other patients, their radios."

They should have told her. Prepared her for the time when he would begin to ask questions. How did it happen? Did I fall? And then, what about Hank P.? How did that one happen?

"And that's not all," the nurse said as she followed Elizabeth back into Henry's room. "We have a surprise for you. Show your wife what you can do," she said to Henry and for the first time, Elizabeth noticed the metal bar hanging above his bed.

Henry reached up, his whole arm trembling, and curled his fingers about the bar. He began to pull himself upright.

Elizabeth slapped her hands against her cheeks in astonishment. "Isn't that wonderful?" the nurse said.

Yes, but it's only an arm, she told herself later as she sat beside his bed knitting a sweater which she planned to send to her sister for the youngest baby. It's only an arm. When she considered how far he was from walking and even then they weren't sure about his right side. "Henry," she said loudly several moments later as he lay panting from exertion. His hearing has not been affected, the doctor had told her, there was no need to yell, but she couldn't help it. It seemed that because he couldn't talk above a whisper, he couldn't hear either. "I have been wanting to talk to you about the farm." Her metal needles clicked out a frantic pace. "I was thinking, the way prices are that now would be a good time to sell."

He didn't respond. She set the knitting aside and went over to his bed. He stared at the ceiling. She sat down on the edge of the bed. Spittle ran from one corner of his drooping mouth. She snatched up a tissue, began to dab at it. "Think of it," she said gently. "Everything considered, we should get rid of the land."

He pulled away. "No," he said, and then louder, "I forbid you to do that." He began to thrash his head from side to side on the pillow. She held his cheeks between her hands, felt the faint flutter of his muscles as he tried to free himself. She felt ashamed, unworthy.

"Henry, please, be still." His head was fragile, as fragile as an ancient porcelain cup that would shatter if you flicked it hard with your knuckle.

"It's all right," she said. "We don't need to talk about it yet." She had dreamt of him one night, that she carried him out and away from the hospital. I'll care for you, she'd said. I'll look after you, make you well. And here she was, upsetting him. He grew still. She patted him lightly on the cheek and felt that peculiar ache rise in her chest. The farm, it wasn't hers to sell. She took up her knitting once again. "The way your exercises are going," she said, "you will be up and around the yard by spring."

He blinked rapidly. "Phone Hank P.," he said harshly. "Tell him I'll lease the land. One year only."

Elizabeth dropped a stitch, squinted and raced to pick it up before the whole sweater unravelled. "I'll tell him," she said.

"He's not being very realistic," John said. "Expecting anyone would even want to lease the land for one year. Especially a guy like Hank P."

Especially Hank P., Elizabeth thought. He would be the one to do it. "You're a fine one to talk about being realistic," she said and laughed. When he was small he would butt his head against her stomach, his crib, the walls, in order to make things happen. In the early grades in school, teachers said that he threw himself on the floor and banged his head when he didn't make one hundred percent on a test.

"But he's not thinking," John said, choosing to ignore her gentle teasing.

Elizabeth shushed him. "He's your father." And John was

his son. There were indelible marks other than his short stocky frame, his bullishness. John was deeply religious like Henry, in an unbending, fierce way that made her feel defensive and inadequate. And yet, father and son had never worked well together.

"You have to realize why your father wants to hang on. What has he got?" A bed, a chair, a window in a shoebox of a room.

John got up from the kitchen table and put his arm around her shoulders. "And what about you?" he asked. "Shouldn't we be thinking about you as well?" If she stood up, she would be a foot taller than he. All his caresses came when she was sitting. She leaned back in the chair and let her head rest against his chest. For the first time since Henry had fallen in the snow, she felt like weeping. He kneaded her shoulders, demonstrative in a way she'd taught him. The way Henry might have been if someone had shown him how. She'd kept house for Henry a full year without realizing that he cared for her. Not until he fired the hired man for making jokes about her size.

"This has been hard on you, we know," John said. "Sharon and I don't know how you've managed to keep everything up."

"It's all right," she said. "I'm all right." She wanted to tell him about her desire. About the greenhouse. When she worked in the greenhouse, the sun's light diffused through the sloping glass roof and its steady warmth on her broad shoulders made her feel secure. The smell of the young moist plants in their flats of peat moss filled her with energy and she walked faster, moved more quickly. She enjoyed reading through all the seed catalogues and meeting the people who came to buy bedding plants.

"It's not all right," John said. "Sharon and I have been thinking—even if Father doesn't get well, you should go away for awhile. Take that trip to Niagara Falls."

"Oh no," she said. "Not without Father." If she went to the falls alone, she might never come back. She'd be swept away by the thundering water. She'd be a speck going over the brink, tumbling in the mist, never stopping. With no one to hold her back, she would lean over the railing with all those other people in yellow rubber raincoats, she would lean just so far and be gone.

"I shouldn't be thinking about trips," Elizabeth said, "but

what I'll do if worse comes to worse. And I've been thinking, if something happens to your father, I would like to sell the farm and live in town."

He smiled a quick anxious smile, sat down beside her and took her hands in his. "Great," he said. "I'm glad to hear you say that. Sharon and I were hoping that's what you'd want. We've made plans and I wanted to talk to you about them. It makes it easier that you want to live in town."

She thought he would say they were going to start a family and wanted her close by.

"We've decided to open another dealership. A bigger one. This time, in Morden."

She hid her disappointment. "Why go to Morden? I thought—isn't business good here?"

She saw the look of annoyance pass across his face. "I'd keep the business in Reinfeld as well," he said. "And open another one in Morden. Because business is good. Now's the time to do it."

"Father always said you spend too much money." She pulled her hands free and began to clear away the dishes.

She expected an outburst, but John got up and began to help her. He scraped food from plates. Sharon had taken a day to go shopping in the city and he'd come for supper.

"We're positive we should do this," John said quietly as he set dishes down into the sink. "We've prayed long and hard and we're sure that this is what God wants us to do, too."

"Well then, that's good. Do it." She was conscious of her voice sounding tight and strained.

He cleared his throat noisily and spit phlegm into the garbage can, just as Henry used to do. "I'll need money to do it," he said. "I've got too much tied up in machinery right now to go to the bank."

"How much money?" Henry had five thousand dollars in their savings account. She had a little from working in the green-house.

"Twenty-five thousand."

"So much? I don't have that much money."

"I know," John said and she knew now the reason for his quietness. He was worried. She felt the knot of braids pull at the back of her head. She ran water into the sink, began stacking dishes down into the soapy water.

"What then?" she asked, fearful, her old sickness bumping there beneath her breastbone, dreading his answer.

"Sharon's father has agreed to lend us part of it. I could sell Dad's machinery," he said. "I could get a good price for it."

Henry's acreage was small, a little over one section, that was all. What kind of a price would she get without the machinery?

"Mama," John said, using his old name for her, a form of endearment. "He'll never work again. I thought you realized that."

It was true. And Mr. Ellis could up and sell the greenhouse before Henry realized it. "And what would I do?" she asked. "If something happened to your father, what would I do in town? Work in the shop?"

"You wouldn't need to work," he said. "If things go as well as they have so far, you wouldn't need to work anymore. Sharon and I would see to that. I think it's a good investment for you. We'd be partners, the three of us, you, me and the Lord."

"How could you refuse such a generous offer?" Irma asked the following day. They carried wooden flats in from the yard and stacked them against the wall in the greenhouse. The time was right to begin transplanting, culling the spindly seedlings and transferring the stronger ones to the flats where they would grow thick and straight. Now is the time to do it, John had said. Now is the time, she repeated over and over while she worked.

"What do you mean?" Elizabeth asked, offended by Irma's tone of voice. Irma Muller is an old woman who tries to look young, John had once said, because the woman coloured her hair blonde and used cosmetics. Elizabeth had not reminded him that she and Irma were the same age.

"Well kid, how could you refuse a partnership with God, tell me? He's got you over a barrel, that one. Smart."

Elizabeth knew what it must look like to Irma, but she was certain John was sincere. "He's my son," she said. "If a son can't come to his mother, then who should he go to?" She said this to slight Irma, who let her only daughter Marlene run free like a stray dog.

Irma let a bundle of flats drop to the ground with a great clatter. "Why doesn't he go to his father?" she asked. "No, he knows better," she said and lifted her little finger. "He's got you right there."

Elizabeth was hanging her overalls in the back porch after work when she saw Hank P.'s truck pull into the yard. She was about to call into the house, Henry, you'd better come, Hank P. is here, and then quickly step out of sight, but. . . . She folded her arms across her chest. She would speak to him on her own. Had Henry somehow gotten a message to him?

Hank stood with the door open neither inside nor out. He seemed uncertain whether he should enter. "How is Mr. Zacharias today?" he asked. His red sideburns grew thick and curly half-way down the sides of his face, making it seem broader than it was. She noticed a button missing from his shirt and his bare stomach, curly fine hairs. So he didn't wear an undershirt in winter either, not like Henry who wore one summer and winter, day and night. Her eyes met his. He was almost as tall as she was. It made her uneasy to stand eye to eye with a man.

"He's the same," she said.

"I'm sorry to hear that," he said, as nice and polite as if someone listened behind the door. He stood turning his cap in his hands, which were sprinkled with cinnamon-coloured freckles (young-looking hands cupping a large white breast). His hair, red, against her own dark hair. That old man, he can't be of much use for you. Was he truly sorry? For her, or for Henry? She knew what he'd gone through when his Anna died with cancer.

"I've come to see you about the cultivator," Hank said. "Mr. Zacharias said last fall, if I fixed it, I could use it."

She nodded.

"So, I thought you should know. I'll be working in the machine shed until it's done." He turned in the doorway and put his cap back on.

He was being so polite. "Wait, Henry wanted me to. . . ," Elizabeth began.

He removed his cap once again and waited.

"Henry said to, he sends his regards," she said and looked away. Blood rushed to her face. I have never made love to anyone other than my husband, she'd told Irma, so that she could taste the memory of him rushing against her. She had written on the calendar, "Today while I was digging among the garbage heap for mushrooms, I found a leper in lovely clothes of hard knotted flesh." Henry had read it, asked her what it meant. It's just an idea that came to me, she said. That's all. Did Hank think she was remembering that afternoon half-way between Winnipeg and Reinfeld? The day she'd gone to get the chicks. "I'm not here most afternoons," she said to cover her confusion. "But feel free to come in and help yourself to coffee. I'll leave it on the stove."

He stared at her longer than was necessary to thank her. He closed the door behind him and she stood rooted, confused and angry with herself because she had not given him Henry's message, because she had blushed so readily and now, after all these years, what did he think?

In March the doctor intercepted Elizabeth as she was about to enter Henry's room. "I'm sorry," he said flatly, "but Mr. Zacharias has contracted pneumonia." It seemed like a strange way of putting it, as though Henry had an obligation to take on this new disease.

Her chest ached as she watched Henry's straining to breathe. Tubes dripped medicine into his veins. A nurse came in and pushed a rubber hose into his throat, switched on a machine and sucked up his mucous. Elizabeth gagged. But when it was over, Henry could breathe easier and so she was grateful to the nurse and smiled at her, stepping out of her path quickly to show she was anxious not to be a nuisance.

Today, she would have told him about the snowstorm, how Hank P. had ploughed their lane so she could come to the hospital. "Snow as high as my waist in the lane," she had written. But such news was of no use to poor Henry. He struggled to speak. "What is it?" she asked, dreading some message, some final command, some last question about chicks and accidents.

"Ruining the land," Henry said.

Her heart constricted. "Who is ruining the land?" Had he heard somehow that she hadn't leased it yet?

His mouth, encrusted with fever blisters, moved painfully slow. "Communists."

Her shoulders sagged with immense relief. She watched the slow drip, drip of medicine into the glass tube for several minutes and then left.

Elizabeth felt the sides of March press in on her as she

listened daily to Henry's feverish ranting. The septic tank froze and she didn't call John. John was too busy with his own life and besides, she really was undecided about the money. She hated to picture them praying every day, or the thought that she really might be the answer to their money problems. She called a company in town to come with their heat lamps and torches to thaw out the septic tank, but they weren't in any rush and so in the meantime, she squatted amid the trees beside the granaries and threw her dishwater onto the yard and bathed at Irma's house in town until it was fixed.

Henry seemed never better, never worse. They took away his exercise bar. He was gaunt and appeared bitter over this new setback. She felt responsible. As though she'd caused it to happen by talking of selling off the land. Since she'd decided not to carry Henry's message to Hank P., she couldn't look fully into her husband's eyes, brilliant with the remnant of his fever, but off to one side. The evasion and the sameness of her life depressed her. March weighed heavily and it was on such a day that she arrived for work to find the "For Sale" sign pushed down into the ground beside the greenhouse. She stared at it, telling herself, this is what you get. This is what happens when you even think such selfish things. She backed the car out and drove home.

When she opened the back door, she saw rubber boots on the mat. She reached up to hang her coveralls and saw Hank's parka. She felt the strangeness of its presence pass through her hands as she hung her clothes beside his. When she stepped into the kitchen he was working with his tools at the sink. The faucet lay in pieces on the counter.

"I thought seeing as how I had my tools with me, I might as well fix it," he said without turning around.

That was what he'd said that summer, pulling alongside her car, offering to fix the tire. "You needn't have gone to so much trouble. John would have fixed it for me." Then knowing she sounded ungrateful, she thanked him, feeling the blood rushing to her face once again.

There was nothing she could do without coming too close to him and so she poured a cup of coffee and watched him work. He was across the room and yet it seemed as though he was there beside her. Bending his red head across her chest, his hand cupping her breast, tongue circling her nipple. Soon he was finished and washing his hands, and she was lying across the seat in the car, thinking, so this is what it's like with another man. She had to tell herself over and over to remember that she'd been disappointed that it hadn't been all that different. He wiped his hands on her good dishtowel and squatted to pack his tools into the toolbox. She noticed the straining of the muscles in his thighs against the fabric of his pants. She stared down at the bottom of the porcelain cup. She used to imagine what it would be like with another man and when she'd glanced down at him poised above her, she'd been amazed at how similar he was to Henry, she thought he'd be bigger, stronger looking. Maybe if she had let herself go more it would have been different, she told herself. Let him touch her all over and smell her the way he wanted to. He stood beside the door ready to leave.

"It's fixed," he said.

"Thank you." She smiled.

"I've also finished work on the cultivator today," he said. "Tell Mr. Zacharias it's working."

"I will." He acted as though someone were looking over his shoulder.

He hesitated. His expression changed. He seemed to be nourishing a cunning thought. "Has Mr. Zacharias ever said what he plans to do?" He spoke with a gesture, indicating with his freckled, sure hands (between her legs forcing them open) the wide expanse of Henry's fields. "We, some of the neighbours, would do the seeding for him. If that's his wish."

"I plan to sell," Elizabeth said.

His thick eyebrows shot up, he recovered and his face became expressionless.

"Would you be interested?" she asked.

Again their eyes met and she saw something else flicker in his eyes, a look of unsureness. She was surprised and then faintly exhilarated by the thought, I have made him feel uneasy.

"I might be."

As the door closed behind him, Elizabeth lifted the cup and pressed its edge against her teeth. Her breath was hot inside the cup and moisture clung to the fine dark hairs above her lip. She watched Hank's truck turn the corner at the end of the lane. I plan to sell, she'd said, as though it was her farm to sell. And saying it made it seem real. I am tired of carrying people around on my back, she'll tell Irma, who will crow and say, well it's about time. She got up from the table and wrote on the calendar, "Make an appointment with the hairdresser."

In the middle of April, Henry had another stroke. "Henry has another bout, quite bad," Elizabeth wrote, the terse calmness of the words denying the turmoil inside. She stayed with him all day now, leaving only to get a bite to eat at a restaurant in town. She stood at the narrow, tall window beside his bed and noticed it was finally spring. Moist warm air rushed into the room over-top the gentle hiss of the radiator. Below in the parking lot, people arriving to visit, wearing light coats, sweaters and also below, Hank P.'s truck.

She emptied the basin of water into the sink beside Henry's bed with shaking hands and turned to face Hank, who had come into the room without making a sound. He nodded to her. His eyes took in Henry's shell-like body, the tubes in his nose, the bag at the foot of the bed that collected his wastes.

"I heard he was worse. I'm sorry," Hank said in a kind way that made her remember that his wife had suffered. Hank was different than the Hank who had laughed while she'd rammed her car into his car, because he wouldn't let her pass, making her angry in a way she never thought anyone could. She was about to thank him but saw that his voice had lied. The same smug expression was there, uncovered, and his desire for her, control-led, he would wait until she couldn't wait. He was passing his lust for her across the inert form of her Henry.

"If you need anything at all," he said. "I'll come."

She nodded. "John can come, too."

Henry sighed deeply and they were diverted to him, to the bed. His chest moved gently up and down and the blankets with it. His sternness was pinched out like a candle; had it ever been real, or had it been a covering? she wondered. Henry hadn't asked her for anything and he had shared all with her. He was a feather now, falling among feathers.

Hours later as Elizabeth came back from eating lunch, the nurse met her at the door of the hospital and said, "Mr. Zacharias has just died." Then they took her to his room and left her alone with him. She pulled out the drawer and dropped his comb and brush into the plastic net bag she carried in her purse.

She collected his partial plate from the cardboard container. She thought she might cry. It was the time for it. She looked around the cubicle for one last time. Henry's final giving out had already been absorbed by the breath of others. She imagined the lane, his residue fading even now beneath the melting snow. It was all done now: his slippers, housecoat, the partial plate. She set the bag down. There was one last thing she wanted to do. She gathered Henry in her arms and carried him over to the window. He was lighter than a child. "See, out there," she said. "It's spring."

When she passed through the large glass doors, she was surprised to discover that it had been raining. "First rain today," she would write on the calendar. She'd signed the papers to release Henry's body to the undertakers with a steady hand. No, she'd said, I don't need to wait for my son to come. But I'll wait. She walked towards his car on the parking lot. A door slammed shut as Sharon came running towards her. It's all right, she'll tell them. I'm all right. She would go to see the falls. She would hold onto the railing or she would let herself go. Whatever she did, she would do willingly.

Katie Funk Wiebe

A Real Live Death

Death came in bunches that year, like grapes on a vine. First, there was the death of our grandmother, but it never seemed like a death, for it was only on paper. A letter from Russia, edged in black, to Mother and Dad, stated what had happened and how it had happened. And what she had said to her children before she died—about getting the milking done, and where the rope was to tie the cow. It was a death for Mother, for it was her mother, but it wasn't really a death for the rest of us, for it took nothing from our lives, even as our grandmother's life had added nothing to them. We had never known her.

Then there was the death of the father of Dorothy, my friend in school in fifth grade, and that wasn't really a death either, for one day her older sister found him hanging by a rope in the old barn by the slough. And he was dead with his tongue sticking out. She had run screaming from the place for someone to help her cut him down, and she only about seventeen. And the next day everyone was talking about it in school before the bell rang and during recess, but Dorothy wasn't there, so she didn't hear us. And then after a while, she came back to school and life went on as before, only she didn't have a father.

One day I attended a real funeral—with a coffin, a body, a few flowers, a sermon and mourners, real ones. The local United Church minister had died—an old man who always wore a grey wool worsted suit—to match his grey beard and hair, I thought. Maybe even his insides were grey—he looked so old to me. He walked all stooped over, as if his backbone had gotten tired. Yet he spoke to me with a kind, gentle voice, as if he were stroking a cat. My parents liked him and his preaching. Now he was dead.

I walked around the grey coffin lined with shiny shirred material and set upon chairs at the front of the church and looked in. An old man who didn't look like the man I had known lay in the box, his eyes closed, his wrinkled hands clasped over his chest as if in silent prayer, like he sometimes held them when he prayed in church. Although the adults around me looked sad and teary, I felt nothing. I looked for the wart on the side of his face that moved when he talked. It was still there. This death and the dying of Mother's mother as it had been explained in that long black-edged letter didn't match. Which was real death? What was dying? What happened before it happened? After? I didn't know.

One spring day Dad told us over our macaroni and sausage that a woman and her husband from the country church had been driving to town. Stories always got told like this, from the beginning. The fabric cover of the buggy had torn loose and its wild flapping had terrified the horse. The animal had jerked forward, pitching the woman over backwards onto the dirt road. Her neck had been broken. The funeral would be Sunday.

Dad took Annie and me to the funeral with him to the Russian church, about seven miles in the country. Frieda, Mother and the others stayed home. Annie and I were used to sitting quietly through long services we didn't understand. We had attended plenty of services that were either all German or all Russian, but today the service did not resemble the usual high-spirited gathering of the Russian services. The strong, sonorant female voices in the choir that usually carried the entire congregation along in jubilant hymns, sang softly, mournfully without even trying. I watched openly as a woman nearby wept in loud gasps, rubbing her eyes vigorously with a handkerchief borrowed from her husband's pocket. A man in a dark Sunday suit and white shirt, face darkened by the sun to the clear line where he wore his cap, sat with two small solemn boys, each scrubbed shiny clean, near the front, all rigid like the statue in the Memorial Park. No one whispered across the aisle as they usually did. The preacher's voice sounded grim, though I could understand only the odd word.

At the graveside—a crude oblong hole gouged deeply out of the virgin prairie—the coffin was opened for the last time. It was the custom. The woman in the church and some others cried in louder even more violent gasps, clutching each other. The man in the dark Sunday suit stood dumbly, staring into space across the grave. Someone had taken the children away. Other men in unaccustomed stiff suitcoats, marked by black crepe armbands, stood near the mounds of dirt by the hole, ropes in hands, ready to do the men's work at the funeral. In the background, a few children played by the cars and buggies, their high shrieks piercing the self-imposed silence.

Annie and I edged close to Dad, who stood near the dark cavernous hole. Curiosity overcame me. I wanted to see a dead person. This dead person. I bent over the hole, over the coffin, with its missing lid, for a good look—and nearly tumbled in. Below me, in the semi-darkness which shrouded the body, I saw my mother lying quietly, eyes closed. Same oval face. Same auburn-red hair, parted and pulled back. Same pale complexion. Same well-defined lips.

Mother! My mother?

My heart thudded and twisted as if it wanted to leap out of its prison. My stomach churned. I felt my body shudder under the assault of this recognition.

Why hadn't Dad told us we were going to Mother's funeral? Was this the way it was done? We had seen her alive about an hour ago at home, sitting in the rocking chair by the dining-room window reading the *Zionsbote*. She hadn't been feeling well, as I remembered.

Dad didn't look particularly sad as he peered into the hole with me, although he looked solemn. But then I had never seen him crying for any reason. Fathers didn't cry. Only mothers and children cried. I wanted to shout, to scream, to force someone to explain to me what was happening before the men lowered the lid and nailed it shut. Mother—my mother! I needed my mother. I wasn't big like my mother who could get along in this country without her mother. I hadn't outgrown her—not yet.

No one listened to my pounding heart, and I had no courage to cry out. The men in the dark suits and crepe armbands lowered the lid, then one man jumped nimbly into the grave and nailed it shut. The others helped him clamber back out. Then I heard the dull thumps of shovelfulls of soil hitting the lid, soil which probably had never been disturbed before, except for Indians riding or walking over it. The mourners and sightseers, restrained yet relieved, turned and left. Annie and I followed Dad to the car, parked on the far side of the church.

Dad guided the car over the rutty dirt roads back to town, all three of us sitting in the narrow front seat. I sat rigid, cold, clutching my insides to keep from crying. Dad drove into the driveway of our yard as he usually did, and Annie and I crawled out before he put the car away in the garage. He closed the garage doors and locked them, then he turned to close the yard gate. There were patterns to our family life—doors were locked and gates were closed at all times. Some gates and doors were used a lot and some were used only a little. Our front door with its small strip of stained glass symbolized a life that might some day come to our family in this new country. We used that door very little, though it led to the parlor where the couch, the piano, the Victrola and the large fern reigned in joint solitary splendor. In winter the door was covered with heavy corrugated cardboard to keep out the icy drafts, and couldn't be opened at all. The back door handled the family and even the guest traffic. It led to Mother, the kitchen and warmth. But we had been away, and now it was time to close the gate and open the kitchen door. I hesitated to enter.

I swung the door quickly. There stood Mother, as usual, in her blue checked dress and white apron, bending over the kitchen stove, cooking something for supper in the blue enamel pot.

"Wie ging es?" she asked, glancing up from the pot she was stirring. It smelled like cocoa. We often had cocoa on Sunday evenings.

I looked at her, wanting to run to her, grab her, hold her, but I stayed in the small entryway where we kept the wood, the snow barrels, and the washing machine and outdoor clothes, took off my coat with deliberate movements, looking at Mother sideways. Mother was not dead, not in that box they had buried in the ground. That woman had been someone else's mother. I still had my own. But some day she would die. Some day I might die, and they would lay me in a box and cover me with dirt. Death terrified me, but not as much as the fear of being buried alive. What if they buried me in a coffin before I was so dead I would never come alive again?

Lying beside my sister in the darkness of the night, I heard the clock strike ten, then eleven—and the story of the two young men in one of the German villages in the Ukraine who had died of typhus came back in many forms. In Russia when a person died, family members laid the body out on boards in the *Sommastoav*, washed it, then swabbed it with alcohol to preserve it until the relatives from neighboring villages showed up for the funeral. On the day of the funeral of the young men, the men who came to take the bodies to the church noticed beads of perspiration on the forehead of one of the bodies. They listened for a heartbeat but could find none. They placed a feather before his nostrils, but it stayed motionless. They argued back and forth what to do. What if he were alive and they buried him? They tried to rouse him, but it was useless. Finally they buried him with the other one, convinced he was more dead than alive.

The thought made me burrow deep into the hollow spot in the mattress of our white iron bed. I imagined the young man waking in the darkness of his narrow resting place and hearing the dirt being thrown onto the lid. Plunk! Plunk! Another clod! Buried alive! His weak shouts had nowhere to go in the small dark space. I could feel his heart racing as fast as my own as the realization hit him. I nearly smothered myself in the tunnel I burrowed for myself in the covers smelling thickly of sleep and human bodies.

And then strangely, I forgot about death.

For many years, each morning before we ate Mother usually read us stories from a German Bible storybook. I liked the Old Testament stories better than the New Testament ones. I didn't like the ones about Jesus being betrayed by Peter and Judas, then whipped by some other men, and crucified on the cross. I tried hard not to listen when Mother got to that section, which was usually before Easter. As she read, I thought my own thoughts about the play we were practicing in school or whom I would ask to play jacks or knife with me at recess. When I looked at the pictures by myself, I usually skipped the whole section about the crucifixion of Christ. I knew what was on those pages—the thief twisted in pain, the sad women kneeling at the foot of the cross where Jesus hung, his crown of thorns puncturing his brow, and blood and water spurting from his side. That death didn't make sense.

Because Easter usually came before the roads to our own

German church across the river opened up in spring, we often attended services at the country Russian church. The Russians were friendly, generous people. On this special day they brought the symbols of the risen Christ with them to the service—big mushroom-shaped loaves of decorated *Paska* resting in baskets lined with colourfully embroidered napkins. When the people met on Easter Sunday, they greeted each other with special words—not "How are you?" or "Good morning" but with *"Christoss Voskress!"*(Christ is risen) to which the one being greeted responded, *"Voistinno Voskress"* (has risen indeed). Occasionally the women would exchange *pysanky,* eggs painted in batik fashion with multi-colored design, as a symbol of the new life.

I couldn't say the Russian words, but the happy chorus of deep and high voices in the small crowded entry, intermingled with human and sometimes barn smells, lifted the gloom of the previous days. I wished I could speak Russian so I could say the greeting to someone also. But always I was glad we could forget the terrible stories of Jesus on the cross for another year. When I was bothered about going to hell, about the world ending suddenly on December 31, I stood in the clothes closet where Mother's nightgown hung limp but secure and said, "Come into my heart, Lord Jesus; Come into my heart, Lord Jesus," and hoped he had by the time I was finished.

If my parents at times clung to Old Country customs, or at least enjoyed the *Paska* and colored Easter eggs, they found some of the new Canadian ones hard to accept. They had grown up in a country where the poor had actually begged door to door for food or starved. Therefore, they had no understanding of the custom of trick or treating at Halloween. The first years we children asked to go out with our friends, Mother's answer was a firm "no" and Dad's even firmer. Go out begging? Unthinkable! No child of his would beg for candy from his customers and friends. He would bring us some candy from the store. We accepted the unpleasant ultimatum for several years, though bug-eyed with jealousy when our school chums came to the classroom the next morning burdened with candy kisses, gum, and apples, while we cradled our little handful of suckers in one palm.

Every Halloween I came to Mother and Dad with the same

question. I wanted to dress up like a ghost and go trick or treating. It wasn't begging, not the Russian kind where a boy or girl in tatters walked from door to door with soulful eyes, pleading for *Khleb* to keep from starving. This was Canada, not Russia. This was fun, a kind of game. No one minded us children coming to their door for treats. Didn't mother give cookies to the children who came to our door? Didn't Dad give gum and suckers to the children who came to the store? Couldn't I go, just once?

One year after first talking it over with Dad in the little upstairs bedroom, Mother agreed to let me go with my friend Mona for "a little while." I found an old sheet, cut some holes in it for eyes, and joined Mona and the other girls under the corner lightpost, a paper shopping bag under my arm. At last. I had made the break. I was one of the gang hollering "Trick or treat" at door after door. Up one street, down another we went. We collected a weighty bag of candy, gum, apples and cookies. The butcher gave us each a wiener. The druggist handed out samples of toothpaste.

My "little while" was nearly used up when we knocked at a small white house, dimly lit, on a side street. I was shivering from the cold already and knew it was time to quit, but we wanted to finish off a few last houses before we went home to show off our loot to younger brothers and sisters. I banged on the door of this small house with new-found bravado—I was doing it like the others—a real Canadian—no longer an immigrant—and shouted "trick or treat!" We never actually soaped anyone's windows if the people didn't give us treats, but this was what the bigger children always said, so we said it too. "Trick or treat!" we shrieked as we waited for someone to answer our knock.

A greying, thinnish woman with deep lines in her forehead, dressed in a limp gingham housedress, opened the door to say brusquely, "There're no treats here tonight. A man's dying in here," and swung the door shut in my face.

My feet refused to move. Dying? How often had she said those words that evening? A man was dying behind that wooden door of the house with the low porch and the broken step we had walked up. Was it her husband? Was he lying on the bed or sitting? What did people do when they knew they were dying? Did they talk about milking stools and ropes or about Halloween treats? Mona and I turned and went home, never saying a word. I never went trick or treating again.

And then one spring, death moved close again in another way. Next door to us lived an elderly couple named Zbitnoffs. I never figured out what Mr. Zbitnoff did for a living, anymore than I ever figured out what many people in our small community did for a living who didn't go to work on Main Street in one of the businesses there like the grocery store, hardware, shoemaker shop, law office, drugstore, bank, cafe, or poolroom. I think he may have been a retired farmer. This congenial couple spoke too little English for me to understand their conversation with Mother, who spoke Russian well.

Mrs. Zbitnoff had a flourishing garden of vegetables with lots more cabbage, dill, and cucumbers than we grew. We children ate the raspberries from their canes that grew over our side of the wooden fence. Our houses, built close together, looked almost like twins. If we had had windows on their side, I could have touched their wall with a long reach through a window—at least using a short stick. The long run alongside the house on our side of the fence, closed off at one end by a rain barrel and a pile of wood, made a wonderful place to hide in the early evening when we children played Run my Good Sheep Run. Mrs. Zbitnoff often knew we were hiding there when we crouched next to the galvanized iron rain barrel as she worked in her garden, but she never told on us, only smiled her quiet gentle smile while her eyes got lost in the crinkles of her skin.

One day Mrs. Zbitnoff told Mother that her daughter Glycera was coming home from her missionary work in North Africa sick with tuberculosis, that terrible disease. TB meant first isolation, then surgery, then a slow death. The doctors in the East (meaning Toronto—always Toronto) had done the surgery, removing a lung and some ribs. Now she was coming home to die. Mrs. Zbitnoff's eyes glistened unusually bright as she talked to Mother, who later relayed the story to us.

Death was coming closer to me and our family. Next door. So close I could touch the trees, the rain barrel, the house, that would shelter it. My skin prickled at the thought.

We met Miss Z. several days later resting on her bed in the small front bedroom off the living room. She didn't mind us children staring at her and at the dozens of bottles and containers lined up on the small table—or even at her clothes lying on the patchwork quilt on her narrow bed. I examined everything carefully, especially trying to get a good look at Miss Z. This dark-haired, dark-eyed woman with the thinned out face and caved-in back and shoulder looked sick in her body, I decided, but her eyes looked like living and like a person who liked living. Which seemed strange. She joked and laughed and then spat into her paper sputum cups, which her mother burned almost immediately in the crackling flame of the kitchen stove. Sputum. I almost like the sound of the word. In Blaine Lake lots of men spat, and the little globs, sometimes stained a deep tobacco brown, looked disgusting as they withered on the sidewalk on Main Street beside the dog turds. I watched carefully where I put my feet when I walked in front of the poolroom. But hers wasn't spit. It was sputum and she burned it in the stove.

Signs of dying were all over her body, I agreed to myself, if you looked hard enough. Paper-thin skin stretched over her high cheekbones. Her legs and arms were really skinny—like chopsticks. She had a strange, slow way of moving her body when she wanted to get up. Her clothes hung loosely, like a hundred-pound flour sack trying to cover only fifty pounds of the stuff.

The signs of death were there. But they had missed her eyes. They sparkled, as if daring death to overtake her. But then, maybe, eyes were the last to die, and some day I would walk over to her house, and her eyes would look like the rest of her or like the eyes of the minister in the coffin several years ago. I decided to watch her eyes. Then I'd find out about death.

We girls visited her often in that small front bedroom of the nextdoor house. Miss Z. assured us there was no danger of catching TB. We should come as often as we liked. The sputum cup was an extra precaution because she had been a nurse.

As she lay in bed she told us stories about working in a hospital for natives in Africa, always with a chuckle or the desire to amuse. Another day she showed us how deeply corroded the underside of her wristwatch had become because of perspiring heavily in the tropics. We stood and marveled at the power of human sweat. In cold Saskatchewan we hardly knew what sweat was, even in summer. She told us about the last trip home on the ship and how the ship's officers had wanted to carry her off ship to shore on a stretcher. She had refused. "As long as I can walk, I will." Sometimes we heard stories about growing up on a farm in Blaine Lake in the early pioneer days and of nurse's training in the city when duty hours were long and strenuous. She brought a new dimension into our lives of a life of possibility beyond the borders of our small town. That her life had ended in TB didn't make the previous years less worthwhile.

Then one day the sparkling eyes looked sad. We were paging through Eaton's mail order catalogue together, ooh-ing and ah-ing over the gorgeous lace-trimmed wedding dresses with long trains and beaded veils cascading down the brides' back in billows of white airy foam. "I shouldn't be looking at wedding dresses," she commented to no one in particular. "I should be looking at funeral clothes." She spat the remark out like the men downtown spat their chewing tobacco.

So it was coming after all. And for a long time I didn't want to go next door anymore.

Shortly after Miss Z. returned to Blaine Lake, her father built a screened-in porch on the upstairs verandah. She wanted to sleep there in the open air, he told my mother. The doctors said it might help. He would humor her.

Each evening through the short summer and late into fall when the snow was already falling gently on the dried grass and the air was getting crisp so that my nose tingled when I walked to school, she had her mother wrap her snugly in wool comforters with hot water bottles and heated bedstones and roll her cot onto the porch for the night.

Early, very early in spring she started sleeping out there again. As I lay in my bed with Annie just a few feet from Miss Zbitnoff on the open porch, but separated now by only one wall and one screen, I thought about her. Glycera. A different name. Not like my plain one. A romantic name. I let it roll off my tongue. There she was alone on that verandah—always the last to see the fireflies flitting in the night air, the first to check out the Big Dipper and to see the brilliant northern lights scramble through the heavens to find the best place to glimmer. In spring she was the first to hear the rain dripping from the eaves, the first to smell the fresh breezes, the first to see the sun rising in the East, the first to hear the meadowlark greet the day. She was dying close to life, I decided. A rather nice way to go.

Glycera wore mules. I had seen the word in a storybook, so I knew what they were. Black satin ones, and a cotton dress that buttoned down the front to accommodate her weakened shoulder and arm muscles where the lung and bones had been cut out. As the months wore on, occasionally she walked to our house in her mules and cotton dress, entering through the kitchen door, sometimes going as far as the dining room to visit with Mother and drink a cup of tea. I decided she always carried her sputum cup with her, so that if death overtook her at an unguarded moment, she could cough its essence into the paper container and give it to someone to burn. I watched carefully for the day to come—and yet once again the eyes sparkled.

One Saturday Mother sent me to Zbitnoffs with some freshly baked crumbcake. I carried the plate carefully so as not to lose any of the buttery-crisp crumbs. Miss Zbitnoff was lying on her bed, dressed in a flowered navy silk dress—one without buttons marching down the front. The mules had been exchanged for solid black oxfords—low and comfortable. A new brown coat with a wolf-fur collar lay on her suitcases beside her. I looked so hard, I stumbled into the doorway and almost lost the cake.

She took the plate from me with a wide grin. Her mother smiled her usual crinkly smile, her dark eyes happy. Then Glycera reached down. Her eyes hugged me first. She stretched her arms out and drew me close. My hands felt the bones stick out and the hollow places gape as my arms closed around her cut-up body.

"I'm going to Toronto to visit some friends—say thanks to your mother for the cake," she whispered. "I'll see you in the fall. You helped me get well by visiting me."

I ran out the door and back home, not stopping to miss the cracks in the sidewalk as I usually did. My heart was singing. Glycera wasn't dying. She was going to live. She had stared into the darkness each night with those dark brown eyes and refused to let the darkness fill them. She had looked out, beyond the verandah screens and seen life. I had looked into the darkness of the hole at the church graveyard that day when the woman was buried and seen death—and been afraid.

Life was a gift, not a hostile force that tried to kill us off, one by one. Grandmother Janzen in Russia had died lying on her thin mattress. She had struggled for life and to stay with those who had to milk the cows, but death had come. Yet there was a rhythm to life that included both the limits of human finitude to suffer and the potential of the human spirit to strike back. Glycera had looked up night after night and found strength to die, and now she was going to live.

"Christoss Voskress," I shouted as I ran to tell Mother the good news. My plate was empty, yet Glycera had just given me a whole mountain of colored Easter eggs. And Easter was still two weeks away. I would listen to the Easter story this year. I understood.

"Voistinno Voskress! Voistinno Voskress!" shrilled a meadowlark on a fencepost.

David Waltner-Toews

The End Times

The old sow, she'd have to go.

Prom pulled at the thin wisps of white hair puffing irregularly out from the sides of his bald head like the white matter out of a bullrush. I'm going to seed, he thought, so old am I. That old sow, can't even remember when I got her.

"Didn't I get her for preaching at the Klopfen Church?" he asked out loud. "Vic Reimer, he's a pig man."

Rachel, her thick black hair greying at the edges, stood at the counter pinching out the balls of dough for zwieback. She was, by now, becoming used to being admitted to Prom's thoughts part way through. It took her a few moments to make the connection from Reimer to the appropriate church to the 'her' in question: the old sow of course. Hadn't had a litter for a year.

"Yes," she sighed. "It was those folks. I think they were trying to tell you in as subtle a way as they are capable of what they thought of your preaching."

"Well I think I better take her over to Thiessen's and get some ham out of her. No use feeding her through another winter."

Rachel looked out the kitchen window. Large flakes of snow were settling softly from the grey sky, as if the clouds were feather-filled quilts that had come undone. "Today?" she asked, simply.

Prom set his teacup down on the white wooden kitchen table. "For every thing there is a season, and winter is the season for butchering."

"There's to be a storm."

"Snow, my lovely, Rose of Sharon, snow is nothing but spring run-off before it's run off. It's children before they leave home." He paused, meditatively, standing beside the table. "You have to work twice as hard to do half as much when it snows, shovelling to the barn, lighting a woodfire under the old truck to warm up the engine, chopping the ice in the water trough, but it's a pure kind of work, warms the aching soul."

Rachel turned to face him, then threw her flour whitened arms around her frail-looking gentleman, this lovable little prophet who had pulled her, single-handedly, out of the slough of her post-divorce despond.

"You really miss those kids, don't you."

"We should phone, tomorrow, to Winnipeg. I think Abe was to be visiting Harry and Sarah." He kissed her on the cheek, lightly, then, laughing, in the old comradely Russian style. "But for today, we have sufficient evils to keep our minds distracted. Today's Thiessen's once-a-week day for butchering. He's got the inspector there and everything."

She returned to her buns. "Think you can handle old Thiessen and his sufficient evils?"

Prom was bending over by the door, pulling on his galoshes. He reached for his parka and his Russian hat with the fur ear flaps. "Well I've heard about his uncle the Menshevik who was thrown down the well by the Bolsheviks right in front of his family often enough that I think I can fill in any details he misses."

Rachel talked down to her dough. "I hear lately he's been going on about our German heritage, how the war spoiled it for people. It's the Jews, he says, first they crucify Christ and now they spoil the German culture."

Prom opened the door. "Ja, well, maybe the old sow will keep him busy today, a sacrifice to bear all the bitterness. I'll be back in a couple of hours." As he stepped into the yard, he realized that the snow was indeed coming down in thick white blankets, but as with so many other things in his life he thought, once committed, follow through. Rachel watched from the kitchen window, her husband of seven years, seven good years, disappear and reappear as swirls of snow passed between the house and the barn. For one moment, she almost thought he'd been assumed into heaven by the pure cold hand of God, but then he reappeared at the barn door. And the seven good years were followed by seven lean years, she thought, and immediately put the thought out of her mind. God had brought Prom all the way from Russia to Saskatchewan. He would not pluck up his little prophet when he was most needed. God had brought Rachel even further, from the higher realms of Winnipeg, where Mennonites had made it and were filling their newly built barns, preparing to eat and drink and defend their consumption with guns—God had brought Rachel from that gilded pedestal to a simplicity of faith where every zwieback was a sign of grace.

Prom started up the truck in the central walkway of the barn, between the gutters, and backed it up to the pigpen at one end. "No pigs in the dairy barn," said the inspector. Where had he been all his life, thought Prom, that he should make such foolish rules. Yet every time the inspector came he said the same thing. And Prom's response, also, would be the same.

"You're going to persecute me? A poor Mennonite farmer? How many cows do I have? Ten. Count them. And how many pigs? One sow. I'm supposed to build a separate building for each? Listen, in Russia we all lived together, pigs, cows and people too."

The inspector would throw up his hands in despair. "One of these times I'll have to report you. Next time for sure. What happens if my inspector checks around?"

"Don't worry," Prom would say, "I'll explain. It's part of my religion, explaining." Well there would be no more explanations necessary. Wouldn't he be surprised next time. No pigs in the cow barn. A barn just like the English, unilingual. Prom pulled the wooden ramp out the back of the truck and opened the gate of the pen. "Come on Tina, time enough for sleep going in the bye and bye." He poked at the thin, old sow with the tip of his boot. She grunted. He gave her a good kick and she stood up. "Mittagschlaf is over," said Prom. "Move thy buttocks." She grunted and complained at every step. By the time he had pushed and cajoled and bribed her with barley into the back of the truck he was out of breath.

When he pulled open the big barn door to drive the truck out he was just about blown over by the gusts of snow. "Some spring run-off," he muttered. "Going to be seeding in the muck this year." He drove the truck out, jumped out and pulled the barndoor shut, then turned on the windshield wipers full speed and roared out into the blinding whiteness.

It was only five miles straight down the road to Thiessen's. At one time, Fred Thiessen's slaughterhouse had been a thriving concern. From killing a few pigs and cows for neighbours in a converted machine shed, Fred had expanded, with the help from the Mennonite Credit Union, into a large brick building. He had bought all the right equipment—scalding tank and de-hairing machine for pigs, overhead rails into a walk-in cooler, drains in all the right places to please the government inspectors. He was butchering five days a week and selling genuine Mennonite farmerswurst as far away as Saskatoon. And then, one day, he just seemed to give up. Some say it was because he had fathered five girls, all of whom married nice Mennonite boys who had farms of their own to attend to. He himself blamed it on government policy and the price of meat, both of which were part of larger, more sinister, plots. Old Fred, the heavyset, jolly butcher with short-cropped white hair topping a red wrinkled face, became suddenly morose and bitter.

In the heyday of his business, one of the girls had answered the phone and taken orders. His wife would have nothing to do with that squealing, bloody business, and Fred himself never trusted telephones. Even then, in the old days, he was suspicious. Now that the girls were gone, no one answered the phone in the little butcher shop office. Fred kept the door to the office locked. He suspected that the government had planted a listening device in his telephone, just to keep tabs on him. A person couldn't answer it and if you tried to unplug it or cancel the telephone service, well, who knew what terrible fate might befall you? Now only if you knew Fred and could contact him through church or by dropping into his place could you get some butchering done. Business was down to only one day a week.

In between, the old man would sit on an upended wooden crate in his slaughterhouse, sharpening his knives, listening to religious radio broadcasts from the United States. It was from one of these broadcasts that he had learned of the Jewish-Communist-Catholic conspiracy, a devilish scheme to rule the world. It was all so clear to him now, it almost made him laugh and cry at the same time. If only you would listen to him, he would explain it to you. If he was butchering your pig, you listened.

The inspector, a young boy barely thirty, paced around in his white coat, black-rimmed safety glasses, white hard hat and large black rubber boots. He tested the scald water with his finger, kicked at the drains, stuck his knife here and there into hung carcasses. Usually old Thiessen and whoever else was around just ignored the boy, as they called him. Only if he pressed his face close to the meat, slicing carefully a lump behind the ear or the blood red lumps along the guts, did the other men pause. It seemed to them that the boy was searching for a written message. "Okay," he would say after he had read it, or "Just discard the head." Then there would be a sigh of relief. Sometimes, rarely, he would gravely stand back from the carcass and, in the manner of a judge, pronounce it condemned. Thiessen would invariably argue, firstly about the quality of the meat, what would such a bursch know about meat and, secondly, in recent years anyway, he would bring up the Jewish conspiracy. The inspector, a United Church boy from Ontario, would shrug his shoulders and stick a condemned tag on the carcass.

"If you don't like it call Saskatoon and have my supervisor come out."

Thiessen would wave his knife around, cursing in Low German. How could he explain to such an imbecile his fear of the telephone? What did he know about the Communists anyway? Muttering to himself, Fred would turn to other business.

The storm thinned and lifted as Prom drove toward the Thiessens. When he pulled into the slaughter-house yard and backed his pickup to the ramp, only a few flakes were settling through the still air. The inspector's old brown Chevrolet, with chains on the rear tires for traction, was pulled up near the front door, as was another truck that Prom didn't recognize.

As he opened the door the warm, steamy, fleshy air of the butchering room pushed him in the face like a wet pillow. The inspector was unbuttoning his white coat and Fred was hanging some metal hooks on the wall in the corner.

"Got time for one more?"

The inspector frowned and looked at his watch. It was already four in the afternoon. The sun would soon be gone, and on these roads, in this weather. . .

"What's it like out there?"

Prom swung the door open and gestured with his hand. "Clear as a piglet's ear."

"Cow or pig?"

"One old sow."

"If it's okay with the old man I guess it's okay with me."

Thiessen put a hand on one hip. "For Koslowski, I've got time. He's got good strong ears, that man. Makes it worth butchering. Bring her in the back. The old sow, ja? Come on, I help you."

Prom came in, pushed the door shut behind him, and the two men walked across to the back door. The inspector attempted to protest.

"You're not supposed to be in here in street clothes."

The men ignored him, went through the rear door and down a walkway which, in better times, had been squealing and bawling full of beasts, and opened a second door. Outside was the ramp and Prom's truck. They drove the old sow back up the walkway, turned up a concrete ramp at the far end of the pens, and through another door which led back into the butchering room, opening there to a rail-enclosed platform. The whole process took about twenty minutes since the sow, sensing something out of the ordinary, kept turning around and attempting to make a fast run between her two pursuers. They were red in the face and perspiring as they re-entered the butchering room.

Only then did Prom notice a wizened, gnome of a man with a white stubbly beard and a pail in his hand sitting on a box in one of the corners. In keeping with regulations, he had on an off-white, torn, blood-stained butcher's coat pulled over his "street" parka. He smiled at Prom, holding up his pail. "I make blood sausage," he said. He grinned, revealing three upper and two lower teeth in an otherwise empty red mouth.

"Nicky P., how are you keeping?" Prom shouted. The Ukrainian grandfather was known to non-Ukrainians only as Nicky P. He was very deaf. If you asked about his last name, he shrugged. "You wouldn't understand it, too long for English." Prom, recognizing the old country immigrant syndrome, was happy to leave well enough alone. He and Nicky P. got along fine and, as Prom removed his parka, hung it on a hook near the door, and picked up a butcher's coat which had been dragged through blood and filth for many years without laundering,

Nicky squawked out a long song about the woes of children who had lost the old art of sausage making and grand-children who moved to Edmonton and didn't even speak God's tongue anymore.

"They are just making good in a new country," said Prom, gingerly pushing the filthy buttons through the appropriate holes.

"Got to be a yid or a commie to make good here," broke in Thiessen. The butcher had loaded his rifle and was standing near the sow, aiming at her head from a distance of about twelve inches. Prom thought of his own children, Sarah a veterinarian, married to a Mennonite medical doctor and Abe, well, who knows what, maybe a preacher yet, but no failure in any case. He thought of Fred Thiessen's five daughters, all of whom were well settled on prosperous farms. He was about to say something when the butcher blurted out, "Take this you old commie Pope!" and fired his rifle. The blast ricocheted loudly around the cement-walled room, startling Prom; even Nicky was brought to his feet.

Nicky P., however, did not rise out of fright. He was after blood. After the pig was shot, regulations stipulated that her throat had to be slit immediately, so that the body would bleed out properly. Tina jumped just as she was shot, startled perhaps by Thiessen's accusation. She managed to throw herself over the low railing between herself and the scalding tank, sending a wave of hot, bloody water across the floor. Thiessen sputtered, wiped his face, and grabbed some iron hooks off the wall. "Koslowski, you want this meat you help me pull her out so we can bleed her." Prom took a hook and the two men dragged the thrashing half-dead beast to the edge of the tank and slung her over the side, head down. Thiessen slit her throat with one quick movement of his arm and the blood spurted out on to his apron. The inspector was standing to one side, knife in hand, a look of dismay and resignation on his face.

Nicky P. scurried out with his pail, chasing the scattering spurts of blood as the sow kicked out her dying spasms, catching the precious liquid, as well as a few chunks of flying manure shed by her feet, in his pail. Prom wiped his brow with the back of his arm, smiled, and looked over to where the inspector stood, whetting his knife on a hand stone.

"Is this regulation?"

The young man pushed his hard hat back up on his head with his wrist, then continued working at his knife.

"I didn't see a thing," he muttered. As the blood-spattered gnome returned with his half-filled pail, face beaming, the inspector shouted at him, "You going to sell that stuff?"

Nicky P. stared at him for a moment, then, as if suddenly understanding, shouted back. "You want some good blood sausage? I make you some."

The inspector shook his head and waved for the man to go. "He won't sell it. It's no business of mine if he poisons himself."

Prom chuckled at the irony of this boy worrying about a man three times his age eating something that might shorten his life, something he'd probably eaten for eighty years.

When the blood quit coming, Thiessen slid the sow's body back into the scalding tank, pushed her under with the tip of his knife and gently rolled her body. Then, with one deft motion he swung her up and out the side of the tank into the de-hairing machine, a kind of horizontal egg-beater which banged and bounced the body around, scraping off the loosened hair. When most of the hair was off, the butcher turned off the machine, returning the room into a stunned silence. He stuck his knife into the tendons behind each rear leg, poked through a couple of iron hooks, fastened them to chains, and hoisted the body up by an overhead pulley. Only then, as he scraped the remaining hair off from around the legs and head with the side of his knife, did he begin to talk.

"For fifty years I voted Liberal," he announced, never taking his eyes off the glistening pork flesh before him. "They let us into this country, a man should be grateful, I thought. But now that's all over." He paused, evaluating the carcass and the work remaining. "Trudeau, he's nothing but a communist. There was even a picture in the paper, him shaking hands with Brezhnev and the next day, you know? He goes to visit the Pope. I ask you, what more evidence do people want. Trudeau wants to go to the United Nations. You know why? You know about the rule of the antichrist? You know how Catholics touch their foreheads with holy water? The mark of the Beast."

He was scraping down the snout now, hard, working into all the little corners.

"And the Jews too. They own the banks. Most people don't know. They finance Russia. How else could that hell-hole stay afloat? Marx was a Jew. Freud was a Jew. Catholics and Jews, they keep the Communists going."

He stood back and appraised the clean, glistening body, picked up a hose, turned on the nozzle and hosed her down, top to bottom. Then he stepped up to the belly and with one clean motion slit her through, crotch to sternum. In another motion he had tied off the rectum, cut and pulled the warm, sausage-coloured intestines down. He grasped another part of the watery snakes, tied, slit and then heaved the whole greyish brownish reddish mass of flesh into a cart.

"Go to it boy," he grunted, waving his knife at the inspector. The inspector was already bent over the cart, carefully slicing various lumps.

Fred Thiessen wiped his knife on a whetstone hanging from his belt. "Ja Prom, we're the last ones. This is the end times. It's down to us against them, the whores."

"And who are the *we* brauda Thiessen, the ones without sin, throwing the stones. Who are we?" Prom spoke quietly.

Thiessen, startled, stopped and looked to where Prom was standing, hands in his pockets.

"What did you say?"

"You heard me."

The butcher attacked the rib cage with a large pair of cutters, cutting down the sternum. Then he reached in and pulled out the heart and lungs.

Prom hesitated. He was never sure what to say in situations like this, to people like this. With so much bitterness and hatred, how, or where could healing start. Where was the window, however tiny, for the light of grace to enter? The old butcher, red faced, sweating, dripping with blood, stood there for a moment, heart and lungs in one hand, knife in the other.

"Koslowski, you know I have done everything right. I have forgiven seventy times seven. I have turned the other cheek. Now look, what do I have. Has the Lord blessed? Blessed the government with my money, that's all." He pointed his knife at Prom. "I'm not throwing stones. I'm just telling it as it is." He dropped the heart and lungs into the inspector's cart, stuck his knife into his belt, and swung down into place a chain-saw hanging by a rope from the ceiling. He pulled it to start and the room crashed with the rattle of its gunfire. The saw whined and smoked as it chewed its way down through the middle of the backbone. Thiessen turned off the saw and swung it away. "It's all yours, boy." He waved towards the inspector, who had been very carefully threading the intestines between his thumb and forefinger. Thiessen walked over to Prom, wiping his hands on his coat.

"The cut with the saw should be the first cut, not the last. If I was working with wood." He heaved out a loud, grunting sigh and sat on the edge of a barrel filled with brine. "I always wanted to be a carpenter, like my father, to make good furniture from wood."

Prom put his hand on the butcher's shoulder. "How long have you been here now?"

"Nineteen twenty-six. I was sixteen. Land of opportunity said the CPR, said everybody. I guess so." He pulled out his knife and began slowly whetting it. "My father had a big shop, lathes, saws of all kinds, the finest woods. It was supposed to be mine." He surveyed the two carcass halves. The inspector was crouched down, poking at the nodes behind the pig's ear. "Saskatchewan's okay, but it's not Molotschna in 1900. Nobody appreciates a good commode here." He shook his head.

The inspector was shaking his head. "I'm going to have to condemn this carcass. She's got abscesses all through her. No wonder she didn't have a litter. Look at this uterus will you?" He seemed defensive, eager to point out all the faults of the carcass, expecting, at any moment, to be verbally abused. But Thiessen paid him no attention and Prom only nodded vaguely in his direction.

"Ja, Prom, the Bolsheviks might as well come and take this too. I don't want it."

Prom had been wanting to say something in a pastoral way, such as, "If these are the end times, how then ought we to live?" or "What credit is it to love our friends only, the Bolsheviks do as much," but the opportunities to say something slipped past him and suddenly, inexplicably, all he could think of was Nettie, his first wife, when the twins were born. A time of life and a time of death. The war was over. Stalin was not dead. It was time, finally, to leave Russia and start over, if not for their own sakes, at least for the child in Nettie's belly. They had clambered over high rocky passes south of Samarkand, where the snow had swirled around them, and had come down into a wet, fog-ridden, narrow, stone-filled valley in the border area near Kashmir.

Miraculously, they stumbled upon a tiny village—three stone and mud huts crouched near a stream—housing taciturn, morose Mennonite families. These were the last remnants of a group that, seventy-five years earlier, had followed Claasz Epp, Mennonite "saviour-prophet," to the ends of the earth to meet their Maker on his triumphant return. Those, too, had been end times.

There, in a straw bed, in the shed rife with heavy odours of cattle and horses, Nettie laboured to deliver Abraham and Sarah. And there, in the hours that followed, her full round face and plump Germanic body grew quiet, and soft and pale as unbaked dough, then cold as hung *Kalbfleisch*. End times and beginning times.

With the babies tucked under his parka, and a supply of warm goat's milk from the village, Prom had packed a horse through the passes, through the Kashmiri war zone to Sprinigar. There, at last, stunned, weary and filled with a great sadness, he had rented a houseboat and a nursemaid for the babies. In the stillness of the grey-blue mist over the lake and the sharpness of the mountain peaks hovering above, slowly, quietly, his soul was healed.

His hand tightened on Fred Thiessen's shoulder. "Life is a series of beginnings, that's all. The endings we know nothing of. We only know how the story recedes into the darkness." He paused. "If these are end times, they are also times for beginning."

Fred Thiessen stood up and slapped Prom firmly on the back. "I only know I am weary of all this and I want it to end. See?" He pointed to the carcass with the condemned tag poked into its hide. "All that work and no ham after all. Just dog food. Better these days to be a dog."

The inspector pulled open the door and stepped outside to his car. As the door opened, a blanket of snow pushed its way in and sifted across the floor, where it melted and mixed with the blood and dung. Fred Thiessen picked up his hose and began washing down the floor. Prom pulled off his butcher's coat and pulled on his parka. He wanted to say something more to the butcher, but Thiessen had reached over and turned up his radio, parked on a small shelf against the wall. "Welcome to the Glory Be Hour of America," announced a cheery male voice over a background of harmonious female singing, "the voice of the end times." The butcher concentrated on pushing a lump of congealed blood and manure toward the drain with a jet of water.

Prom opened the door and stepped out into the biting wind. He was still immersed in thoughts about Nettie, and his life before this life in Canada, and Abe and Sarah, and now Rachel, waiting for him in the warm kitchen at home. He started the truck and pulled out of the laneway, barely aware of his physical actions. It seemed, in the thick white of this dusk, as if the world were luminescent, and if only he could think hard enough, everything would suddenly become clear. Somewhere, just beyond his grasp, in these glorious ever-changing whorls of cold light pluming up before his headlights, in the blinding, numbing blizzard out there, lay the pure meaning of his life's patterns, of Fred Thiessen's life, of all lives.

The enveloping whiteness totally obliterated any visible vestige of road, so Prom drove by the feel of the ground under the truck, not exactly hind-sight, but, as it were, now-sight. In any case, the only sight available. Even after he realized that he had driven into the deceptive, snow-filled ditch, and that the truck was spinning its wheels deeper and deeper into the soft gulf, he turned off the motor and sat quietly for several minutes listening to the silky snow-voiced wind hiss past the windows. Then he climbed out and began the long, cold walk home.

Sandra Birdsell

Judgement

It was early morning when Mr. Thiessen died, and wreaths of mist still hovered above the river in pockets, trapped by the shadows of overhanging willow branches. His corpse lay in the porch of a small white cottage. The cottage sat on the edge of a town beside a road that led over a hill and down the other side of it and came to an end in the river.

The expression frozen into the dead man's face was one of determination. His nostrils were packed with wads of cotton, making his nose his salient feature. When he'd been alive, his predominating feature had been his eyes, blue as snow when the sun has just dipped into the winter horizon. He always seemed to be looking beyond into something that was invisible to others. Even at the hotel in town, where he once walked late at night to sweep rubble from the parlour floor, his blue eyes contemplated a scene beyond the smoke-filled parlour, something amusing to make him stop sweeping and chuckle suddenly, or something sombre and dark which he would take to the cottage with him to think about while he puttered in his flower garden. But his pale blue eyes no longer looked into the ridiculous or the profane. They were opened, staring up at the rafters which were strung with bundles of dried basil and sage leaves and spirals of flypaper thickly coated with the husks of insects.

Outside the cottage, an old woman sat on a bench and leaned against the narrow slats of the porch. The back of her head was almost level with his where he lay inside on the couch beneath the screened windows. She looked like a lizard sunning itself in the early morning on a moss-covered rock. She didn't wear her dentures and so her caved-in mouth made her nose jut forward from her face and her chin recede into her neck. She sat shapeless and colourless with her sun-spotted hands idle in her lap. The narrow slats of the porch wall pressed into the woman's fleshy back but she didn't notice. She was listening to the wind passing through the screens in the windows above her kerchiefed head. She thought that the sound of it was not a hopeless sound. It was the same sound as the river rushing along its course to its irrevocable end in a larger body of water. The wind had come early that morning, before the sun, and had drowned out the fluttering sound of her husband's breath struggling to free itself of the liquids in his lungs. She blinked rapidly and folded one pudgy, spotty hand over top the other.

She scratched at her ankle with her slippered foot. The town was so still that she could hear the humming of electricity in the wires along the road and the sound of blood rushing in her veins. Birds cried as they circled the air above the river. Get up, she told herself. Put on your workboots and go into the back garden and pull the potatoes. All summer she had plucked beetles from the leaves and squashed them between her fingers. She had banked the plants with mounds of black dirt. Now is the time to pull the potatoes, she thought and then she caught herself. What am I doing? My husband is dead and I think of potatoes. But the idea of work to be done was restful. Instead of jumping up and running to the potting shed to take the bushel baskets down from the wall, she would rest. There was still time to sit. The town hadn't begun to stir and the doctor had yet to come and administer the six o'clock injection of morphine. She had this time of grace before she needed to accept the finality of her husband's stiffening blue-white features.

She bent down and picked at a loose thread on her plaid slipper and watched with fascination as the chain stitching unravelled. She looked about for a place to put the unravelled thread. She gathered it between her fingers and rolled it into a ball. She leaned back against the porch and through the slits of her half-closed eyes, she watched the sun rise. It was a fire-ball that swept from north to south above the trees that lined the river bank below. Back and forth it wheeled. She sighed and ran her tongue across her shrunken gums to erase a sour taste that nestled there like the orange sprinkles of beetles' eggs on the underside of a potato leaf. If only Eve hadn't sinned, she thought. Then there would have been no beetles to squash between her fingers or weeds to be hacked away. Because of Eve, each time her monthly bleeding had stopped and she'd been pregnant, she'd faced that nine months with dread, longing for a way around the curse. But there was no path around the pain of childbirth. You had to go through it before you could experience relief. It was all part of the curse, she told herself, beetles attaching themselves to her potatoes, childbirth and the silence in the porch.

She stared unblinking at the fireball above the trees and rolled the thread between her thick fingers until it was moist. Then she let it drop to the ground. She bent over, searched the other slipper for a loose thread, found one and pulled. What was worse for her now, she wondered? Loose threads or twenty-eight jars of watermelon pickles?

She saw them suddenly, the jars lined up on the shelves in the cellar, side by side, shining with the inner glow of the pale pink fruit, jewel-like and perfect. Of all the times he had to choose to die, it would be this time when the cellar was full of preserves. Yesterday he'd asked her for a dill pickle and she'd refused because they weren't sour enough. What did it matter whether the pickles were sour enough or not? What did it matter? Watermelon pickles or not watermelon pickles? What does anything matter now, she asked, but felt saddened by the look of her slippers. The tongues had been loosened when she'd pulled at the threads. They made things too cheaply. She forced her plucking hands to lie still in her lap. What am I to do now? she asked herself. What am I going to do with twenty-eight jars of watermelon pickles? She recited them:

> two dozen peaches in heavy syrup
> three dozen quarts crabs
> two and a half pints pears
> fourteen jars plum jam with wax seals, seven with tops
> one dozen two-quart sealers dills

And I couldn't even give him one.

The fireball climbed higher in the sky. The sound of the wind changed. It carried within it another sound. It was the sound of dried corn stalks when her skirts brushed against them.

It was the sound of a man's hoarse whisper, urgent.

"Anna."

"Yes, what is it?" she asked. She had always promised herself that if an angel should speak, she would say, here am I, Lord.

"Water. Please. I want a drink."

She rose from the bench slowly. She climbed the three stairs. She entered the porch and passed by the bed of the dead man without looking at him. She went over to the treadle sewing machine where there was a tumbler and a jug of water. She tried to lift the jug. Her hands were two spotted stones dangling uselessly from the ends of her arms. She knew her husband was dead. She'd pulled the plaid blanket up around his chin and felt the unyielding heaviness of his cold arms when she'd placed them beneath the blanket. Could it be grief that caused her to hear voices where there should be none?

"I can't lift the jug. You don't really need water, do you?" Dried leaves stirred on the windowsill where his potted plants were lined, now just brown stalks in hard earth, neglected because of his illness. It was as though her words had lifted the leaves into motion.

"Ahh," his voice was expelled slowly. "Why would I ask you for water if I didn't need it? I'm so very hot."

The snake of fear uncoiled in her chest. Hot. He was hot? "Where are you?" she asked. She had warned him and warned him. All through the long night she had read the Bible, first the Psalms and then the New Testament, and had come to the parable of Lazarus and the rich man, when the sun first sat upon the trees. Send Lazarus to touch the tip of my tongue, she had read. The flames torment me. For those who didn't believe in a real hell, this was the place they should look, she was going to tell him and then noticed the absence of his rattling breath. She'd set the Bible aside, gotten up swiftly and knelt beside him and listened. His nose had stopped bleeding and the cotton wads in his nostrils were stiff with dried blood.

All night long he'd plucked at the cotton with his nicotine fingers and his sin had glared in the early morning light as she knelt beside his cooling body. His stained fingers were evidence of his sin, his habit of slipping into the potting shed every hour to roll a cigarette. The indelible yellow stains were proof of his imperfection. Where are you, God had asked Adam and Adam had answered, I hid because I was afraid; and that was what he'd done too, shutting himself away inside the potting shed to smoke his cigarettes, as though God couldn't see. She'd knelt and prayed that God could overlook this one thing, but she doubted that He would. She saw her husband's nosebleeds, his coughing and spitting of blood as judgement of guilt. She'd warned him every single day for sixty-two years that this could happen.

"Where I am is not your concern," he said.

"Just so. Don't blame me if you're hot. What more could I do? I bathed you every hour. Now tell me, what else before I go? The potatoes are ready for pulling."

He looked past her with his steady contemplative blue gaze. He looked into each far corner of the porch and then up at the dangling spirals of flypaper. "What else? A smoke. Mother, make me a cigarette."

She was beyond anger. There was an immense sadness flooding into every part of her large body. "The body is the temple of the Holy Spirit. You would defile it with nicotine, even now?"

He sighed. He closed his eyes. His mouth was cracked from his fever. He ran his tongue across his chapped lips. She wondered if she should dip a hanky into the jug and moisten his lips for him and then she remembered that he was dead and she was standing there talking to a dead man and he was answering her, which was as far as she was willing to go, because he was not an angel.

"I never told you this," he said after a short time.

She stopped breathing.

"Never mind. It doesn't really matter."

"What? What?"

"It's nothing. I was going to say something about the way you look. But it doesn't matter."

She looked down at herself. There was nothing wrong with her appearance. She felt comfortable in the shapeless dress. She dressed in the manner fitting for an older Christian woman. Nothing between mid-calf and the neck was revealed. She even wore heavy cotton stockings during the summer.

He was casting stones at her to draw attention away from

his own wrong-doing. "I'm running here and I'm running there," she said. "You make yourself sick, I have the running around. I wonder what you would look like if you followed me through the day? And what else? I stayed up and prayed for you all night. The girls come every day and I do the cooking. I haven't had time to fix my hair for three days and so I wear the scarf."

"I didn't mean that."

"What then?"

"It doesn't matter."

"Say it."

"I meant that—oh, I don't know if after sixty years it helps to say anything about it, but—you're too fat."

"I?"

He nodded his silver head.

She slammed the porch behind her. Her slippers smacked loudly against the stairs. She suddenly hated the colour green. He'd painted the bench she'd sat on and the platform that held the rain barrel on the south corner of the house facing the potting shed and the three steps leading into the porch, the same vivid green as the fruit trees. He had never asked her, what do you think of green? Do you think green would be a fair colour? He'd never asked her whether she thought fruit trees across the back of the garden were a good thing. The first thing she would do would be to walk into town to the hardware store and buy a can of paint. Grey or brown, or something the colour of a potato beetle. And who would have to bring in his glad bulbs for winter storage? She would. Even though her vegetable garden had been placed in the back field farthest from the rain barrel and beneath the fruit trees (wood ticks in spring and three part rows of corn lost to the shade of the fruit trees) and even though his flowers had gradually taken over half of the vegetable garden, she'd never complained. A continual dropping on a very rainy day and a contentious woman were alike, the Bible said, and that was not her sin, being quarrelsome. Not that it would have helped to complain. Complaining would have just sent him into his faraway expression more often or into the potting shed. She would bring his glad bulbs in and she would also bring in the potatoes.

She sat back down on the bench and let her hands fall into

her lap. She half closed her eyes once again, lulled by the sound of the wind in the screens. Even so, she told herself. Watermelon pickles or not watermelon pickles, what does it matter? Once more she viewed the sun through half-closed eyes. It became a fireball that jiggled and darted off to the right. She felt the warmth of it in her broad cheeks. It filled up all of her eyes. If she could turn her head right around, the fireball would make a full circle around her. She turned her head as far as it would go. The fireball followed. She turned her head the other way and heard the clatter of clay pots knocking against each other in the potting shed.

"And listen here, Father," she said. "And not only that. I told you and told you it wasn't a good thing to feed that cat. It's back here again. It's knocking over your plants. And who's going to have to clean up that mess, I wonder?" Hah, let the cat reach above the door where he hid his papers and the tin of tobacco and let the cat form a cigarette for him. That was what tobacco was good for. It was good for animals only. Poison for stray cats. She searched about in her dress pocket and found a peppermint candy. She rolled it about her mouth. She felt some of the tension begin to leave her body as its sweetness was released and slid down the back of her throat.

"Mother. Oh Mother. Are you still there?"

"I am here."

"Make me a cigarette, Mother. Just this once."

"Never. I won't be a part of you willfully harming your body."

"But you do it yourself."

She withdrew the diminished peppermint from her mouth and examined it closely. "That's foolishness," she said and put the candy back into her mouth. "God gave us food. If we didn't eat, we'd die."

"You refuse to make me a cigarette?"

"I refuse." She wouldn't have that on her conscience. She'd never made it easy for him. She hadn't permitted him to smoke his weed in the house. She was positive that he had her to thank for his eighty-one years. I have fought the fight, she told herself, I have won the race.

"In this case, I must obey God rather than man," she said and smiled gently, a toothless innocent smile. She waited for him to reply but heard instead the sound of a car moving slowly up the road. Six o'clock already. The fireball danced crazily. She arranged her skirt to cover her knees. The doctor's car entered the lane slowly and came to a halt. He got out of the car and walked across the yard and stood in front of her.

"Look," she said, and pointed to her feet. "My slippers are coming apart. They make everything too cheaply in this country."

"Nothing lasts forever," the doctor said. "Tell me, did Mr. Thiessen have a good night?"

"A good night, yes."

He was short and squat, wide enough to block out her view of the sun. She didn't like this man because even though she had never seen him smoke a cigarette, or smelled tobacco on his clothing, she suspected that he did smoke because he'd never reprimanded her husband for smoking or advised him to stop.

"And how about you?" he asked. "How did it go yesterday? Did your daughters come over and help out?"

"They come over every day," she said. "It's a little extra work cooking meals for them. But I don't mind."

"It's unfortunate at a time like this, but we do have to eat, don't we?"

"That's what I told him. God intended that we should eat."

He shifted his black bag from one hand to the other. "Some more than others." Then he set the bag down on the bench beside her, opened it and took out the stethoscope. "I may as well have a look at you too, while I'm here."

"There's nothing the matter with me."

"Give me your arm, please."

She held up her arm. He felt for her pulse. He frowned. He placed the stethoscope against the pulse in the crook of her arm, listened for a few moments and put the instrument back into his bag. "I'm not fussy about the sound of that," he said. She caught a fleeting glimpse of the syringe of painkiller that he'd come to inject into her husband's thin veins.

"Well," the doctor said. "Tell you what. It might be a good idea to have one of your daughters bring you into the office for a check-up. Do you think you could arrange that?"

"The potatoes are ready for pulling."

"The potatoes. I suppose so. But couldn't you get someone

to do it for you this year?"

She stared at him.

"Well, never mind. We can talk about it later. I'll just have a look in on Mr. Thiessen right now."

"He's in the porch."

She heard the sound of his feet as he walked up the three green stairs. She heard the porch door squeak as it opened and closed. Her time of grace was over. She got up from the bench to follow the doctor. She heard the sound of pottery breaking in the potting shed.

That cat. She would have to go and chase that animal away before it broke every last one of her husband's pots. Why didn't he think of those things? He fed the cat and left her to take care of the consequences. She took the broom down from its clasp on the wall beside the rain barrel. It was the outside broom, used to sweep dust and snow from shoes and for chasing animals. She raised the broom and walked lightly along the pathway to the potting shed. She was looking at the bottom of the door for the cat to come scooting out and then she would lower the broom. She saw her husband's shoes first. He was wearing his brown walking boots. Then her eyes travelled up the length of him until his blue eyes looked straight into her own.

"You! I thought it was a cat."

He'd pulled the cotton wads from his nostrils and his nose was back to its normal size. He wore his tweed cap low onto his forehead and his black serge jacket, the one he wore when he went to work at the hotel, was buttoned neatly. He clutched two earthenware pots, one inside the other, to his chest.

"Don't worry," he said finally. "I cleaned up the mess."

She lowered the broom and stepped to one side as he pushed past her on the narrow path. She caught a glimpse of a flash of yellow inside the pot which he held to his chest. It was his tobacco tin. He'd hidden his tobacco and papers down inside the earthenware pot.

"What are you doing? Where are you going with that?"

He walked away quickly, looking straight ahead. He passed by the green bench, strode jauntily down the lane to the dirt road.

"Father, wait. Leave the tobacco behind. Someone might see you." She followed him but the distance between them widened. She began to trot. What would people think if they saw him? She panted with the effort to keep up. The sound of her running pounded thickly inside her head. He was leaving her behind. "Wait for me. I want to come," she called one last time. But she knew it was useless. Once he'd made up his mind, there was no use talking. She sat down heavily on the bench and wiped perspiration from her forehead. He walked swiftly down the road to the bottom of the hill where the road flattened out towards the river.

He hesitated at the edge of the river and then turned around. He shielded his eyes with his hands. "Look here," he called to her. "I'm not coming back, so don't think that I am, because I'm not."

Tears burst and ran across her tanned broad cheeks. "And who is going to bring in your glad bulbs for winter?" she asked, hoping wildly to sway him with his beloved flowers. "I can't. The doctor says that maybe I should get someone to pull the potatoes."

He waved her question away. "Where I'm going there are enough flowers to go around and I will have my own mansion, white, with a flat roof like the houses in Mexico." He turned his back to her, faced the river and vanished. In the shadowy pockets along the riverbank, the wreaths of mist uncurled and evaporated in the sun. A crayfish scuttled along the muddy river bottom sending a swirl of yellow bubbles to break at the surface.

She felt the seconds fleeing from her. She had to do something, but what? What to do now that she was a widow? What would she do with ruined slippers and twenty-eight jars of watermelon pickles? She heard footsteps as the doctor descended the three stairs.

"He's dead, I'm sorry," the doctor said. "You should have sent someone to get me. I would have come."

She got up from the bench and wrung her plump hands and began to pace up and down. Father, oh Father, she said to herself, you should have let me come with you for once. What am I to do without you? She searched quickly through one pocket and then another until she found a peppermint. She popped the candy into her mouth and rolled it about her tender gums. She felt the relief of its sweetness meeting her stomach. Then she felt the doctor's warm hands, leading her back to the bench.

Her breasts jiggled as she sat down. What could she do? A man always did that. They always left women with the consequences. He made the decisions, she was left with the mess. And all because of Eve.

The doctor sat down beside her and stroked her arm. "I would have come," he said once again.

She shrugged free of his touch. "And what difference would it make to call you? You couldn't have stopped him. He wanted to go and so he went."

"I suppose you're right," the doctor said.

"And to think of it, one dozen two-quart sealers dills," she said. "And I couldn't even give him one."

She watched as far above her the fireball wavered and began to lose its shape. Then the top of it sank to meet the bottom and the sides of it spilled out into the morning sky.

Rudy Wiebe

Sailing to Danzig

My name is Adam Peter Wiebe. As far as I know, there hasn't been an Adam in the family since the name Wiebe was first recorded in 1616 in Danzig, which is now of course Gdansk, Poland. The first Adam Wiebe was Dutch, and in Danzig he had two sons, Abraham and Jacob. Oddly enough, my own father, who was born in Chortitza Mennonite Colony, the Ukraine, was called Abraham Jacob, which in the Russian Mennonite tradition of naming meant that his father's name before him was Jacob. My oldest brother, who was born in a Mennonite village in the foothills of the Ural Mountains, was named Abram Abraham, my second brother Daniel Abraham, the Daniel coming from my mother's father. How is it then, I asked my parents years ago, that I, the last son, was named Adam Peter?

"Actually you weren't," my mother tells me without hesitation. "In the government papers in Saskatchewan, wherever they have them, your name was Heinrich."

"Heinrich?"

"In the papers, yes, and Abraham your second, like always. You were Heinrich Abraham."

"I'm not Adam?" At age seventeen I am about to discover my name?

"Of course you're Adam," she says calmly. "That was just those government papers. But we were living so far in the Saskatchewan bush when you were born it was seven seeks before your father got to town and he registered your name 'Heinrich Abraham'."

My father, across the kitchen table from me, has continued to study his *Mennonitische Rundschau*; his reading glasses, bought at a counter in Eaton's, tilt at the end of his long, almost patrician nose. He sits this way every Sunday afternoon, the only day of the week he does not have to feed cattle on the farm where he will work as a hired man until he is sixty-nine, another seven years, never able to find the one Canadian dream he still has: a job where he can work inside and be warm all winter. He says nothing now, not even at my mother's teasing irony which, we all three know, will prick him eventually into some response.

"He had the day wrong, too," my mother continues suddenly. "He remembered it was a Saturday but he got the date wrong a whole week and when we got the registration when he was going to become a citizen Mrs. Graham said to me, 'My Lloyd was born the same day as your Adam, the midwife came from you to me, how come your day is wrong?' and then I noticed that, too."

"It was eight weeks after, not seven," my father mutters finally; as if correcting her fact will balance his.

"But my name, you didn't remember my *name!*"

He seems particularly intent on the *Nachrichten*; he will never understand more than the barest English and it is in the weekly *Rundschau* that he learns what he knows of the news of the world.

"Mr. Graham wrote the names in then," my mother says," 'Adam Peter' and so we corrected both the date and your names."

"When was this?" I ask.

"Well father, when was it, you became a Canadian citizen?"

"1941. You want my registration number too?"

My mother is knitting and ignores that, easily. She knows he memorized the number immediately in case he was ever forced to cross the border again; when they got to Canada at last on March 5, 1930, he vowed he would never leave of his own free will and he never has.

"But you always called me . . . ."

"Yes, we always have."

"So how come you called me that, Adam?"

"Oh," my mother looks up from her knitting, dreamy like the look I now see again on my daughter's young face, "there was a little boy, a Penner, he was a little Adam and he died just before you were born, he was so beautiful, always singing and only four and so good, laughing in the children's room in church and playing with all the babies to make them laugh too, it was so sad when he drowned in the slough behind their barn. That was a nice name, he was an Adam, so good."

"Well," I say bitterly, "you tried your best, with the name."

"Adam," my mother says softly, and touches me. For an instant her voice and fingers seem about to find tears behind my eyes, but my father says gruffly,

"Where did you find out about this Adam Wiebe, in Poland?"

"In a book."

"Books, books, all your books they'll ruin you." If I only had the chance. What's ruined him? Being born in 1889 in Russia he always says, a Mennonite hauled into the Czar's forests in lieu of compulsory military service and he had finally finished his four years and come back to his village to marry my mother when World War One erupted and he was dragged back again, another four, or three rather because the glorious October Revolution ended all that, they got so busy killing themselves, all those Communists, and playing games with him forever, what could anyone do but do what he was told? But finally, at forty, he did one thing: he left what little he had, they were poorer than Russian meadow mice, and took his wife and six kids to Moscow to try and get out of there; forever. Astonishing, he did one thing, after a Mennonite father and four older brothers and over seven years of the Czar's army and then ten years of Communists, the Communists, o he had learned to do what he was told.

"What was this Adam?" my mother asks.

Adam/Peter—ground/rock, surely a name significant enough for anyone. Adam/Peter/Abraham—ground/rock/exalted father of a multitude, dear God more than enough, all earth and exaltation, with Wiebe a solid Friesian name to anchor it; a people stubborn and implacable as water. In a class I taught years later at the University of Groningen there was a long blonde Friesian girl name Wiebke den Hoet, her father the dike master on a new polder slowly forming itself out of the North Sea. But I could not know this when I was seventeen, did not know Wiebe was a Friesian given name transformed by deliberate centuries into a patronymic, my mother knitting mittens for poor children on a hot August Sunday in Alberta. That first Adam Wiebe sailed from his Dutch fishing village of Harlingen on the North Sea for Danzig in 1616 because that Hanseatic free city needed a water engineer and he was the best in the world. Harlingen is still a village; its labyrinth of dikes and canals, many of them probably built by Adam, still thrust it out in alternating loops of earth and water against the gray sea. The aerial (KLM) photo I have shows it almost as neat as the 1624 copper engraving of Danzig which in the top left corner features the city's coat of arms and the top right a portrait of Adam Wiebe himself.

"Look," I say to my mother, and read for my father's benefit, since he won't look up, "Wybe Adam von Harlingen."

"That's your father's nose," my mother says, and so it is. But a higher forehead, heavier eyebrows in a narrower face; an unstoppable genius who served Danzig thirty-two years and before he died had streets and gates and even squares named after him.

"Where's my long nose?" I ask.

My father laughs then. "It got lost for a turned-up Loewen. Her mother's family."

"Does your book have pictures of a Loewen?" my mother asks.

If I could answer her now, I would tell her the Loewens were Flemish believers from the other great Hanseatic city Antwerp, probably jewellers who escaped religious persecution and arrived in Danzig even earlier than Adam Wiebe, but perhaps now rather than parade all my dubious facts of history I would ask her to sing, that beautiful soprano now lost forever except in the folds of my memory. Any of the songs she sang when the leaves came out green as frogs in the Saskatchewan poplar May and she began to cook on the stove outside to keep the house cool for sleeping. It would be a song from the *Dreiband*, their pocket-size hymnal without notes but of course a person who sang in a church choir then knew at least five hundred songs from memory, and my father across the yard somewhere within earshot would answer her in tenor harmony, their voices floating like lovers hand in hand high in the bright air. By some genetic shift more drastic than my nose the two musical rocks of Flemish Loewen and Friesian Wiebe have faulted into my tunelessness: though I can recognize any melody, I cannot reproduce or mirror one either close or at a distance. Not even the overwhelming choir of thirty-six Peter Wiebe descendants in Gladbach, West Germany last year helped me to one tuneful sound, the over two dozen children from two families finding hours of melodies in that tiny apartment, their heads filled endlessly with identical words and notes.

"Peter Wiebe," my father would have slowly raised himself erect. "That was my brother, the rich one with us in Moscow in 1929, he always . . ."

"Leave that old story," my mother would have said quickly. "We have to forget such things."

"Forget!" my father's thick worker hands are crumpling the paper. "You forget when your own brother who's as rich as the dead Czar keeps saying to you, 'How do you think you'll get out to Germany, you and your Marie and six kids, when you don't have three kopecks to rub together?' How do you forget that?"

"Abraham," my mother murmurs, "God needs money for nothing."

"And the Communists don't either, thank God," my father laughs sardonically at his own wit. "Having money in '29 was the end of any going, no beginning."

"So forget that old story, it . . ."

But I would have to interrupt her. "This isn't your brother Peter, Pa, it's his son, he was in Moscow with you too, young, he . . ."

"Peter Wiebe is in Germany now? Did he buy his way out, now?"

"It's your nephew, not your . . ."

"That young Peter was nineteen in '29," my mother says dreamily. "Short, very thin, and very bright eyes. Such an open Wiebe face."

And he still has it the first time I see Peter Wiebe. In 1982. He was coming towards me through several thousand Mennonites at their annual reunion in Germany to celebrate their seventies escape at last from the Soviet Union; exclaiming, "That's a Wiebe face, a Wiebe face!" and for that moment he appeared to be my father reincarnated in a slight, short body, his thin blond hair which would never turn grey and that patrician nose and square jaw, limping towards me through the crowd that turns to stare and then laugh aloud at our happiness, at our embrace and enfolding double kiss. I might have been holding my father, alive again after seven years; though he had never in a lifetime held me like that.

"I never wanted a Peter in my family," my father says. "An Adam I didn't care, but a Peter, another Peter . . ."

My mother is singing. She will be singing not to avoid my father: they did not live sixty-one years with each other that way; rather, that wordless sound suspended by her voice, a broadening colour which does not hesitate at sadness or laughter, or break because of anger, unforgiveness: it is a sound which slowly, slowly threads brightness over the glowering, stifling Sunday afternoon. It is like the story young Peter Wiebe, now seventy-two, will tell me of his second arrest and his second transport to the Gulag in the last fierce days of the dying Stalin. He will say:

"We had religious freedom, of course, it was official, guaranteed by the Soviet Constitution of course, but no more than three people could talk politics together and the police must suspect everything so when our village met every Wednesday evening for Bible reading, faith became politics. I had the only Bible and the room was full, always tight full and I read in German, no one ever said a single word not used by Luther— where would you get a Russian Bible? This German Bible from my father was the only one in the village, and even if we had spoken Russian, who knew what person had been pressured by what police, and why? Your own sister or cousin or even husband would never dare tell you if they *had* to inform to prevent something worse. That was the way they controlled us, fear, and if *you* had to inform at least you knew how to protect yourself because you knew at least something they knew because you'd told them—well, why would Soviet police or party members believe us when we told them again and again we never spoke anything at all but the words of Jesus, and sometimes his words, well the way you say them can sound like something a little slanted and people will smile as if they know something, just for a second they know and can think, something. So that time they came in as I was reading John 15: 'I am the vine, you are the branches. They that abide in me . . .' they were pounding loud on the house door, and of course it takes a while to get the door open and there's always so many big men and women around the door that they can't actually get in for a while and when the knock came I had to leave the room, like I'd done two times before but this time they are smarter: two of them greet me by the kitchen door as I come out. 'We just want to ask you a few questions, nothing more, don't worry, Katerina Petrovna, he'll be back for night.' Of course, but which night? Four years later, when Stalin is dead three years and Khruschev reviews all the ten or eleven, maybe it's thirteen, million political prisoners' records, I am released just as quick, I can go not even into free exile as they call living anywhere in the Soviet Union except within five hundred kilometres of your home village, I can go, go home. I am alive only because I am small, and because I can keep books. Even sitting on a stool in a heated room all day you get barely enough food to keep a body as small as mine breathing year after year, but if you have to labour in the mines or the forests in the terrible cold, especially if your body is big like yours, you do not last a month; the smaller people last longer, sometimes almost half a year, but me they would have stuffed with black bread gladly forever, sometimes even a fish-head in the soup because every camp administrator has to have a bookkeeper who will keep him ahead of his boss—you cannot imagine the unbelievable records that have to be kept, every turnip peel weighed and written down to whom it went and to have a prisoner in camp who can add and is honest, well, honesty is so unbelievable that every camp boss I ever had kissed me and cried when he had to let me go. By God's grace there I am, four years of a twenty-five year sentence, the food ration is the same whether you have to meet an impossible quota set in the Kremlin of trees cut in waist-deep snow or add numbers all day, columns like forests down page after page growing themselves green in your head until you are an adding machine, your eye sliding down their wrinkled bark and clicking so exactly even the unexpected Kremlin inspector with machines can't do anything faster, leave alone find a mistake in books stacked to the ceiling, thank the dearest God who gives you this year after year mind of numbers and denial, nothing more, 'No, I did not . . . No, I never said . . . No, I know of no one . . .' the

84

unending questions that come to you at any time of any night
and only the numbers are constant, solid as rock and the frozen
spruce piling up like corpses around the camp you have no idea
where it is buried in the taiga but you know exactly how many
bodies there are, trees or people. You become numbers; soon an
axeblow no matter how feeble in the farthest swamp is already
written on the paper of your mind, eleven to seventeen chops
per tree up to thirty centimetres in width for a fresh prisoner,
seventy-six to ninety-three for the same tree for someone who
will be dead in her bunk rags tomorrow, the skin stretched stiff
across her torn teeth and you have another statistic: longevity
calculated in relation to declining rations, in relation to quotas
not filled, how long can rations be cut for the prisoner coming in
weighing thirty to forty kilos, forty to fifty kilos, do women last
longer than men even though their initial production is never as
high and they have the same quotas, same food ration? The
largest men always die first. But I am small, I work inside where
it's warm, I last four years; until Stalin is dead. It is Wednesday
evening again when I get off the train and walk to my village
along the empty farm roads and I open the door of our house,
the same door where they took my father in 1936, and the
woman inside who is reading stops and she gives me back my
father's German Bible and I open it and read as if I had never
left, aloud in that room crowded with the same white, silent
faces the words of Jesus, '. . . they that abide in me and I in
them, the same bring forth much fruit, for without me you can
do nothing.' That was my second return, the first time was in the
war when I was falsely accused and our collective farm worked
two years to get me out. But my father never came back the first
time. They came for him in 1936, and Stalin still lived then for
almost twenty years."

This story, and all the other stories I will hear from Peter
Wiebe are already there in my mother's song as she sings until
my father joins her, their voices singing this story which has
already taken place but which they will never hear nor speak
about sitting at the worn kitchen table in Alberta, Canada, my
memory of them like their memories of Moscow, like Peter's
memories of his father, my uncle Peter Jacob, the rock and the
deceiver, my father's brother having to live on in the Mennonite
village in the Ural foothills to which he and his family are

returned from Moscow in 1929 while my father and his family travel to Germany and finally Canada. My uncle has to wait seven more years until that knocking on the door he has always known will come finally comes, and he disappears into the winter darkness leaving only memory and his German Bible, a tall, strong man like my father who has no mind for numbers either but can chop down a thirty-centimetre tree in nine strokes of an axe, easily, and so fill his quota. At least for the first three or four days. With the square Wiebe face we all have, but a nose unlike mine; a patrician nose like Adam Wiebe in 1616, the year Shakespeare died and Adam sails to Danzig to lay the city's first wooden watermains and set artesian wells in its squares and drain the marshlands along the Radaune River by building dikes and canals and wind and horse-driven mills that lift the turgid water up into the slate-gray sea.

"What is this," my mother says, pointing with her knitting needles, "these strings here?"

She is studying the gray picture of the copper engraving of Danzig, the coat of arms in its top left corner, the narrow, energetic face of Adam in its top right. Below the coat of arms is a line drawing of a high hill labelled Bischoffs Berg, the centre is low sagging land along the river and marshes with the church spires and gates of the city beyond; but below Adam's picture on the right there is an elevation almost as high as the hill: it is labelled Wieben Bastion. Adam built that fortification to protect the city from the army of King Gustavus Adolphus of Sweden, and he constructed the city walls and the bastion above the swamps of the river by using earth from the Bischoffs Berg. The strings between the two my mother is puzzling over is the double cable Adam Wiebe strung on poles so that, by means of an endless stream of moving buckets attached to this cable, the earth could be carried over the river and the swamps from hill to bastion. So exactly were these buckets designed, so precisely were distance and weight calculated that no power was needed to make them move: the weight of the filled buckets at the top of the hill carried them down across the valley to the bastion while returning the empty buckets back up to the top. And though the gigantic Gustavus Adolphus and his mercenaries destroyed much of Europe for hire and the unending glory of the Protestant Church, they never got inside the walls of Danzig, leave alone near its central bastion, because in 1622 my ancestor invented the cable car to defend a defenseless city.

"When did this Wybe Adam von Harlingen die?" my father asks abruptly.

"1652. Pa, he built all that for them, and Danzig never even made him a citizen."

It is then my father looks up. "Yeah, yeah," he says, heavily, "that's the way. It always is. When those Communists hammered on our door in Moscow and told me to get on that train to Germany, they gave me a yellow card. 'Stateless refugee,' that's all it said. A hundred and fifty years in Russia and they send us out, a piece of yellow paper and fill in your own name. 'Stateless refugee'."

I had not known that either. I suppose it doesn't really matter. After all, over how many lakes and rivers and parts of oceans, across how many fairgrounds, up how many mountains on how many continents have I sailed through air suspended somehow from a cable and not known about my ancestor Adam Wiebe? My ignorance has, of course, never made any of those cables less real, any sailing less beautiful. Or potentially dangerous.

And in my memory my parents sit at our kitchen table in Alberta suspending the thin thread of their songs across the marshes and bitter rivers of their memories building what bastions? Against what fearfully anticipated or remembered war, against what knock at what door, "We just want to ask you a few questions, come, you'll be home for night"? Slight, bent Peter, the rich Wiebe's son having to live a sort of a life in the Soviet Union, I the poor Wiebe's son living a different sort in Canada: which would one actually prefer? Peter Jacob who vanished in 1936, Peter Peter bringing that Bible to Germany when he is too old even to keep other books and still so immovably honest and absolutely immovably stubborn and he is told to go at last, go, who wants you, you old bastard, you troublemaker—these are facts, were already becoming facts one August Sunday afternoon long ago when I was a teenager and discovering that my mother and father could tell me so little about the names I had, could tell me only small facts that explained nothing; facts like intermittent poles sticking up out of sinking ground, holding up cables no one could explain what genius, what vision had once made them possible so that all that solid earth could be moved so beautifully over swamp from the Bischoffs Berg to build the Wieben Bastion.

Wybe Adam von Harlingen, where are you now? Your cables are gone. Only the memories of songs remain.

II. Outsiders

Sara Stambaugh

How Lena Got Set Back

Lena's first husband, Isaac, hadn't much in the way of material goods. As Lena's cousin Sike said, he was pisspoor. But he soon made up for his earthly poverty by inheriting a heavenly mansion, though he left behind a daughter, wife, and no hopes of setting them up.

Lena did better on her second try. She was in her thirties and still had a sparkle which even plain clothes couldn't dull. She pulled her hair back into a bun under her covering, but she made sure that it waved nicely over her forehead. Though her skirts were over her knees, a shapely calf showed through her dark stockings above the black shoes, and after several years of widowhood her tidy print dress (usually in an attractive lavender sprig) worked itself into a lace-edged V over the properly caped bodice. The other ladies gaped at first, but after the first Sunday showing the younger ones began to imitate the Widow Burckhardt's innovation. It wasn't long till she'd got herself a second husband.

This one was well set up, though the church people whispered to each other at how an old, godly bachelor could be caught so easily. She'd chased him on a bus tour, they said, and only caught him when his donkey stumbled half-way down the Grand Canyon, where he had no one from the community to turn to for help.

But get him she did, and shortly the Widow Burckhardt was Mrs. Jacob Eby and set up with her daughter Lillie in a fine house in Strasburg. And Jake too, of course, since it was his house and crammed with furniture from his family: a set of six arrowback chairs to go round the extension table when some of the eight extra boards were put in for family dinners, extra chairs from his grandparents in miscellaneous patterns, and two special ones painted in Gaudy Dutch, yellow with tiger stripes and big pink roses over the back. That was only for the dining room, mind, and the rest of the house was filled with comparable treasures.

As for the house, it was in the village, brick and substantial and verandahed. Lena saw that Lillie had piano lessons in the front parlor and smiled over the other ladies while she sat on the woman's side during church.

Then Jacob died. Lena switched to blacks, but aside from her natural bereavement, she wasn't overly crestfallen when she arrived at church the first Sunday. The ladies in the cloakroom passed her down their row of ample bosoms, one past another, kissing her cheek as she went. Gleaming in her new mourning, she prodded Lillie and moved lightly down the line of solid women and dutiful pecks, then sat through Sunday service while the preacher of the day made special mention of her tribulation and called for prayers.

It was only with the funeral and reading of Jacob's will that her vision of the world changed. Jacob left all his worldly goods to the local Mennonite school, and she and Lillie were penniless.

Lena's first reaction was incredulity. At fourteen, Lillie was too young to realize what had struck, but Lena did. The church ladies came by and patted her on the hand, smiling smugly and staring at the wave in her hair and the scandalous neckline. Lena stared back and accepted their condolences. Then she made a trip to town and hired a lawyer to break Jacob's will.

She and Lillie were dutifully in the front parlor when the delegation arrived from Church. Lillie was practicing and broke off in the middle of *The Poet and Peasant Overture* when the knock came. The girl rose at her mother's nod to answer the formal knock at the parlor door. A knot of self-conscious men straggled into the room, the four preachers who circulated about Strasburg, Kinzers, Paradise and Hersheys, Deacon Eby and Bishop Sam Hershey leading the way. Self-consciously, they eased themselves into Lena's satin parlor furniture and the extra chairs she and Lillie brought in from the dining room.

Bishop Hershey stared at Lena. He was a vigorous elderly man who had retired from farming several years back after his son settled enough to take over. The other younger men were cleanshaven, but he carried the authority of a full grey beard, though his lip was clean. Mennonites didn't wear mustaches.

Bishop Hershey sat himself carefully in one of Lena's yellow satin chairs. The other men stared at her patterned carpet, but he looked her up and down, from her waved pompadour to her shapely black ankles. Then he cleared his throat, "Sister Lena," he said, "I and these godly men have come to speak to you."

"Lillie," Lena said, "maybe you'd better see to the kitchen." Glancing over her shoulder, Lillie moved to the varnished swinging doors that opened to the back of the house. "And see that the beans don't burn," called Lena, as her daughter disappeared.

The men around her gave a collective sigh, and Lena turned to Bishop Hershey. "Now tell me what you're after," she said. The other men kept their eyes fixed at the floor, but Brother Hershey again cleared his throat. Focusing on her eyes, he leaned forward. "Sister Lena," he said, "some dealings of yours have come to our attention. The congregation has sent us to investigate what may be a serious, indeed a most serious backsliding."

"Oh," said Lena. Reacting to the pressure from the Bishop's stare and the careful breathings from around the room, she pulled her ankles back against the rungs of her chair.

"You know, sister," the bishop continued, his eyes trained on her waved hair, "that we are enjoined against certain actions."

"Of course, Brother Hershey," Lena breathed, drawing her legs in further and fidgeting with the crocheted edgings on her hankie.

"It has been brought to our attention," continued Bishop Hershey, his voice rising as Lena's limbs retracted, "that you have considered raising a civil suit against a member of our congregation."

Lena pushed forward in her chair and flashed out her ankles. "He's dead," she retorted. "And how else am I to look to that child out there?" and she nodded towards the varnished door.

The men around the room looked at her, then once more

forced their eyes against the carpet. Bishop Hershey again cleared his throat.

"God's way is separate," he said softly, and another sigh went round the room.

Lena stared up now, moving her legs as though she were a calf tied against the beams by the hind legs. "I know all that," she said, "but what else can I do?"

"Follow God's way," said the bishop. Lena looked at him, then she laughed. The godly men who crammed the room glanced at her furtively, but the bishop rose from his yellow satin chair and thundered. "Lena Eby," he cried, his voice resonating from the upright piano, "you have turned from the congregation and set your face to the ungodly. You have set yourself back from the congregation and henceforth will not join in the communion of saints until such time as you repent of your ungodliness!"

Lena rose too, as the words were pronounced, then followed dumbly as the group of men led by the bishop solemnly moved through the front door and out to the porch and beyond. As soon as they disappeared, the kitchen door swung open. "What does all that mean, Mamma?" asked Lillie. "It means I've been set back," Lena replied curtly, "Now look to those beans."

The beans got scorched and so did Lena. She continued to go to church faithfully, but the ladies in the cloakroom drew back and stopped their conversation while she hung up her coat and bonnet. Lillie continued to sit with the other girls in her Sunday school class, but Lena proudly walked the length of the church aisle, flashing her ankles at the men who huddled on the right, and sat by herself on the last bench on the woman's side. At least her cousin Sike, for a few weeks, anyway, was seated opposite her on the men's side. When the sermon sounded too much against backsliders, he looked over and winked, and they grinned at each other across the aisle.

But while she was being ostracized Lena's lawyer kept busy. "If you hang on we'll break it," he said, when she visited him in his fancy office. She didn't know he was worth trusting, but Lena held on, even when Lillie complained that her friends didn't whisper to her during prayers and ran from her in the break after Sunday school.

"That ain't nothin," replied Lena, and went on to her next appointment with her lawyer. Her cousin was welcomed back to the congregation in a ceremony between Sunday school and church, when the bishop kissed his cheeks and said how fine it was to see true repentance. "And he got it for drinking," muttered Lena, but she combed out the waves in front of her covering and continued to march proudly up and down the church aisle.

Finally her lawyer called her to come to court. Lena crossed her legs smartly, and the judge found against her husband's will. Lillie wasn't there to applaud, because Lena wouldn't allow her daughter to witness a breach of church rules.

But Lena stopped by Bishop Hershey's on her way home from court. "Bishop Hershey," she said, "I'm willing to admit my backsliding."

The bishop beamed upon her while his wife stared from behind the door and clucked her tongue.

Lena was welcomed back to the congregation the following Sunday. She crossed her ankles and smiled at the preacher from the front bench, and when Bishop Hershey asked did she repent, she replied, "Most heartily." The bishop's wife had to bend down and give her the kiss of peace.

Warren Kliewer

Uncle Wilhelm's Love Affair

Reverend Schultz never did mention the love affair in a sermon, even though some people thought he should have and even though one man circulated a petition which was signed by twenty-one people, and he dropped it into the collection plate one morning. To be sure, the preacher may have had the incident in mind one Sunday when he said, "Speak not to me, my brethren, of the wickedness in Winnipeg. Who knows how many sins are committed every day in our own city park? Yes, in our own park here in Waldheim."

But perhaps it was just as well that Reverend Schultz did not preach a sermon about it, for Wilhelm Engeler, or as he was usually called, Uncle Wilhelm, would have neither heard nor heard about the sermon. For retired now, so old and arthritic that he couldn't work and indeed could do very little more than feed and dress himself, so old in fact that he was not even the deacon any more; he spent his days in walking from his tiny, one-room house at the edge of town, past the cemetery and the clapboard walls of the German church, past the railroad station where he would stop and gaze off at the tracks running on and on into the forest, past Kroeker's Shoe Repair Shop, to the small square park in the centre of town. He usually arrived at his favorite green, cast-iron bench at about seven-thirty in the morning and stayed there until six in the evening, except for the times when he walked back to the depot to watch the train come in at two-thirty or the rare times when someone took him to the Red Rose Cafe to buy him a cup of coffee, which he would cool by pouring it into his saucer and blowing on it. And it was from this favorite bench that he first saw her, the girl that people said was seventeen years old and that they said he had a love affair with.

Of course the people of Waldheim didn't blame the old man for the love affair; they blamed his son, Sam Engeler, who was the Sunday School Superintendent and who, people said, thought he was too good for everyone else because he had attended the Bible Institute in Chicago for two years. Or was it one year? Anyway, he had been gone for two years. And they blamed Sam for letting his father live in a house that was no more than a shack. And they blamed Sam because Uncle Wilhelm was dirty. That is, all the people blamed him except Reverend Schultz's wife who, at least once a month, had to explain the situation to old Mrs. Wiehens.

"That Sam Engeler," Mrs. Wiehens would say, "some Sunday School Superintendent he is. Won't even give his pa enough money to get a shave. Won't even give him that much, when he ought to take him into his house and take care of him."

"Well," Mrs. Schultz would say, "there's more to it than that. Sam's a good boy in some ways."

"That's what you always say: there's more to it than that. But Mrs. Becker says the same thing I do."

"But you know it's partly the old man's fault."

"And Mrs. Kroeker says the same thing Mrs. Becker and I say. That's three of us."

And then Mrs. Schultz would patiently and at great length explain that Uncle Wilhelm had never learned how to speak English and that Sam refused to speak German. And that was why the two could never get along.

"That Sam Engeler," Mrs. Wiehens would repeat, "some Sunday School Superintendent. Can't even learn German just to please his pa. And all us German people living in Waldheim and going to his church, and he can't even learn German."

"But he does know German. He says the prayers in German. He sometimes gives the sermon in German, doesn't he? And look at Uncle Wilhelm. He's been living in Canada for over sixty years, and all this time he has refused to learn English."

"Ya, that's true," Mrs. Wiehens would say. "I even had to learn English to buy some things in the stores." And there the argument would end. Of course Mrs. Schultz would have lost her point if Mrs. Wiehens had ever asked why, since he already knew the language, Sam refused to speak German with his

father, but this observation would have required more shrewd-
ness than Mrs. Wiehens possessed.

"No no," she would simply say, "those Engelers. Such a
family."

But when the details of Uncle Wilhelm's love affair became
known, not even Mrs. Schultz could defend him. For what was
going on was all too obvious.

At first of course, that September when Uncle Wilhelm first
saw the girl from his park bench, there had been no subject for
gossip. Uncle Wilhelm had been sitting with Pete Kroeker on the
morning when the girl turned the corner onto the main street,
followed Uncle Wilhelm's usual route past the depot and the
shoe repair shop, said "Good Morning" to the two old men, and
then walked toward the north end of town and disappeared.
They followed her with their eyes, saw how even the light
breeze that day whipped her thin gray dress around her knees,
saw the hole at the elbow of her green sweater. Neither of them
had seen her before, neither knew who she was, though Pete
Kroeker had heard several days before that there was some new
woman in town who had come from down south, Minnesota or
North Dakota or somewhere like that. But they knew no more
about her than that. And every day for several weeks after that
Uncle Wilhelm saw the girl, who followed the same route each
day, walking at about ten-thirty in the morning down the main
street from the depot to the north end of town.

Naturally the people did not begin to talk when the girl
first began to stop and try to carry on a conversation with Uncle
Wilhelm—he speaking German, she speaking English, and
neither understanding the other—though of course the people
did notice it. It was Maria Becker who first saw the two trying to
talk, and who did not notice the discrepancy since she was deaf,
and who then told her mother. Mrs. Wiehens heard it from Mrs.
Becker and then told it to Mrs. Schultz, who passed it on to her
husband. But the love affair had still not become the subject of
conversations. Nor was there much gossip when the people
noticed that Uncle Wilhelm began to walk down to the depot at
ten each morning, and wait until the girl met him, and that
the two would walk together all the way through town and
carry on the bilingual conversation which neither understood.
Nor was there talk when the people noticed that the old man

supported himself by holding the girl's hand or arm or shoulder, though again Maria was the first to see and Reverend Schultz the last to hear.

"Gottfried," Mrs. Schultz said to him, "You can't do anything about those two, can you?"

"Yes, yes," he said, his red face breaking out into a smile, "him who the Lord loves, He chastises."

"How can she see anything in him, that's what I'd like to know."

"Her seed shall bruise his head, the prophet saith. And he shall bite her heel."

But it was not until spring that the scandal broke, for the girl's walks stopped suddenly in the last week of October on the day of the first snowfall, though Uncle Wilhelm waited for her at the depot morning after morning until November had ended and even he could no longer stand the wind. When she did appear again in May, it is not likely that Uncle Wilhelm noticed how poorly her gray dress fit even though dark streaks showed against the faded material at the seams where she had let the dress out. But the women noticed. Mrs. Kroeker turned pale when she told her husband about it, for Uncle Wilhelm had been the one who had taught her the catechism. Mrs. Becker cried about it. For hadn't it been Uncle Wilhelm who had converted her son Johnny? It had done some good too, for a while, even though Johnny had run away to Winnipeg a year later and had gotten into bad company there in the warehouse where he was working. All the good that Uncle Wilhelm had done, the people of Waldheim said, and then he had to go and do something like this. It got so bad, in fact, that Sam Engeler was afraid to appear in public, and he called off Sunday School and told the people he had laryngitis.

But most upset of all was Mrs. Wiehens—so upset that when she hurried across her garden to the place where her backyard touched the parsonage yard, she did not notice she was dragging her feet along a row of newly sprouted onions and knocking them down.

"Oh," she wailed all the way to the back door of the parsonage. "Mrs. Schultz. What shall we do? what shall we do? Oh. Those Engelers. Oh."

She sat down on a kitchen chair panting and fanning her

face with the bottom of her apron.

The minister's wife tried to soothe Mrs. Wiehens, but it was no use.

"Think of it," Mrs. Wiehens said, "that nice old man, our used to be deacon, and then he went and did that."

"Now, now," Mrs. Schultz said.

"Eighty-eight years old he is already—eighty-eight. And now he has to get married."

"What? He's going to get married? I didn't know about that. They didn't tell me he was going to get married."

"I didn't say he was going to. I only said he's going to have to."

"When he's eighty-eight years old?"

"Yah. You'd think a man like that'd know better, wouldn't you? And when he's a deacon too?"

"But when he's eighty-eight? You don't really think that's his child, do you?"

Mrs. Wiehens nodded. "You don't never see her with any other boys, do you? All the people say that she's Uncle Wilhelm's girlfriend, don't they?"

"But that can't be! That just can't be! Who ever heard of an eighty-eight year old man becoming a father? That's impossible."

"Well," Mrs. Wiehens said, "if you don't believe it, go look at the girl's belly."

"But eighty-eight!"

"Do you suppose she'll want a church wedding? She can't wear a white dress if she does have a church wedding, can she? She hasn't come to see the preacher yet, has she? She ought to pretty soon. But she probably won't want a church wedding. Especially since she isn't a German. Of course, she could say she's a German just to get on the good side of the people, but she can't prove it because nobody knows what her name is. Not even Uncle Wilhelm. Mrs. Kroeker told me that Uncle Wilhelm said to Pete that he didn't even know what her name was. Oh, my! What're those Engelers going to do next?"

"Eighty-eight years old," Mrs. Schultz whispered.

Naturally Mrs. Schultz told her husband and asked whether he couldn't do something about it, talk to Uncle Wilhelm or Sam Engeler or something. "People always expect the preacher to talk to somebody when a thing like this happens."

"Yes," he said, his red face smiling, "yes, the Lord's chosen prophet, like the lamb from the flock."

"Maybe you could get Sam to talk to him."

"Ah, yes," he said nodding, "the Lord will provide for his servants. Yes."

But as it turned out, a week later, Reverend Schultz had not spoken to Sam Engeler, and so Mrs. Schultz did. Wisely, she made Sam promise before the end of the conversation that he would speak only German to his father and that he wouldn't start a quarrel by trying to speak English. And before Sam left the parsonage, Mrs. Schultz shoved a small paper sackful of cookies into his hand. "That's for your pa," she said, "or maybe for the girl, if she's there. If she wants some. I know I shouldn't send anything along for a person like that, but I guess I can't help it."

It was the very next evening that Sam went to his father's house. He found the girl there too, sitting in the rocking chair which squeaked every time she moved. Seated next to the table and near the dim, untrimmed kerosene lamp, she was trying unsuccessfully to thread a needle, for the needle would slip or fall, the long strands of the moistened thread would bunch up, or the thread would miss the hole. And so Mrs. Schultz's admonition became unnecessary, for it would have been necessary for Sam to speak German in any event to conceal what he was saying from the girl.

Without a preliminary greeting, Sam blurted out, "When are you going to send that girl home?"

"Oh, my, my." The old man smiled. "You still know German."

"Naturally I know German. If you'd ever come to church on Sundays, you'd hear me talk German."

"Yah, but you know. . . I can't sit still that long. You know that."

"All right. All right. Now I want you to tell me about that girl."

"My, my, my. It's so nice to hear you talk German."

"Yes, Pa. We'll talk about that later on. Now I want to know about this girl. Do you know what the people are saying about you?"

The old man looked around the room for a moment, squinting his eyes as he looked toward the lamp. "You mean this one?"

"Yah. This one."

"I'm teaching her to talk German. She can already say '*Ohm Willi.*' Say '*Ohm Willi*' for my boy here." When the girl only giggled, he continued, "Sometimes she does good."

"This is shameful," the Sunday School Superintendent said.

"Huh?"

"Shameful."

"Who is? She?"

"No, you. The way you talk to her."

"No, she's not shameful. She's a nice girl." Then turning to her, he added, "Aren't you a nice girl?"

Again she giggled.

"What's her name?" Sam asked.

"What? My hearing's not so good any more. You got to talk loud to me."

"What's that girl's name?"

"Oh." Uncle Wilhelm ran his forefinger over his lower lip and closed his eyes as he thought for a moment. "I don't know," he finally said. "I asked her once, but she didn't know what I was saying. She doesn't always know what I'm saying."

"You don't even know her name?"

"No. No. Sure would be nice if I did, though."

"Where does she live? Do you know that?"

"Live? Oh, she stays here sometimes."

"Over night?"

"Oh, yah. Sometimes. Sometimes not."

"Where does she sleep?"

"What?"

"Where does she sleep when she stays here over night?"

"There. Over there." He pointed toward the bed.

"And you sleep there too? With her?"

"Me?"

"Yah."

"No, I never sleep. You knew that. I always sit in that rocker at night for three, four hours. I haven't slept in bed for many years. Six. Eight, maybe."

"What do you mean, you don't sleep?" Sam sat down suddenly, his hands tightly gripping the arms of the chair.

"You knew that. I told you. I can't sleep any more."

"For six years?"

"Yah, sure. Oh, I sleep a little. Off and on. Not in the bed, though. I told you that."

"No, you didn't. Never. Are you sick pa?"

"Sure, I told you. I thought I did. I know for sure I was going to tell you. I even wrote it down here somewheres." He opened one of his cabinet drawers and pulled out two handfuls of odd-shaped, yellow sheets of paper. "I got it here somewheres."

"No, no, Pa. Let that go now."

But the old man continued to shuffle through the papers, picking up one after another, examining each one carefully on both sides. "You just wait. I got it here. I even remember what it says. It says, 'Tell Sam about that I don't sleep'."

"Give them here. I'll find it myself." Sam took the papers out of his father's hands. "We'll talk about that later on. Now we've got to talk about that girl. What're you going to do when she has her baby? Just what're you going to do? At your age? Just think how that looks to people. Just think what it does to me. I sometimes feel so ashamed I can't even walk downtown."

"If you'd just give me them papers, I bet you I could find it right away."

"Pa, you're not listening to what I'm saying."

"Oh, yah yah. You just keep right on talking. I'll listen. It sounds so good to hear you talk German."

Sam grasped his father's hand which was vainly fumbling toward the stack of papers. "Pa, what're you going to do with the baby?"

"What baby?"

"That girl's."

For the first time in the conversation Uncle Wilhelm could not immediately answer. He simply stared. His mouth hung open. "So she's got children, huh?" he finally said.

"No, no, she doesn't have them yet. She's going to have one."

"She's got children," Uncle Wilhelm repeated. "I wonder why she never told me."

"Pa, listen to me."

"Maybe. . . . What about that? You don't suppose she did tell me sometime? In English? Maybe she did."

"Pa, listen to me. That girl does not have any children. But she is going to have one. She's pregnant. Are you listening to me?"

"Oh, oh. She doesn't have any yet. Only she's going to. That's what you said?"

"Yes, Pa."

"Oh, now it's all clear to me." He nodded vigorously.

"You understand now, Pa?"

"Oh, yah. Yah."

"Another thing, Pa. The people all say that it's your child. You ought to hear the way they're talking."

"Mine?"

"Yes, Pa."

"Oh, yah," the old man said, nodding. "It's mine. It's mine."

"But, Pa, that can't be. You're eighty-eight years old. A man eighty-eight years old can't have children. I don't believe what the people say. But you shouldn't hang around with her, because people will keep right on talking every time they see you together."

"Yah, eighty-eight years. I'll be eighty-nine next September. Your grandfather only lived to be eighty-two. And here I am—eighty-eight. Almost eighty-nine."

"Pa, that isn't your child, is it? Tell me the truth now."

"Eighty-nine. Almost ninety years. That's a long time."

"Pa, listen to me," Sam said, shaking his father's shoulder.

"What?"

"Is that your child she's going to have?"

"Oh, yah, yah, yah, sure." He was silent for a moment before he added, shaking his head. "Ninety years."

"Well," Sam said, "I don't know what to say. My own pa, doing a thing like that."

"You say that girl's going to have a baby?"

"That's what you said. You said it was your child."

"You don't suppose, Sam, do you. . . ." He caught himself before he finished the sentence. Then after gazing long at the girl he continued, "You don't suppose it might be a boy, do you?

And that maybe she'd call him Wilhelm?"

"Don't talk nonsense like that. Then it's really true what the people say, that you're going to marry her."

"I sometimes think you should've called one of your boys Wilhelm."

Sam did not reply but only waved his arms as he stood up and walked toward the door.

"That sure would be nice."

"You're really going to go through with it?" the younger man asked, his hand already resting on the doorknob. "Listen to me, Pa. I don't want to quarrel with you now. But I want you to come up to my house tomorrow morning. You hear? Tomorrow morning. I'll get the preacher up there—you remember him? Reverend Schultz?—and we'll talk about it some more. Can you remember to come up to my house tomorrow?"

"Little Willi," the old man whispered, still gazing at the girl. "That sure sounds nice."

"Tomorrow," Sam said as he closed the door.

And Uncle Wilhelm nodded. "Yah."

But he did not appear in the morning. The two clergymen were there at seven-thirty, Reverend Schultz sitting in the over-stuffed chair with his hands folded and Sam Engeler walking to the window every few minutes to peer out beside the drawn shades. They maintained their strict vigil until ten o'clock when Mrs. Schultz brought them two doughnuts apiece and coffee in a thermos jug.

She said, "Maybe he forgot, Sam."

"I told him three times. I told him to come to my house in the morning and Reverend Schultz would be there and we would talk about it. But he hasn't come."

"Well," she said, pausing to think about the situation, "maybe he doesn't know where your house is. Has he ever been here?"

"No, he hasn't ever been here. He never comes to visit me. He doesn't even come to church when I preach the sermon."

"Then how's he supposed to know how to find your house? Why don't you go and get him?"

"Not know where I live? You mean to say my own father doesn't even know where my house is?"

"Have you ever invited him over here?" she persisted.

"No, no," Sam said, "I wash my hands of the whole thing."

"Yes," Reverend Schultz said, his red face smiling. "Shake the dust from off thy feet, thou generation of vipers."

"But we ought to wait just a little longer," she said. "He might come yet."

And so Mrs. Schultz sat down in a straight chair to wait with the men. At eleven-thirty, when Uncle Wilhelm still had not come, she saw two boys walking past the house, and she sent one down town to see if he could find Uncle Wilhelm sitting on his park bench and the other to tell Mrs. Wiehens to bring them some dinner. The second boy returned with Mrs. Wiehens and her dinner basket, but the first did not.

"That proves it," said Sam. "He wants to go on living in sin with her."

Mrs. Wiehens' eyes began to fill with tears, and even Mrs. Schultz had to blow her nose hard.

"Yes, yes," the preacher said, smiling, "the lost sheep come home to the fold."

"We must pray," Sam said, "pray for the lost one gone astray—pray for the sinner in our midst. . . ."

"But Sam," Mrs. Schultz said, "the dinner'll get cold."

"We must pray," Sam repeated twice as loudly. "We are four of us now. We will hold a prayer meeting for our lost brother. We will throw ourselves on our contrite knees and hold intercession for my lecherous father." And nimbly slipping to his knees, he began, "Our Heavenly Father, Who dost love each and every creature, numbering the hairs on our heads, watching even the very sparrow that falls from his nest. . . ." Reverend Schultz nodded as he and his wife knelt, and Mrs. Wiehens groaned and her knee cracked as she slowly inched her weight downward.

They prayed in turn until four o'clock when Sam intoned a long "Amen" and pulled back the drawn shade to peek out.

"Don't you think we should eat dinner?" Mrs Schultz said.

"Pray without ceasing," Sam said. "Prayer and fasting. We will pray until sundown for the sinner."

But Uncle Wilhelm did not appear, and after Sam had read them the passage from the Book of Revelation concerning the whore of Babylon, the Schultzes and Mrs. Wiehens walked home in the darkness.

"Oh, my," Mrs. Wiehens said, "there's so much sadness in that Engeler family and so much sin."

Reverend Schultz agreed.

Mrs. Wiehens quickly added, "There's so much goodness too. Do you think he'll go to hell for doing that terrible thing, when he was such a good man all his life?"

"Yes, yes," the minister replied. "The Lord will provide for his own."

Andreas Schroeder

The Roller Rink

I will admit at the very outset of the following history that parts of it may be untrue. Unfortunately, I can no longer tell which parts—I have been reworking these notes for such a long time now that my own fabricated sections have become indistinguishably blended with the original facts. I am not even certain precisely how I first stumbled into the environs of the story, though I seem to recall it was while I was stranded in a small village in southern Germany many years ago. I remember nursing a particularly vicious headache at the time and attending to several impressive bruises (unfortunately I have no idea where I might have sustained these knocks) when, for some reason, I noticed a long, oval building standing fairly far back from the street. There was a jagged hole broken through one of its walls.

Normally I wouldn't have paid much attention, but directly below the hole I saw the imprint of a body which presumably had fallen through the hole and lain for some time on the grass below. From the hole itself I could hear the smooth rush of countless ball-bearinged wheels against a background of lilting electric organ music.

The oval building was a Roller Rink, and a very popular one it appeared, for when I approached the front booth for my ticket I was given a card indicating my application had been noted and instructing me to take a room in one of the nearby hotels until my turn came up. I took a room as directed and settled in for a wait which lasted many months and often threatened to drive me quite mad with boredom, had I not had the company of others who were also waiting to take their turn. I soon discovered that virtually the entire village was comprised of hotels and boarding houses, all of which were constantly filled to capacity with persons waiting to be admitted into the Rink.

After almost three seasons had passed, an errand boy brought the message that I was to present myself the following morning at the front ticket booth to complete certain formalities prerequisite to my entry into the hall. I spent that night with my waiting companions celebrating the good news, accepting the tearful goodbyes and good wishes accorded those about to take their turn. In the morning, after a hurried breakfast, I paid my bill and headed for the Rink.

My excitement was such by this time that I paid scant attention to the "formalities" and am consequently unable to reproduce them here, but I do remember being ushered assiduously into the Dressing Room, a large, high-ceilinged, almost clinical looking chamber with white walls and a bevy of brisk girls in white smocks always available to help newcomers into their skates.

My enquiries about the hole in the wall—my initial reason for seeking entry into the Rink—were politely but firmly ignored, and I was entreated to hurry with the putting on of my skates to make room for others who had waited as long as I and were understandably impatient. I realized there was little I could do for the present and decided therefore to have a closer look at the hole once I was mobile and able to inspect this mystery on my own.

To maintain one's balance in this Rink implied learning to skate from scratch, regardless of any former skating experience, and irrespective of the skater's age or native abilities.

At first, people landed on their knees, slid about on their backsides or completely disappeared; others, though not immediately recognizable as themselves, suddenly flickered into view and bounced heavily across my vision. At times, then, more and more often, they struggled by, eventually streaked by, pieces of wall stood firmly for a moment, then glanced away hesitantly, soon casually, and I began to lose sight of the individual boards and sections of rail. Later, possibly much later, people receded swiftly in perspective, about-faced, dipped and rolled smoothly away, and the business of maintaining my balance became a matter of personal, not public, survival.

By the time I was secure enough on my feet to think about destinations, many more months had passed, and I had almost forgotten what I had entered the Rink to find. Almost as an afterthought, one day, I set course for the far wall where I had seen the hole.

The hole was not there. The hole was no longer there. There was no hole. There had never been a hole broken through the wall of this Roller Rink.

Standing against the railing alongside the wall, I couldn't decide which statement was the true explanation for what I couldn't find. A long, smoothly dove-tailed, highly varnished barrier receded unbroken into the distance, where it curved slightly and disappeared. Wherever it might have been, the hole was no longer anywhere in evidence.

Though I was badly disappointed with this conclusion, there seemed to be little I could do to change it. Standing as I was on the edge of the main stream of traffic, I suffered several near-accidents as the skaters, unaccustomed to stopping or circumnavigating others who had stopped, collided with me from behind and nearly pulled me down. I soon realized that stopping virtually anywhere on the course was extremely dangerous, and that the safest thing was to keep moving at a steady, moderate rate, regardless of any irregularities which aroused my curiosity. This way, at least, there tended to be no surprises.

Of the following dozen years there is little to tell. I skated incessantly, round and round the enormous oval hall, gradually losing all sense of a time before my entry into the Rink. From the continual circling I developed a mild but perpetual dizziness which dulled the senses in a peculiarly pleasant sort of way, so that I stopped even my formerly habitual jotting down of notes.

There seemed little point to it after all; what minor changes occurred in the daily routine were hardly sufficient to warrant mention.

Not that my subsequent life became completely uneventful; there were enough clashes and quarrels with other skaters to provide an often disagreeable overtone to my life in the Rink. Most of the squabbles occurred when I began to tire of the persistently monotonous pace and attempted to skate in reverse or engage in a little racing. Invariably, the ripples of indignation and even fear which passed through the crowd soon forced me to re-align myself in the proper manner and subside. The skaters clung to each other timidly, carefully balancing their proprieties before themselves in sober ritual. Confrontations for any reason whatsoever were considered entirely unacceptable. Instead, the singing of hymns and patriotic songs was encouraged, effectively masking the sounds of argument or dispute.

In retrospect, now, I doubt that I would have lasted many more years in that Rink had I not been offered, by the Rink directors, a course in roller rink management. I was informed that, though my rebelliousness has compromised my position to some extent, the directors were willing to consider the past a period of adjustment, and that I would be given this unusual chance to redeem myself.

My studies would encompass the entire area of skate mechanics, the styles and techniques of the skill, the different types of music and their effects on the skating masses, also designs of rinks, the various kinds of flooring, different brands of varnish, paint, leather padding and the variety of layouts available for lobby and rest areas. I was to study the arts of timing and pacing, the various rhythms, the tension of centrifugal and gravitational forces played off against one another for balance; in short, the entire problem of the man on wheels.

Though I balked somewhat at the tone of the offer I decided to accept, realizing that I had been in the Rink too long to remember how to survive elsewhere, and hoping this would make my life in the Rink a little more interesting or at least endurable. Under diligent direction I began to spend hours every day repairing torn buckles and straps, replacing lost bearings, exchanging worn wheels and tightening loose or damaged screws. With my manual in one pocket and a small set of portable tools in the other, I spent whole weeks cruising the skating floor, helping hapless skaters who had run into difficulties. As time passed I worked with increasing desperation, feeling always on the edge of disillusionment, always on the verge of betrayal, hoping somehow that a deeper involvement would result in a more secure commitment to the idea of the Rink itself. For when I stopped to think about it, I could feel it slipping from my grasp like a smooth round elusive stone, the belief in the skaters, the Rink, the skating round and round the interminable oval, the never-ending repairs to equipment which stumbled along for a short while, then collapsed again. It began to make less and less sense to me how I could have abandoned all that I had been before (though I had to admit I could no longer remember with any certainty just what I had been) with little more than a shrug of the shoulders and a vague curiosity about a hole in a wall which I couldn't even locate anymore.

The more I realized this, the more I tried to smother my uneasiness in additional work, driving myself with a fiercely clenched mind, deeper and deeper into the tendrils of a vocation leading to Supervisor of Those Who Skate.

When, ten years later, I had chased myself through the entire course, I took up my post as administrator of the large, well-worn Rink and settled in for a term of helping the skaters through their paces.

The Rink, by this time, had been growing too small for my taste and I made immediate application for permission to undertake major renovations throughout the hall. There was bickering, grumbling, and much frustrating pedantry, but the permission eventually materialized and the work was launched. By spring of the following year the renovations were almost complete, with work going on solely in the main rink of the skating complex. This area was, as you might imagine, my special concern.

Through my studies I had begun to realize that the secret to a happy congregation and a long-lasting Rink was to position its walls in such a way as to make the skater believe he is moving constantly in a straight line. With this in mind I laboured long hours over the walls and floor to ensure absolute smoothness and continuity. As I sanded and polished each board again and again, it seemed to me that I was not only smoothing the way for others, but straightening the compromising curvature out of my own life.

When the renovations were entirely completed several weeks later, a great inauguration celebration was proposed.

It was decided we would begin the ceremony by all skating once over the entire area of the Rink. At the signal of the juke box operator (who had recorded a new piece of music designed especially with the new walls in mind) we would begin, with myself in front and the whole skating pack following in neat, orderly rows behind.

The planned celebration was to last throughout an entire week and drew much attention and excitement among the masses which gathered in the Rink lobby on the first day of the feast. It took much effort to prod the entire crowd into its correct position for the beginning of the journey; confused skaters stumbled about everywhere, falling against railings, losing their balance to crash into already assembled lines which promptly lost their cohesion; there was much quibbling over which rows were the most desirable and who should warrant skating where. When everyone was finally in his place, I raised my hand and waved for silence.

The juke box operator gave the sign. Smoothly, as if driven by electricity, I glided off, pulling my assistant supervisor after me. Row after row set off, until soon the entire herd was in motion, swaying leisurely, easily, from foot to foot to foot. Old women smiled at old men who grinned and nudged each other playfully; the atmosphere was high-spirited, contented and free.

A little time passed. I began to increase the pace bit by bit; the floor was so smooth and the wall so continuous, there was nothing by which anyone could gauge their speed—so there were no complaints. I tried to count the boards in the wall to keep track of our progress but we were soon skating so fast that the boards blurred as we rolled by and I found it difficult to decide where one board ended and the next began. Someone behind me had begun a hymn; I remember being annoyed for an instant that someone should have started the singing without my prior consent, but there was no sense in making a scene on such a special occasion and, besides, we were now speeding along at such a rate that my turning around would have meant placing the balance of the entire skating assemblage in jeopardy.

Suddenly, I thought I felt myself beginning to edge very slowly toward the right, toward the wall. Surprised, uneasy, I looked down at my skates; everything seemed in order, the wheels were spinning along quietly, the leather straps were tight and the metal clamps for the toes seemed secure. It was when I pushed a little harder with my right leg in an attempt to reposition myself into my former place, that I heard the click. It sounded as if a bearing had chipped.

Puzzled, I looked up to see that I was still moving very slowly toward the wall. Trying to ignore the noise in the bearings (which was becoming more and more pronounced) I strained once again toward the left. My skates resolutely refused to shift—and suddenly it dawned on me that we had reached that section of the wall at which the curve began.

I turned my head, glanced back—nothing but elation, singing, horseplay—no one noticed the drift of the curve.

A flood of anger, exasperation and resentment poured through my mind as I began to realize the implications of this trap, but there was no longer time for thought; I struggled bitterly now, closer and closer to the speeding wall; my skates making a terrific racket but everyone singing so loudly that no one could hear. My eyes began to hurt; I saw nothing but smooth continuous boards streaking past my pupils back into my skull—stooped down in a grasping effort to undo my straps, thinking possibly to leap out of them, more image than idea—a split-second later I felt my shoulder brush the wall, my right skate screamed along the varnish, dug in, my body swung around and slammed into the wall, I saw an enormous blackness and then there was nothing. . .

Total silence. Or a gentle hissing sound around the edges of a hole which may not even be an exit, which possibly exists in outline only, in the imagination of a skater just escaped into the confines of a larger surrounding rink. There is room for argument of course, and some evidence that there was, in fact, an actual hole. But it may perhaps be appropriate to point out that it is not as uncommon a thing as it might appear, for a man to construct his past in ramp-like fashion to launch himself into a future he might not otherwise be able to afford. It is possible, for instance, that this gaping story is itself the hole through which the man in question fell, or that it is a substitute for the hole he never found. Another possibility may be arrived at by superimposing the identities of the man at the beginning and the man at the end, placing them on opposite poles of the story's own oval configuration.

Of course it may be that none of these possibilities apply, being suggested, as they are, by the author himself who has admitted from the beginning that an undeterminable part of this fiction may have been fabricated and therefore be untrue. For one thing, it must be pointed out that such feinting is characteristic by persons attempting to make good an escape by confusing their pursuers with false leads and half-true information. But of course this warning, too, is suspect, having been made by the presumed escapee himself. . .

Victor Carl Friesen

Old Mrs. Dirks

Old Mrs. Dirks lived on the outskirts of a small prairie town. Her house had but two rooms, had never been painted, and was not very warm in cold weather. Each winter she banked snow against the gray walls to increase the insulation. From a wood-pile behind her barn she hauled huge loads of unsplit firewood to the house. For this purpose she used an old round tub to which she had fastened a short length of rope. Even piled high, the tub slid easily over the snowbanks so that Mrs. Dirks, without too much trouble, could keep her house warm. In fact, she usually kept it hot, stuffing one piece of wood after another into the Quebec heater which served the two rooms. Rosie Dirks was seventy-five years old and, like most elderly people, she needed extra warmth to be comfortable. When she was not working, she sat beside her stove.

Her husband, one would have thought, might have done the outside chores. He was still living—but not with her. And he had not been for forty-eight years.

Mr. Dirks had grown up a very shy young man. Merely talking to a girl, or *of* a girl, made him feel ill at ease. Then when he was twenty, the woman who was to become his wife had smiled at him after a church service. He had felt more ill at ease than ever, for it seemed to him that he was obligated to marry the woman. His shyness might have prevented his carrying out any such decisive act, but she took the lead and made things easy for him; she was five years older than he.

Rosie had smiled at several young men before Mr. Dirks came along and, since nothing had happened, she had been getting worried. In her day twenty-five was considered middle-aged. In a land just emerging from a pioneer era, children stopped school in their early teens and started working as adults. By the age of sixteen a girl was marriageable.

Rosie had been marriageable for nine long years; she had not been what the neighbourhood women called "pretty." As a young woman she had a bad complexion, noticeable particularly on her forehead. Her nose, although not ill-shaped, was rather long, and she had a protruding lower lip. When she smiled this lower lip might have made her look sensual had she been pretty otherwise, but as it was it made her look as if she were complaining. And an observer would readily assume she was, for until her twenty-fifth year, no man had paid her court.

Rosie had not given up hope—keeping herself slim, avoiding the matronly stoutness that wives soon ate themselves into after marriage. Rosie had not been over- or underweight, but her figure, like her legs, tended to lack shape. One thought of straight, smooth tree trunks when one saw her legs. But she was physically strong—still an admirable quality in a wife.

Rosie's courtship with Mr. Dirks quickly ended in marriage. The bride with her blushing groom moved into a neat little home, and for a while they were quite happy. Rosie worked hard, cooking and washing and sewing. Tending to a husband was a pleasure for her; she sang as she clattered pots and pans in preparing meals.

Mr. Dirks was overcome with all this attention. He felt like a rich man even though he had no steady work. A good-paying job would come, and meanwhile he had his Rosie. He sat about the house with his shoes untied and waited for his meals.

Mr. Dirks' shyness vanished in time, and his wife could not have foreseen the result. He began to talk freely with people that he met in town, including the women; women are drawn to a recently married man. These women were attractive, more attractive than his wife, and he came to enjoy bandying words with them. When he ventured to say something naughty, they laughed and were embarrassed. He began to think that he had charm and wished he had not married such a homely wife.

In time his flirtations turned to philandering. He came home late at night and did not bother making excuses to Rosie; he did not say anything. Then one night he did not come back at all. A short time later Rosie had a letter from him, with no return address, saying that he had sold their house and that he was going away. She never saw him again.

Rosie Dirks by this time was not unhappy to be rid of spineless Mr. Dirks. But a small kernel of bitterness was there, bitterness that she could not keep her man. This feeling she was determined not to show and pushed it back into a dark corner of her mind. Her lower lip, however, protruded more than ever. Her complaining look became fixed.

Shortly afterwards Mrs. Dirks moved to her present home on the edge of town. "Life is real, life is earnest," she had read in a poem somewhere. There was not anything in life to smile about, she had decided. She had a living to make, and she set to do so in earnest. She kept a cow, a red and white Guernsey which each summer she picketed in a nearby ditch to graze, and she kept chickens and geese. The cow's milk which she did not use herself she poured into one-gallon syrup pails and sold in the town. She soon had a few regular customers. They felt sorry for this solemn woman who appeared before their door every day.

The chickens and geese were Mrs. Dirks' greatest blessing. They provided eggs and meat, but it was the companionship they gave which she most valued. They gathered about her when she flung out grain from her held-up apron. Whenever she went out, even to walk into town, a few chickens would come running up. "I've nothing for you now. Go 'way," she chided them. But she liked their attention.

On a warm summer's day when she left her outside door open, a hen might hesitantly put one foot on the sill and, moving her head slowly to one side, then the other, with bill agape, try to fathom the mysteries of the interior of a human dwelling. With much deliberation the hen would eventually step over the sill and step down inside, still looking about, as if awed by her own accomplishment. Mrs. Dirks would laugh out loud in spite of herself, and the chicken would scurry out.

The geese were the aristocrats of the barnyard, waddling about like fat burghers, necks stretched out, heads looking down on their world. They were very class-conscious, always together, usually apart from the chickens. Sometimes in the evening Mrs. Dirks would stand outside her kitchen door and sing, not from happiness but from habit; she used to sing when Mr. Dirks was still around. At such times the geese would tilt their heads upward, wondering at this strange sound.

The townsmen also listened—and shook their heads. Mrs. Dirks did not have the pleasantest of voices; her songs sounded like the wail of the world's suffering, keening high over the town. "Poor, lonely Mrs. Dirks," they thought. They did not know that she laughed at her chickens—her face was so grim when she was uptown. They did not know that she had geese to sing to.

Mrs. Dirks was too practical-minded to allow herself to become sentimental about her fowl. When she wanted a chicken dinner, she carried a squawking hen to the chopping block at the woodpile. When she wanted to sell a dressed goose to the town's butchershop, she tucked a fat goose under her arm and, bending its neck into a loop, cut through the loop with a few powerful strokes of a sharp butcher knife.

So passed the years. Mrs. Dirks grew old, and her townsmen grew old with her. She continued to live aloof from them, not caring that most of them now drove cars instead of horse-and-buggies. She walked before; she walked now.

She did not care about contemporary fashions. Her dresses were longer than the mode, invariably gray or brown, and cut from heavy, coarse cloth, even in summer. She sewed them herself, generally making them too large so that they hung shapelessly about her.

Her hair she did herself too. Once a week she opened the bun at the back of her neck and combed out the long hair, now streaked unevenly with gray. The hair hung down almost to her waist and made her look like a pagan crone. She did it up carefully each time and set in two brown combs, a present from her husband many years ago. She had lately started to wear them again.

When she was uptown, the townspeople did not notice her hair or her combs. They noticed her thick dresses and the rest of her clothes. Ever since she got old, Mrs. Dirks had taken to wearing men's long underwear the whole year through. These she bought unashamedly in the town's general store. She was not going to catch her death of cold, she told the clerk. Over the legs of the underwear she wore brown cotton stockings and on her feet a pair of felt slippers. She never wore shoes, not even when she went shopping. "Poor Mrs. Dirks," the townspeople thought. "She should really have someone living in the house to look after her."

It was in her seventieth year that a strange thing happened to Mrs. Dirks—strange when one considered her general appearance. She began to imagine that she was sexually desirable and that she always had been. When men peered after her on the street, noting her outmoded clothing, she thought they longed for her; wanted her. "You dirty old men," she said to herself as she straightened her posture and strode off as briskly as she could.

One day some town women paid a call on Mrs. Dirks. One brought some jam and fresh buns. They felt sorry for the old woman and hoped to cheer her up. Mrs. Dirks did not often get company, particularly such happy company. She did not quite know what to make of it—of the small talk and the social laughter. She looked astutely at the faces of her guests and wondered if they had some ulterior motive. Could they know about their husbands' desires for her, she wondered.

On another day some teenage boys crossed the corner of her yard. They had hoped to find something usable in the junkyard behind her barn, but none of the boys had wished to ask the old woman for permission to look. Now they were looking without permission. When Mrs. Dirks saw them, she hurried outside, shaking her apron at them angrily. She had her suspicions about teenage boys anyway, and here they had come onto her yard. One was bareback; another was wearing only walking shorts. "What do you *want*?" she shrieked out. "Have you no shame?" The boys fled in dismay, not understanding the import of her question.

At night when strange noises occurred outside her house, perhaps the wind rattling a loose eavestrough, or a tree branch brushing against a window, Mrs. Dirks thought that some men were trying to peep under the blinds at her. She kept her door locked and a good fire going in the heater. Warmth always gave a feeling of security.

Sometimes when she was already in bed and under warm blankets and she heard a thumping noise outside, she fancied that her long-gone husband was passing through town and was trying to play a trick on her. Then she would sink off to sleep.

One summer afternoon a vagrant appeared at Mrs. Dirks' door. He was an old man and had the run-down appearance of most derelicts. The one-day's growth of white stubble on his hollow face was set off by what seemed a permanent sunburn. When he smiled, his face was creased with wrinkles; he had no teeth. His clothes, denims rolled up at the cuff and an old suit coat, were dirty and had probably been slept in. He was asking for work to earn a meal. "I'll split some wood," he said.

Mrs. Dirks peered knowingly into the man's face. "Men!" she thought, "you're all alike," and she remembered the ones in town who stared after her. She stood firmly on the threshold of her house and grasped each side of the door frame in her old hands. She had the entrance to the house effectively blocked. But Mrs. Dirks had no intention of turning the man away. She was far too crafty for that. She would get some wood split and let the man inside for a meal, but that would be all. She grew excited with her little scheme.

When she was back inside, she could hear the thumping sound of the axe striking the blocks of wood. She got busy herself, heating coffee and frying some eggs and potatoes. Walking between stove and table, she stopped to look at herself in the mirror on the wall. She patted the bun at the back of her neck firmly as she thought of her scheme, then absently smoothed the wrinkles in her forehead. She set the table for two.

"Don't bother to close the door," she told the man when he came in. "It's hot today." As the meal started, neither said anything, each awed a little by the other's presence. He had not counted on eating with her; she was trying to figure him out. Had he heard about her from those men in town, she wondered. "Men!" her mind was saying, but what she said out loud was, "You been here long?"

She continued with other casual questions, but as with most women no small talk is ever really casual. Mrs. Dirks was proving to herself her supposition that this man had designs on her. But he would not fool her. She had her own scheme, and she looked through the open doorway.

The man thought his hostess was simply being friendly. He had more eggs and potatoes, then sat back to finish his coffee. He pushed his chair back from the table.

She got up quickly and poured him some more coffee. It

was a long time since a man had sat opposite her at table. Strange how the years had gone! She glanced at the doorway again. A hen was approaching. "Where did you say you were from?" she asked.

As he answered her, she without thinking handed him the little wine glass, used to hold the toothpicks. She stopped short. They both looked at each other a little dismayed and then started to smile—he laughed outright—for of course he had no teeth. Mrs. Dirks' lower lip protruded as ever in her smiling. But she was embarrassed. She looked at the open door, and—thank God!—the hen had started to enter. Her little scheme was working.

"Ach! my chickens!" she cried, jumping up. "Shoo! away with you!" and she ran after the surprised fowl. The bird tried to take wing, then scuttled for the flock. "Hey! hey!" Mrs. Dirks called, fluttering her apron, and then ran and hid behind the barn. She had got away from that man safely.

The man watched the commotion through the doorway. He thought the woman was looking after the fowl behind the barn. When she did not come back after a while, he stepped outside too, and saying "Thanks for the meal" to the empty yard, he walked away to the centre of town.

In the beer parlour he asked some of the men there who the woman was who lived on the edge of town. He remarked on her friendliness and her sense of humour. "Tried to give me a tooth-pick," he laughed, and he opened his mouth wide for the onlookers so that they could see his shrunken gums.

Word spreads quickly in a small town, particularly when news is broadcast in its most democratic institution, the beer parlour. The townspeople had not been aware that old Mrs. Dirks had much kindliness or a humorous side. Perhaps they had never tried to see these qualities.

The next time Mrs. Dirks came uptown, the people stared at her harder than ever. Was this the same Mrs. Dirks? She seemed to walk with a renewed vigour, or had they just never noticed it before? Her dress too was different. It did not seem as shapeless, and in this surmise the people were right. Something had prompted Mrs. Dirks to wear for once a dress made when she was younger—and slimmer. It fitted her better now than when she had made it, for she tended always to cut her dresses so that they hung in folds about her.

"How that woman has persevered!" the townswomen remarked, nodding to each other. "Still managing to take care of herself! She probably has become quite happy in her home over the years."

The men had to agree with the womenfolk—after these matters had been talked over at home. They observed the old woman with fresh eyes when they saw her. Mrs. Dirks' scrutinizing glance at each of the men's faces spoke of an alert woman who was still keenly interested in life. "Hello, Mrs. Dirks," they said with reawakened cordiality, smiling broadly. "Nice day today." Some of the men tipped their hats.

Mrs. Dirks wore a strange smile in greeting, but she did not say anything. "Dirty old men," she thought again, and she strode off home. She could feel her long underwear under her dress, and she was thankful for that.

At home, Mrs. Dirks sat at her table for a mid afternoon lunch. Through the open doorway the sun shone in warmly. Some hens stepped inside over the sill as they were wont to do when their mistress was eating, for she would toss a few crumbs to the floor for them to peck at. It was a homely scene; an old woman with some chickens about her. Mrs. Dirks did feel quite happy then, for the sedateness of the chickens when they came inside the house always made her smile.

But sometimes when the door was closed, so that no one would possibly see, and Mrs. Dirks sat at her table—she wore a different smile on her face. Her lower lip protruded more than ever; and she was not thinking of chickens at all.

Sarah Klassen

The Letter

When Amelia came home from work, there was a letter in the mail. She held it almost reverently in her gloved hand, hurried up the two flights to her apartment. She couldn't remember when she had last received a letter. Or written one. She suspected vaguely that there must have been letters here and there which she had neglected to answer.

Mail, of course, was always copious. There were bills and brochures and offers of discount dry-cleaning and election notices. A fistful of paper to be sorted daily and stuffed, most of it, into the trash can where it ceased to be mail. She wondered how often she had inadvertently destroyed a real letter.

Well, at any rate, this one was real. Her name and address neatly written in blue ink: Ms. Amelia Coppinger, 483 Twenty-third Street, New Milford. The return address was Grantville. That was not familiar, and she studied it a moment, but no memory of people or events connected with that place came to her assistance.

She shrugged her faded tweed coat onto a chair and reached into the large vase for the paper knife. The vase held, besides the paper knife, a spare key, several quarters and nickels, and a collection of small objects that she could not immediately identify. They had been placed there at moments when it became urgently necessary to tidy her handbag or a tabletop. ("Amelia, maybe the reason you can't find important documents when I ask for them is because you just stuff them into drawers without any system," Mr. Gaines, her former supervisor used to say. "It's so inefficient." His displeasure had become increasingly impatient.)

One object felt smooth and cool to her touch. Curious, she lifted it out of the vase. It was a small jade turtle. How it came to be in the vase, she could not imagine. Its place was the knick knack shelf in the sitting room.

As she stroked its hard surface, she recalled reading that Chinese empresses liked to hold jade pieces in their hands to feel cool on a hot day. For the Chinese, the turtle was a symbol of longevity. At twenty-nine, Amelia preferred not to concern herself with that. She simply hoped that she would reach a normal old age, whatever that was. ("You look quite a young woman, really, Amelia," Mrs. Simpson at the pet shop had said this morning. "Perhaps a little attention to hair arrangement. . . and. . . tomorrow I'll bring a stain remover. For your blouse.")

The turtle reminded her that today was Aunt Ellen's birthday, and she had promised to bring her a lemon pie. She put down the turtle, the paper knife, and the letter and went to the refrigerator to take out a lemon. She placed it on the table beside the turtle. Just as she picked up the paper knife, the doorbell rang.

Mrs. Manlius from the next apartment didn't usually come on a Monday night, but there she was, her blue and green duster like a peacock's plumage around her small form. It seemed to fill the doorway.

Amelia knew there would have to be tea, so she made it almost immediately. She allowed her guest to chatter while she busied herself with the tea kettle and cups. She was glad that Mrs. Manlius liked her tea clear. No sugar bowl and creamer and teaspoons to wash up later. She decided not to offer biscuits. Biscuits always encouraged Mrs. Manlius to stay and talk for a long time. The sunburst clock above the table told her it was nearly six o'clock.

"They say he used a paper knife," Mrs. Manlius was saying, and Amelia realized with a touch of guilt that she had shut out her neighbour's voice. She found herself doing this frequently, and not just with her neighbour. This morning Mrs. Simpson had explained the invoice forms they would be using. Amelia had been unable to fix her attention on the small print and the many blank spaces. The persistent pecking of the blue and yellow bird in the ornate cage had distracted her. In the end she had stopped hearing Mrs. Simpson's voice. Tomorrow she would have to find some way to get Mrs. Simpson to repeat her explanation of the invoice procedure.

"Where did you say this happened?" she asked, rather anxiously, hoping to capture missed details.

"I didn't say," was the reply, "But it was near Grantville. That's east of here. The suicide happened in January. The coldest day."

Grantville. Amelia glanced quickly at her letter. Coincidences always gave her goosebumps. She forced a laugh and said, "Why would anyone want to commit suicide with a paper knife when there must be better tools in the house. Bread knives, butcher knives."

Mrs. Manlius said nothing. She picked up the paper knife and turned it round and round in her hand, her gaze impaled on its point, her body hunched around it like a white-crested, gaudy vulture. Grotesque, Amelia thought. She shuddered a little and glanced at the clock.

"Have you any new recipes for lemon pie?" she asked quickly, trying to distract her guest. She realized at once that her question was silly. One exchanged new recipes for black cherry torte or trifle, but lemon pie did not change. It was easy. A recipe should not be necessary at all.

Mrs. Manlius seemed not to have heard. She picked up the letter and brought the paper knife close to it, as if she were about to open it. Her fingers were pink and wrinkled, Amelia noticed, and her clean nails were neatly filed to a small point. Amelia moved forward instinctively, but stopped short of saying anything when she saw the woman put down both knife and letter beside the lemon.

A smile appeared at the corner of Mrs. Manlius's mouth and drifted slowly across her face. "Lemon pie," she mused. "It was lemon pie my grandmother always served after the mock turtle soup. My grandfather adored it. So did I."

Amelia wavered between impatience and uneasiness. Her eyes itemized the objects on the table: teacups, letter, paper knife, lemon. Where was the turtle? Her eyes moved automatically to the other woman's hands. They lay empty on the peacock duster, innocent as two pale doves.

"I had a pet turtle when I was a young girl," Mrs. Manlius was saying. "In summer I let it swim in the cattle trough. Sometimes for hours. Then I'd come back for it. Put it in the glass bowl. One day it disappeared from the trough."

Amelia was relieved to catch sight of a green lump lodged behind her guest's teacup. The shell was patterned with neat, symmetrical shapes. Two small circles were carved into the head for eyes, and the wide mouth seemed to be smiling, like Mrs. Manlius. How could she hasten this stupid visit? Push it to a conclusion.

"I don't think the cows would have swallowed it." Mrs. Manlius was still securely lost in the past. "I used to imagine that a hawk swooped down and carried it away. There were always hawks."

Amelia wasn't listening. She felt it was time she knew what was in the letter from Grantville. Mrs. Manlius had mentioned the place. West of here, she had said, or east. Maybe nothing good could come from Grantville. Still, it seemed a real letter. Someone's hand had written her name on the envelope. The "A" had a charming roundness and the "C" was elegant. Someone had sat behind a desk, oak perhaps, and had written her name. With a silver pen, she wanted to believe. She couldn't take her eyes from the letter.

"Why don't you read it?" said Mrs. Manlius. "I'll just finish my tea. Lovely tea. A lovely teacup."

Amelia felt foolish at being so transparent, but she longed to read the letter. On Mrs. Manlius' next visit, she would take more time. She would serve cake on the cut-glass plate. She would bring out the brocade napkins, the ones with the pale blue flowers in the corner. They had been her mother's. And they would have a real conversation. Amelia would ask about the brother in Toronto who had the heart condition, or was it arthritis. And she would entertain her guest by telling her about the new parrot in the pet shop, the one who refused to say anything except, "Leave me alone. Shut up."

Her hand moved to take the letter just as Mrs. Manlius reached for her teacup. Quite a lot of tea spilled, most of it on the letter When Amelia came with a cloth, she saw her guest smiling. Maliciously, she felt sure. Anger rose in her, a surging wave of it. She wiped the table with vigorous sweeps. Her mouth was clamped shut. It seemed as though control of her kitchen, of this day, was slipping from her, like spilled tea.

When the telephone in the hallway rang, she didn't want to leave Mrs. Manlius in the kitchen. But she went, wondering when she'd get the pie baked. She cast a passing glance at the shrivelled woman sitting like a small empress on the kitchen chair. She wondered if it would have been wiser to take the letter with her. From the telephone she could not see her guest, but she would keep her ears tuned to the kitchen.

It was Aunt Ellen, cheerful as a canary, and "just wondering, dear, if you'd had a good day at the office." Amelia bristled. "Not the office, Auntie. I'm working in a pet shop now, remember? I told you. In the bird section. Happy Birthday. I was going to call you." She didn't mention the pie. She knew it was the real reason for her aunt's call, and this irritated her.

"And about the pie, dear, don't even think of making it if you're too tired after work. But if you do decide to make it, remember that I don't care for those cream kinds. Just old-fashioned lemon meringue. Just thought I'd mention it, dear." Her voice chirped on and on. Amelia tried to gain entrance into the flow of words, to explain that she was busy with a guest, but there was no opportunity.

From the kitchen she could hear breathy laughter. She imagined Mrs. Manlius plunging the paper knife into the lemon and squirting juice on the letter. When would she get to read it? Would it contain good news, make her happy or excited? She wondered what time it was.

". . . in Grantville." The voice at the other end of the line had not yet come to roost. "A cousin twice removed. Really a sad, sad story. We live in a world of suffering and confusion, Amelia, suffering and confusion. But we must make the best of it, mustn't we, and encourage each other."

Amelia pushed aside the temptation to pursue the Grantville reference. "I'm working on the pie, Auntie," she interrupted, finally. "Expect me tonight. We'll have tea together." And talk about Grantville, she thought.

She realized that her re-entry into the kitchen was completely without dignity, but she could not prevent her feet from rushing her down the hall. She felt a little breathless.

"I took the liberty of opening your letter," Mrs. Manlius was saying. In her voice there was not the slightest trace of apology. She held the envelope in one hand and the paper knife in the other. Her eyes were round and very bright.

Amelia felt a helpless fury at this invasion. It was a few moments before she could speak. "Well, where is it? Give it to me." Her voice was loud and rather desperate. And rude. Even with the full right to be angry, she felt embarrassed at her brusqueness. And foolish in her helplessness.

"Oh, the envelope was quite empty. People sometimes forget to insert the letter when they've finished writing it. It happens regularly to my brother in Toronto. I have a whole flock of empty envelopes from him." She gently placed the envelope and the knife on the table.

Amelia began moving the objects on the table, defiantly, while Mrs. Manlius, defiantly, said nothing. The teacups, the paper knife, the lemon. Where was the turtle? The green symbol of long life. For a crazy instant it seemed that on its presence hung her own hope of continuing. But continuing what? To control her kitchen? To make tea? Bake lemon pie? ("Amelia, try to look less frantic when clients come in," Mr. Gaines had frequently suggested. "And smooth your hair.")

Amelia raised both hands to her bran-coloured hair. She thought she must appear as though she were signalling surrender. There must be, surely, just the right gesture or action for this moment in her life. There were appropriate words to be spoken. Something was required of her. But the right actions, suitable words eluded her. Slowly she lowered her hands.

"I really must go." The peacock duster was rising from the chair. A kaleidoscopic blur, a rustling and shimmering of plumage. An enigmatic smile, moving toward the door.

In panic, Amelia started after her. She stretched out her hand as if to grab a corner of the gaudy fabric. The little empress turned, remorse replacing the smile.

"Oh, Amelia, I almost took your turtle. I was just holding him, because he feels so cool. And he reminds me of my lost turtle. Here." She placed the jade animal in Amelia's outstretched hand. Then she was gone, closing the door with a click.

Amelia stared at the turtle. She thought he looked pale, as though the green had faded. And he was so heavy in her hand, she had to put him down on the table. She moved to sit on the chair, from which the faded tweed had slipped to the floor. All she needed was a moment or two of quiet. To blot things out. Maybe a fresh cup of tea. But first there was a pie to make. She reached for the teacups and rose to carry them to the counter. It was past six-thirty. Aunt Ellen would be phoning again soon. She found a recipe book and began turning pages.

Sara Stambaugh

Old Eby

Willis Wilson didn't like his landlord. When old Eby drove to the village the first of every month to pick up the rent, Wilson made a point of being out until Eby's black buggy had time to disappear back into the countryside. When Wilson hadn't left his wife enough cash to pay (Eby wouldn't take checks), Wilson didn't come home until nine or ten.

"He said he'd be back Monday," his wife would say, "and if you want the cistern cleaned and the roof fixed, he said the rent is low enough that you should do it yourself."

"Cheap flathat," Wilson would mutter and add a few more remarks about Mennonites, especially prosperous and particularly conservative ones like his landlord. "The house is falling down around our ears, and all that old cheapskate wants is his money. One of these days I'm going to tell him what I think." But he made sure he had the money when Eby came around next.

Eby's principles were strict even by Mennonite standards. He kept a buggy when the deacons and bishops had shifted to black Fords, and he never spoke English unless he had to. A grizzled widower, he lived on a farm east of Strasburg with a tenant family on the other side of the house. Word was that he'd never gotten over the shock of his three daughters marrying men who couldn't speak German. "As if English isn't good enough when he wants his money," Wilson would grumble, and look around for jobs so that he could raise money towards the next month's rent.

Wilson worked at whatever jobs he could get. After they finished the railroad underpass at Bird-in-Hand he was late on his rent a couple months until the electric company hired men to put up poles and string lines through the county. By spring of 1928 the towns and villages had electricity, but the farms around the countryside still used wind pumps and lit kerosene lamps in the evenings. Farmers who weren't Amish wanted the lines to go through, looking forward to the convenience. Even the Mennonite church in Strasburg was wired for electricity.

Wilson was happy enough to be on the crew helping to dig and set up poles, and his wife, who came from steadier stock than Willis, liked having a regular time for supper, not to mention the steady pay. It was dependable work, even if at first the crew tangled with some Amishmen who didn't want lines going up on their property. But word came from their bishop not to obstruct the civil authority, and work went on.

Until the crew worked its way east and hit old Eby's farm. White-haired and planted like a locust tree, the old man was waiting for them on his property line. "I won't have electric lines crossing my property," he said.

The crew boss said, "I'm sorry, Mr. Eby, but we're coming through anyway. It's a matter of eminent domain."

"Vas is das?" asked Eby.

"It means the government has first claim on all the land in the nation," said the crew boss, "and the law says you have to let the lines go through whether you like it or not."

Eby raised a white eyebrow. "If the law says this is so," he said slowly, "I can't stop you, even if this goes against everything I was raised in. I've worked this land all my life and paid the taxed on it. But if the government can do this, then they're saying the land isn't mine. Caesar is Caesar," he said as he turned away, "and he's taken my land."

The old man slowly walked across the field, while Wilson watched, gleeful that his landlord had got his comeuppance, till the boss said, "Start digging," and Wilson was too busy to think about old Eby.

That job lasted three months. On the first of each Eby drove to Strasburg in his buggy and collected the rent from Wilson's wife. When Wilson came home, she mentioned that their landlord seemed older and was beginning to look frail. Her husband grunted that it served him right when Eby wouldn't clean out the cistern and fix the roof.

"He said he made the rent low because he expected us to make repairs," his wife said, but she didn't say more.

Wilson was late with his rent the fourth month. Then, through a second cousin who was postmaster, he was hired to help collect back taxes. He drove the tax man to half a dozen farms before he was told to get thirty-five dollars worth of stock from old Eby.

The morning he drove up the lane to Eby's farm Wilson had mixed feelings. He wasn't happy at having to confront his landlord, but he smirked that the stingy Mennonite had to answer to the government. The countryside had been hit with a week of rain, and he'd had to get up in the middle of the night to move the bed from under a new leak in the roof, then try to sleep while the drip plunked into a bucket beside his ear. By the time he and the tax collector drove up Eby's muddy lane, Wilson was in a mood to lead the cheering section while the old farmer's barn burned down.

He pulled up beside the barn and blasted on the horn till he saw Eby at the stable door. Carrying a pitchfork, the old man waded towards them through the mud and peered through the truck window while rain poured off the brim of his black hat and ran down his shoulders. "Mr. Eby," said the tax collector, "our records show that you haven't paid your taxes this year. That right?"

"If that's what the government says, I guess it must be," Eby answered. When the tax man asked whether he was going to pay the thirty-five dollars he owed, Eby's face relaxed into what was as close to a grin as Wilson had seen on him.

"I reckon not," Eby said softly. "If you want taxes off me you'll have to take them yourself." His hat and coat were shining black now from the pouring rain. He thumped the handle of his pitchfork into the mud. "As a matter of principle, it seems to me I can't give the government anything when it already owns all I got," he said. "They told me I don't own my land, so I guess I don't owe any tax money for it." He pulled up the fork, turned deliberately, and sloshed towards the barn.

"You know we gotta take some stock then," Wilson shouted after him, but Eby disappeared into the barn. "What'll it be," Wilson asked the tax man, "a pig or a calf?" The tax collector studied his list and said that a couple of stoats should settle

Eby's account.

Wilson jumped from the truck. "Hey, kid!" he called to one of the hired man's children, who was staring at him from under the barn overhang. "Where's the pigsty?"

The boy said something in German through the stable door. "It's there," Eby said, head, shoulders, and pitchfork appearing at the door. He pointed his chin towards a small building on the far side of the barnyard. Wilson turned up his collar against the rain, opened the barnyard gate, and trudged towards the shed, the mud from the barnyard sucking at his galoshes.

Wilson's cap didn't protect him as much as Eby's black hat, and the rain poured down his neck while he unfastened the top of the double door and looked inside at the animals, two sows, a boar, and a dozen odd little ones. The sows heaved up to stare at him, and the piglets squealed and ran for the far side of the shed where the boar slept. Wilson didn't like the looks of those sows, but since he hadn't much choice, he opened the bottom door and stepped inside. There was a warning grunt from one of them as he sidled past her, grabbed a piglet, and backed towards the door, the animal wriggling and kicking.

It was raining harder now, and Wilson got soaked as he ran with the pig to the truck, where he shut it inside a crate before he started back for the second one.

When he got back to the shed, the piglets were milling and squealing, and one of the sows was waiting. As Wilson opened the door she charged and knocked him flat in the barnyard mud. Flinching at the rain, she backed into the sty, but not before half a dozen of the brood had burst through the door and galloped over Wilson while he flailed at them from the flat of his back.

"Get the gate, Elam!" he heard old Eby shout in German to the boy. Wilson sat up and looked around the barnyard. Piglets leaped around him. Frightened, they squealed like wounded rabbits and made frantic hops like bucking mules, then sank into muck up to their bellies before giving more leaps and falling back into the mud.

Wilson struggled to his feet and made a lunge at one bemired piglet a yard or so away, but it jack-rabbited into the air, Wilson's foot slipped, and he fell on his face. He struggled to his feet, wiping the mud out of his eyes. The first thing he saw was old Eby standing under the barn overhang, leaning against his pitchfork and laughing.

Wilson slogged across the barnyard towards the old man, so angry that he could hardly talk. By the time he was facing Eby he'd let loose some choice names for his landlord, and Eby had stopped laughing. Wilson pressed a finger against Eby's chest, sputtering mud in his rage. "You laughed at me!" he shouted. "You got me into this because you're too stingy to pay your taxes, and then you laughed at me!"

"No," Eby said, but Wilson wasn't stopping now. "You and your principles! You're too much of a skinflint to pay your taxes, and you're too tight-fisted to keep the house I live in from falling around my ears, but you're not too holy to take my rent every month—that's how many principles you've got!"

Eby's face was as much a mask now as Wilson's under the mud. "That's not right," he said and had his mouth open to say more when Wilson wheeled away. Coated with mud like a mountain man stalking a chicken coop, he made his way towards the barnyard gate, pounced on a piglet sheltering in a corner, and rushed to his truck. He wouldn't talk to the tax collector and nearly tore out the gears before he rocked clear of the mud and careened down the lane. When he went home to clean up he didn't tell his wife what had happened.

Wilson was sprawled in the front room a week later when she stuck her head through the door to say that old Eby was in the kitchen and wanted to see him. He told her to talk with him and didn't leave his chair until he'd heard the door shut ten minutes later.

His wife was at the dish bench scouring pans. She didn't say anything, and Wilson had to ask her what Eby had wanted. "Something about taxes and the government," she said, "and about you bringing him to examine his ways." She dipped a pan in the rinsewater and commented that Eby was looking better than he had for a time.

Finally she wiped her hands and turned to her husband. "He said that you'd brought him to examine his principles," she said. "If the government owns his farm, it owns all he has, including this house. That means he hasn't any more right to it than we have. We might as well stay here as anyone else, he said, but if he's to follow his principles, he has to wash his hands of it. And he can't take any more rent."

Wilson stood for a full minute taking it all in. "Why the cheap flathat," he finally exploded. "He's taken my rent all these years, and now he's fixed it so I still have to clean the cistern and fix the roof!"

Andreas Schroeder

The Late Man

(one)

On the morning after the storm, the fishermen got up earlier than usual to survey the damage and repair what could be saved. Unusually strong winds and rain had scattered the nets and flattened gardens, bushes, even trees. Fishing boats lay strewn about the beach like broken teeth. Everywhere an exhausted silence hung limply; even the occasional seagull screech seemed blunted and uncertain. Across the mud-flats the faint rush of breakers seemed to fade, though the tide was coming in, slowly and without apparent conviction.

At this time in the morning the fishermen rarely spoke. They arranged their lines, oiled pulleys, checked over their engines and wordlessly pushed out to sea. To break the fragile silence of the first few hours would have been like putting a fist through someone's window or a boot through their door; it was tacitly understood that a man needed more time to clear away in his mind the rubble and destruction of the preceding night, than was available to him between his getting up and the launching of his boat. Even after they had cleared the beach and set their course for the large fishing-grounds farther north, the fishermen rarely raised their voices—as if in instinctive respect for the precariousness of the human mind launched before sunrise on an uncertain sea.

But someone broke the silence that morning. As the last remaining boats poled into deeper water to lower their engines, a young fisherman pointed to a single unattended boat lying on its side amid the beach debris and asked in a low voice: "Where's he?"

The man being addressed looked startled, then shrugged his shoulders.

The young fisherman risked a further offence. "He sick, d'you think?"

There was no response. The other man slid his oar into the water and pushed them off.

(two)

A man opens his cabin door and steps into view. He is the late man, the man whose boat still lies untouched on the beach below the cabin. There is nothing obviously unusual about this man except, perhaps, a certain reticence in his manner—the reticence of a man for whom the world has become untrustworthy, suspect—and for whom, since that time, a glass on a table has become less and less a glass on a table and more and more a thing too strange and amazing to grasp by name. As he stands in his doorway, his hand rests gingerly on its frame, as if constantly ready in case of attack.

About fifteen minutes have passed since the last boat was launched and the late man stepped from his cabin. Now, his boat ready and his outboard spluttering half-submerged, he pushes off and follows the fleet toward the fishing-grounds.

A few hours later the fishing village begins to yawn, stretch and get up; children and women clutter the streets and tangle the air with punctuation marks.

(three)

When they return in the early evening and pull their boats out of the water above the high-tide markers, the late man is not with them. During the interval of time between the last fisherman's ascent from his stranded boat to his waiting dinner and the late man's arrival at the launching site fifteen minutes later, silence holds the beach like an indrawn breath. The sound of his prow on the pebbles, therefore, sounds like a large freighter being dragged over a granite reef. He has caught fewer fish than the other fishermen.

The next morning the late man appears at his cabin door half an hour after the fishermen have left the beach. Their boats are already vague in the distance when he finally manages to haul his boat to the water-line, which has by this time fallen far below his landing place with the receding tide. He seems weakened, older, leaning wearily against the tiller. When the fishermen return that night he is an uncertain speck on the horizon, half an hour behind the last of the fishing fleet, and when the catch is scored, he has caught fewer fish than the day before.

(four)

Around noon the following day the boats were anchored in clusters to share both lunch and small-talk on the fishing-grounds, and the conversation turned briefly to the late man. "Can't figure 'im out," a yellow macintosh mused, digging thoughtfully into his tomato sandwich. "Won't tell nobody what's wrong."

"Ain't sayin' a thing," another agreed. "Asked him yesterday, I said, what's the problem there, speak up man, but I'd swear he wasn't even listening."

There was a pause as if to let the spoken words disperse.

"Sea can do that to ya, if ya don't look out. Catches up to ya, sometimes." A greybeard shrugged and threw his orange peel overboard, then absently ignored a deck-hand who had asked him what he meant. The deck-hand finally turned away; he was new in the fleet and often found himself unanswered. He was already on the other side of the boat when the old man muttered his answer to no one in particular: "I dunno what happens. I just know it does. Ain't nobody can spin the world by hand."

The next morning the late man launched his boat some forty-five minutes after the fleet had left the beach.

(five)

Little is known of the late man's history, though this doesn't become apparent until he first begins to attract attention by his mysterious dislocation of schedule. Suddenly everyone is rummaging around for old impressions, suspicions, predictions. Little substantial information is collected. Most agree that this relatively young man has been hard-working and "well-disciplined enough, though perhaps just a little too introspective for his own good." Never much of a joiner, and no great community booster, he has, on the other hand been known to help a complete stranger when no one else would. Someone a little more observant points out his peculiar tendency to touch things around him very lightly, almost suspiciously, as if he didn't quite believe they were really there, or that they really were what they seemed to be. This remark is received in uncertain silence. Many frankly admit they haven't the slightest idea of what to make of the whole business, and that he's probably just going through some passing confusion. But then, how to explain (as someone quickly points out) his very methodical, plan-like deceleration of pace in relation to the village's daily fishing schedule—by this time he's reported leaving the beach a full three hours after the last of the other boats has been launched.

(six)

By the time the late man pulls his boat from the water, the sun is little more than an almost-submerged leer on a mindless horizon and the waves have jelled to heavy, slowly swirling mimicries. Night winds begin to cover the eastern part of the sky with a thick, cumulous ceiling of ridicule. Sardonic chuckles ripple along the water-line where the undertow pursues its endless deception of the beach gravel. The late man stands motionless, looking as if he belongs neither to the water nor the land; his face is a ploughed field but his eyes dart about the beach like frightened piranhas. His boat, a tilted sneer on its side in the pebbles, has rope dangling from its prow like corded spittle. Wave upon wave of curling laughter lampoons the beach. Everywhere, everything grins.

The late man no longer defends himself. He has begun to haul up unmistakeable evidence of a treasonous collusion between his mind and its surrounding ocean—a mind he has always thought indisputably his own, and implicitly loyal. A mind to which he has entrusted all his strategies, his stealthy casts into the nature and composition of himself, and whatever else it is possible to apprehend. A mind that has always seemed prepared to take him to any depth, regardless when or where, to set and trawl for the mysteries in all waters.

But a mind, it seems, has other loyalties as well. A loyalty, perhaps, to the greater biology of living things. To the directives of our deepest, unreachable instincts. A refusal to be used against itself.

And a mutinous mind, once discovered, will not be content merely to be cast adrift. As if to ensure that it can never be put into such a compromising position again, it baits confusion, clutters the haul with monstrosities, red herrings, snags, seaweed, garbage or nothing at all. Tightly reefed tenets and principles have come slack; endless qualifications have jammed simple premises, hopelessly entangling sentiments, certainties and articles of faith. Above all, the horror has clambered up the rigging of the late man's brain that all this is beyond his control, and that like a retaining pin pulled from a spring-loaded wheel, this destruction will continue relentlessly until it has unrolled the tension from the spring.

There appears to be little he can do but to hold on until all is done, and to hope that he does not become so weakened as to fall prey to a useless madness.

(seven)

In a matter of months the departures and arrivals of the late man and the fishing fleet have diverged to such an extent that the returning fishermen see the late man's boat heading toward them at dusk, on its way north toward open water. He stands huddled over his tiller, staring unseeing at the darkening horizon as if in purposeful blindness. The fishing fleet parts to let him pass. Though no one appears to understand, everyone sees the desperate undertow in his eyes and says nothing. When all the boats are secured and the gear stowed away, the late man is a dissolving blotch against black evening. A few moments later he is gone.

The late man had returned the previous morning with no fish at all.

As he sat down to dinner, the young fisherman who had asked about the late man on the morning after the storm suddenly spoke of him to his wife. "This is driving me foolish. No one knows anything, or they won't say anything. Everybody pretends to ignore him. This can't go on."

His wife said nothing.

He looked at her curiously, then threw down his knife. "Well damn me, here's a man digging his own grave in plain view of the entire village, and nobody has the guts to look into the matter."

His wife remained silent, but a worried look began to unsettle her face. The young fisherman stood up abruptly. "Then I'll find out," he said, reaching for his squall-jacket. "If for no other reason but self-defence!" he added as he opened the door. His footsteps receded from the cabin. Minutes later, the sound of his outboard began to move across the bay toward the fishing grounds and open water.

(eight)

For a time the young fisherman pilots his boat through almost total darkness. A bulging cloud cover muffles the moon, and the night everywhere sways and sidesteps blindly, ponderously. The occasional clear splash falls short among the sluggish gurgle and sagging cough of deep-water waves beneath the keel. The young fisherman peers intently across the bow, but steers his boat by instinct.

As he moves farther and farther into deeper water, the night begins to thin out; his eyes detect edges, outlines, occasional glimpses of phosphoric glitter. Eventually the moon disentangles itself from the clouds and trudges high into the sky, spraying a fine shower of faint light over the fishing grounds. Now he can make out the darker shape of the late man's boat, lying at anchor on his starboard side. The booms on the boat before him are out, trailing thin glistening lines into the water. The late man is fishing.

The young fisherman sits unmoving at his tiller, uncertain what should follow. Possibilities dart in and out of his mind, unwilling to bite. He waits, his brain idling slowly, his thoughts slack.

A creak from a rusty tackle interrupts the silence. A glass-float dips and scrambles; the late man comes alive and begins to reel it in. A strike.

The young fisherman straightens up and strains to see. The glass-float tugs and splashes at the end of a stiff line; the late man's figure curves against the gunwhale, his arms taut with exertion. The young fisherman feels an instinctive excitement thrill through his body as if the strike were his own. Something huge is on the end of that line.

The glass-float is almost at boat's edge, momentarily calmer. The late man reaches for his fish-net and plunges it over the side, scooping carefully. His back is turned to the young fisherman, obscuring the float as he brings it to the boat's side. The fishnet rises from the water, then stops.

Surprised, the young fisherman leans forward but sees only the hunched back of the late man leaning over his net. A fierce rippling movement shakes the arm holding the handle as something twists and writhes in the meshes, but the late man makes no move to pull it into the boat. Ten minutes pass. The late man still stands bent over his net, gazing at his catch. The young fisherman is unable to see his face.

Finally, in a slow but deliberate movement, the late man empties his net into the sea and straightens up.

The young fisherman watches, still dumfounded, as the late man repeats the same procedure moments later when another line snaps alive. This time his demeanor seems to indicate recognition or less interest; a short look suffices to make him empty the net again. After a short pause a third float begins to bob and the late man reels it in. Half an hour later he is still engrossed in the net's contents, ignoring all the other lines which are jerking at the boom. Bent over the gunwhale, his hair blowing about his head like spray in the wind, the late man stares at his catch in silence, then throws it back into the sea.

(nine)

As a faint paleness begins to tinge the outermost edges of the dark, the young fisherman stands up stiffly, a nervous flutter in his stomach, strangely excited yet uncertain why. He feels almost intoxicated with discovery, though he has no idea what he has discovered or realized.

Carefully pulling out his oars, he mounts them in the oarlocks and prepares to slip away. By the time the sun appears he will be back in the bay and his cabin. Then there will be time to think.

A small sound from the other boat stops his raised oars short. The late man has emptied his net and stepped back against his mast. As he half-turns to re-apply bait to one of the lines the young fisherman catches a glimpse of the late man's face. He almost drops his oars.

The late man's face is totally disfigured. Crumbled skin, twitching lips and bleached white hair.

He is suddenly old—an uncertain fool barely able to hold his balance in the rocking boat. The young fisherman is stunned. The late man was of the same generation as most of the others in the fishing fleet—chronologically about thirty years old. Now he looks three times that age.

But there is no time to lose; the horizon is becoming a thin pencil-line of light across the dark and he will be discovered. Stealthily moving his oars, the young fisherman pulls away toward the south and the fishing village.

As his boat moved into the bay, he saw the first cabin doors opening and fishermen walking down the beach toward their boats. Several of them look up, surprised to see his incoming boat at such an odd time. Obviously his wife had said nothing. He steered toward an unused part of the beach and ran his boat aground.

There, his boat bobbing slightly to the rhythm of his fading wash, he sat on the bow and twisted a piece of rope between his fingers; confused, almost certain, unsure of himself again. The spreading sun warmed his back as he sat, but his stomach remained cold and unsettled. He felt the desperate urge to run, to hit something, to tear something to shreds, but somehow he was numbed or simply too overwhelmed to move. So many things he had come to know but had never paid much attention to abruptly seemed to demand this attention now, to insist on being confronted unequivocally, to be drawn into a larger picture. As they whirled in ever-tightening circles about his head, the steadily mounting pressure threatened to explode inside him like a surfacing deep-water fish.

Then the faint growl from a distant engine punctured the silence and the tension drained away with an almost audible hiss. The young fisherman looked over his shoulder and watched the late man's boat increase toward the bay. Several of the other fishermen paused and shaded their eyes. For a short while everything seemed to hang in suspension. . .

Suddenly the late man's boat is in the bay, its engine silent, drifting toward the beach. As its prow gouges into the sand the late man struggles feebly to climb over the gunwhale onto the gravel, half-falling several times in the attempt. Then, hoisting the bow-rope over his shoulder, he attempts to pull his boat higher up onto the beach.

(ten)

Later, after the late man had been buried and the fishermen returned to their boats, the young fisherman was heard to say, somewhat bitterly, that in a totally paralyzed landscape, the only moving thing had been the late man trying to beach his boat. (That remark was received in uneasy silence.)

They had watched him for an incredibly long time, trying to raise the bow above the gravel, and when he finally collapsed, still no one seemed able to move. When they eventually began to climb down toward the fallen figure, the landscape stretched and expanded in every direction, and they walked for hours before reaching him. They found him lying on his back, his face contorted with a mixture of agony and amazement; it was the oldest face they had ever seen. So they buried him, quietly and without looking at each other, and the young fisherman beached the boat.

The next morning, due possibly to the tiring events of the preceding night and day, the young fisherman slept a little longer, and eventually launched his boat some fifteen minutes after the rest of the fishing boats had cleared the bay.

III. Coming of Age

Sandra Birdsell

The Day My Grandfather Died

I remember the day I bought a small bottle of Evening in Paris
cologne. I was on my way home from school at lunch time and
took the long way home, going down Main Street and past the
drugstore instead of cutting through the coulee as I usually did,
because I wanted to see the display of cologne in the window.
My friend Claudette Gagnon had seen it earlier and told me
about it. Claudette wore a cardigan sweater that had poodles
and pom poms on it and a black "Frederick's of Hollywood"
type brassiere beneath her sweater which gathered her breasts
up into swollen jiggling shelves of jelly. She also shaved off her
eyebrows and painted them back on in a thin coquettish black
arch. Wherever I went with her a residue of attention, like
dandruff, fell on me. But for me, the attraction of Claudette was
more than that. Claudette was French, as was my father. I had
even picked up her accent and went out of my way to say things
such as, "The car, she is parked in the drive-way," and, "H'it's
going to rain."

"For Pete's sake," Mika, my mother, would say, "your
English is worse than mine. You sound as bad as the Lafrenieres." Which made me smile because to be like the Lafrenieres,
my father's people, would make my rebellion complete and
finally take me out and away from the rest of the family.

"From Bourjois of Paris and Montreal," the display card in
the drugstore read. Blue bottles the shape of uteruses nestled
down inside the blue satin-lined boxes. I unscrewed the cap
from the sample bottle. The smell of cologne was like almonds.
It made me ache in "that place" and I would have like to have
touched and gentled myself until the bud flowered. But the

warning I'd received from Mika was profound and clear. "Play with yourself and you'll never want a man," she said. And I knew that I wanted a man, eventually. At that time, I was still like a dog chasing a car, barking and nipping at boys' heels, not knowing what I'd do if I ever caught one.

I stood there in the drugstore, getting off, as they say, on the smell of Evening in Paris cologne. It reminded me of a mystery novel I'd once read. It was a story about a short bald man who murdered beautiful but cruel women who laughed at him. The women were either blonde and cold or brunette and very shallow. They all had long hair and wore skin-tight black sheath dresses and rhinestone jewelry. They smoked cigarettes using a holder. I liked the bald man. He had impeccable manners and manicured fingernails. I thought that killing people for laughing at you was justifiable homicide. According to the novel, he would smile a sinister smile as he took a silver box from his pocket and flicked open the lid. The woman continued to laugh heartlessly through a curl of cigarette smoke while he offered her a deadly candied almond. Then it was his turn to laugh as death came slowly and the victim's contorted features made her ugly in the end.

The smell of the cologne reminded me of my mother walking to the corner to catch the Greyhound into Winnipeg. She carried a shopping bag on her arm. She wore her navy suit which displayed her trim figure, a pink frilly blouse and a navy pillbox hat. I carried a box for her, filled with mittens and scarves which her women's church group had made. All winter they'd met weekly in each others' homes. I despised their fervent good works and their complete lack of adornment. It made them seem unnatural and grimly severe. They seldom smiled. My mother had been elected to take the results of their labours into the city and deliver them to a mission. I swung the box up into the baggage department.

"She's one 'eavy box," I complained. My mother stared at me and then laughed. Her laughter was seldom an expression of joy or good humour. Her laughter said things such as: see, I knew that would happen, or, trust me, the world's a dirty place.

One time, her laughter was spontaneous. I was walking across the yard towards the house and she was standing, framed by the window, looking out at me. For a terrible second I had the feeling that I was looking into a mirror and seeing my own reflection in her face and so I didn't watch where I was going. I stepped on a rake that had been left lying and it sprung up and bonked me between the eyes. My mother began to laugh outright, a deep belly laugh. When I came into the house she was still laughing. And I learned that the way to make her happy was to hurt yourself.

The bus driver swung the baggage door closed. Mika hid the remainder of her laughter behind a pink glove. Just as I was turning away, stinging and angry, she touched my arm. "What would you like me to bring you from the city?"

And I said, "Candied almonds."

When she came home that night, she had them with her and when I opened up the bag, the sight of those lilac, pink, yellow and white candies affected me strangely. I sat cross-legged on the couch with the bag in my lap and played with the seed-shaped candies. The texture of them was like that of a very fine toadstool, pebbly and cool to the touch. They made my heart ache. In the same way my mother pinched her babies to express affection, in the same way my berserk hormones made me want to laugh and cry simultaneously or dream beneath musk-scented sheets of caressing and being caressed, and then recoiling in anger and hitting out when someone tried to touch me—I wanted to crush the candied almonds underfoot. I couldn't help but think about the images that the mystery novel had evoked, and about the possibility of some demented grey person in Eaton's candy department slipping a few poisoned almonds into the candy bin. And so I shared my gift, offered the candies up to my mother and to my sisters instead of eating them myself. While they sucked, I watched for the signs, the deep pain in the stomach, the sudden clutching and pitching forward, their expressions when they became aware of their own finality.

The smell of the cologne in the drugstore that day was like that act. It was power, it was anger and knowing something that no one else knew. And so I bought a bottle.

I took my purchase to the clerk. She rang it up on the cash register and slipped the cologne into a bag. Then she looked at me as though she'd only just seen me. "Have you been home for lunch yet?" she asked. She searched my face with a prying, knowing look. She was over forty years old and so I'd never bothered to remember her name. I knew her only by her breasts. They were enormous. The boys called her Tits Wiggle. I handed her the money. "No, I haven't, why?" What's it to you? Drop off, eh? Flake off, peel off, bug off, take a flying leap.

"It's not for me to say," the clerk said. "You'd just better get going. Go straight home."

I left the drugstore slowly, so as not to let her know that I was concerned. But as soon as I was clear of the window and her sight, I began to run. I knew something terrible must have happened if she wouldn't say what it was. And when I got home, I found out my Grandfather Thiessen had died.

"Guess what," I said to Claudette. "My grandfather kicked the bucket during the night."

"Yeah, so I heard. That's tough."

"He was eighty-one years old; it was no surprise."

We'd met at the Scratching Chicken Hotel cafe during the noon break. My mother was away, sitting with my grandmother. Claudette didn't take her lunch to school as most of the farm kids did. Claudette wasn't farm. She'd been expelled from the convent school at Grande Pointe where she lived with her parents who owned Gagnon Chevy-Olds garage. I'd never been to Grande Pointe, but the kids said if you didn't speak French, no one would talk to you. I always ate my own lunch at home and then rode my bike downtown so that I could sit with Claudette while she ate hers. She was talkative, flashy and demonstrative, traits that I then attributed to her French-Canadian identity only because I didn't see these traits in my mother or my grandparents, who were not French, but Mennonite, a fact that I detested. Being Mennonite was like having acne. It was shameful, dreary. No one invited you out. How to be French, I didn't know. My father was seldom home and when he was, showed no interest or energy, I didn't know which, in perpetuating any of his own traditions.

"I had a cat once," Claudette said. "She was my cat for twelve years. Slept on my bed every night. When she passed off, I really felt bad. I'ad her since I was a kid." She nudged me with her elbow. "You'll be okay. H'it takes time."

We'd all buried animals. I remembered my dog, Laddie, a collie stray. My grandfather had persuaded my mother to let me keep him. He used to take my hand in his mouth and walk me to school. Claudette's sympathetic nudge unsettled me. I squashed a drinking straw flat, rolled it into a ball and flicked it across the counter into the chocolate bars. "I had my grandfather since I was a kid too," I said.

"I guess, eh?" Claudette said and snickered. "I like you, you're bad." She pushed her plate of chips aside and ran her fingers through her thick black hair which she wore short and which met at the back of her head like a feathered duck's tail. She had tiny features and large eyes. We sat side by side with our arms resting on the counter. I was tanned deeply, a dusty dark brown, and she was very fair. I was the only Lafreniere to have black hair and I felt special, set apart. Today, people mistake me for Jewish or Italian.

"I guess he died of old age, eh?"

"Cancer. I think. I kind of lost touch."

"Jeez. Tough. I guess you'll miss him."

I didn't feel one thing or another. My face was a little numb as though I'd just been to the dentist, that was all. I shrugged. "He was sick for a long time. The only thing I really remember about him was that he ate a lot of sunflower seeds. Every pocket, full of seeds, and he'd spit the shells out through his mustache into his hand. His hands were always moist. I didn't like it."

"No kidding." Claudette had grown tired of the topic. She played with the silver cross at her neck and her features had a painful bored expression. Coffee gurgled down from the tops of the coffee makers into the glass urns below. The waitress came over and began to clean up the dishes.

"Let's cut." Claudette said. "This place stinks."

We walked down Main Street, passed by the corner where we should have turned to go to school. "What's up?" I asked, surprised.

"On the day your grandfather died, you shouldn't have to go to school," Claudette said. "My parents, they went into the city for parts today. We can have the place for ourselves."

We cut school that afternoon. We walked, instead, to the outskirts of Agassiz and stuck out our thumbs. Two rides and we were at Grande Pointe. The town was a disappointment. I was looking forward to something more than the jumbled collection of buildings and houses on either side of the wide dirt street that cut away from the main highway and rejoined it a mile later. I wanted more than street signs written in French. Gagnon Chevy-Olds was the newest-looking building on the street. As we drew near, I saw an old man sitting on a painted chair.

"Who's that?"

"It's just my father's uncle," Claudette said. "My father lets him hang around the garage. He's got nothing better to do. Don't worry, he won't say anything about us being here. Half the time he doesn't know what day it is."

He wore a straw hat and grey wool pants and a white shirt, unbuttoned at the neck. The kind my father wore around the house. He beckoned to Claudette and began speaking to her softly, haltingly, in French. His wide face was calm, gentle, no will to harm in it. If someone said to him, tomorrow the world will end, he would reply, so be it.

Claudette leaned over him. "Speak English," she said loudly. "Can't you see I've got company? This is Lureen Lafreniere. She's a girl from school."

He looked at me, took off his straw hat and rested it on his knee. My mouth tingled. If I smiled, my face would be forever frozen in that position. I thought I'd recognized that gesture, the wide sweeping of his hand. He spoke again, and to me his voice was like the sound of newspapers being swept along the street by the wind.

"He thinks he knows your old man," Claudette said.

"Oh yeah?" My heart lifted.

"Wants to know if you're Prosper's daughter," she laughed. "Prosper Lafreniere was an old hermit, older than him. He died last year. I told you, the old guy's cuckoo." She made a winding motion at her temple.

"Tell him that my father's the barber at Agassiz. His name is Maurice. He used to play the fiddle."

She told him. I held my breath. I needed to know something of who I hoped I was.

"I don't remember your father. Was he of this place?"

"Told you, screws loose. Come on, forget it," Claudette said and began to walk away.

The old man lifted his hat, waved it at me. "Adios to youse

girls," he said and laughed. I liked him and wished that Claudette hadn't spoken to him with so little respect.

I followed Claudette between two buildings to the back of the garage. There were sounds of hammering coming from the garage. Through windows in a door, I could see bright splashes of sparks from a welder. Claudette stood on her toes so that she could see inside. "Good," she said. "Jimmy's working today."

"Who?"

"Jimmy Nabess. He works on and off for my father. He's cute." She winked. "Maybe later, I'll invite him to come up."

We went up a flight of stairs. She unlocked the door, stepped inside. A gold crucifix hung above the door. She led me through a small kitchen into the living room. A trestle table rested along one wall; along another, pine bookshelves with knick-knacks on them, a highback wooden bench, and beside the bench a pine couch with burlap cushions. A spinning wheel sat in the corner by the window. Above the couch, there were dark paintings of a fort and Indians huddled around a fire, tepees in the background. Another painting: a cobblestone street leading to an old church and tall European-looking buildings with narrow windows, lining the street.

"Nice," I said.

"You think so? I don't. I think it's crap. My mother had a vacation in Quebec and came back with it. It's like living in a coffin," she said. "Be back in a sec." She went into the kitchen. A moment later she stuck her head around the corner. "Do you like your beer warm or cold? I keep a case under my bed if you want a warm one."

I took her love for beer as being part of her French identity and so I said I'd love a warm beer. I went over to the front window and looked out over the town. There was more to Grande Pointe than I'd first seen. I could see the peaks of houses across the river, where the town unfolded in neat rows among lime-green groves of maple trees. It looked like Agassiz, no different. The same muddy river that divided Grande Pointe ran along the edge of Agassiz as well and the same flotsam on that river, the bloated bodies of cows, broken trees, tin cans, passed through their town as it did ours. Claudette came back with the beer.

I watched as she tipped the bottle, there was a gurgling,

and one quarter of the beer was gone. "They put beer in babies' bottles, the French," my mother said once, referring to my father's relatives. "So that they can go out to dances, they take the kids with them, fill their bottles with beer so the kids will fall asleep in the car, and they can have all the fun they want."

"And so, what's wrong with that?" Maurice said.

And she said, "If they could only see, realize, the damage they're doing to their children."

I tipped my bottle, parted my lips the way Claudette had, but the beer didn't flow down my throat. It foamed, backed up into my nose, stinging. My eyes watered. Claudette laughed and brought me a Kleenex. I asked for a glass and drank the first beer and talked about the other kids at school, some of the boys in our class; and I was surprised that the boys I had gone through elementary school with and now high school, and who I thought were disgusting, she thought attractive. I liked the homestead old feeling of her rough, wooden living room and she wanted a modern one like mine. A feeling of disillusionment was setting in along with a slight light-headedness. Claudette yawned, looked at her watch. "Be back in a sec," she said again. "I'm going to talk to Jimmy. Help yourself to another beer."

I went into Claudette's bedroom. There were clothes scattered about on the bed and cosmetics over the top of her dresser. I looked into the mirror. "Goodness, who is she?" Mika had said once when I was changing, my features rearranging themselves weekly during puberty, giving me at last a broad face, a too-thick nose and deepset eyes, too small; I tried to do tricks with cosmetics but it didn't help.

"She doesn't even look like a Lafreniere," Mika said and it was true. Several times I'd seen my father's brothers, and they were both short and fat and small-featured. I pulled my hair up and away, held it into a pony tail, tight, so that my eyes became slanted. Sometimes I thought I was Oriental, or Eskimo. I saw Claudette's blue bottle of Evening in Paris cologne. I dabbed some behind my ears and then took another beer out from under her bed.

"And this," Claudette said, entering the bedroom suddenly, "is my friend Lureen, the one I told you about?" She introduced me to Jimmy Nabess. Jimmy was Indian. He was short and slender; his hair, almost shoulder-length, was caught back behind his ears. He wore a baseball cap, a satin-looking blue jacket with his name on one shoulder, and dusty blue jeans.

"Hi ya," he said. His expression said that he didn't care if I lived or died.

"I told him we're having a party, and he wanted to come too. Hurry up and finish that beer. Parties are more fun if you're drunk."

For the next hour, we drank beer steadily, almost dutifully, as Claudette worked hard to fill each awkward silence, the trailing off of conversation. Jimmy and I sat side by side on the couch. I grew quieter and quieter because I sensed his dislike for me. Finally, despairing, Claudette said that what we needed was some music and went to her bedroom to get her records. Jimmy moved forward on the couch as though he were about to follow her and then changed his mind, took off his jacket and began squeezing bottle caps. I noted that our arms were almost the same colour.

"You from Grande Pointe?" I asked.

"Uhuh."

I didn't know if this meant yes or no. "It seems like an okay place."

"It's the same like any place."

"Nabess," I said. "Is that French?"

"No."

I didn't want to ask him what it was. "Lafreniere is French. My father speaks French."

He shrugged impatiently. "So what's the big deal? Lots of people talk French. Claudette," he called. "I'm dry."

"Coming, coming," Claudette said and put a record on the player. She clapped her hands and began to do the twist. The beer had made her face flushed, her eyes shine. "Hey come on," she said. "Let's dance."

"I hafta get back to work. Your old man will be the first one to kick my ass if I don't."

"Just one," she said.

They danced for a full hour. I watched for awhile. They were caught up in their dancing, in each other. Occasionally Claudette would suggest that he ask me to dance, but only half-heartedly, and when she turned the record over, she went back to him. I got up from the couch. The room tilted. I walked over to the window. I saw the old man, he was crossing the street slowly. He walked, choosing each step as though it were his last. He stood in front of the cafe, shielded his eyes and looked in the window, searching for someone. Then he began walking down the street to the corner.

I willed his faltering steps, each rising and falling of his feet. He belonged in the picture above the couch, an old man walking along a cobblestone street. It seemed to me that he was no ordinary person, but larger. I wanted to walk beside him with my arm under his and claim him as my ancestor. I leaned with my forehead against the glass and the cool window-pane felt good against my stiff face. My breath was reflected back to me. I smelled sour beer and something else, the Evening in Paris cologne.

The smell of the cologne reminded me of fruit cake, almond paste and my grandparents standing with a tray loaded with chunks of dark fruit cake at their fiftieth wedding anniversary. Grandma wore a loose-fitting white dress made of some light material that did not show her large body, but hid it so instead of looking fat and awkward, she seemed to float. She wore gold leaves in her white hair and so as they approached me, I thought she was a vision, a fairy godmother who had the power to grant wishes. And I would have asked her to take away my aches and pains. I was never without sore limbs, "growing pains," my mother called them, and an uneasy stomach. I did not think they were growing pains. I felt that my bones were going to crack and splinter because of some inner pressure. I would have asked my grandmother to make me feel happiness. But she frowned at the tray of cake my grandfather carried and said, "Nah, Papa, look at what you've done. You've cut far too much cake. It will only be wasted." And the fairy vision vanished.

"Give it the children, then," he said. And it came to me how their conversations always seemed to centre on food, the growing of it, the preparing of it and the eating. That was all that mattered. To me, their lives had been narrow and confining; even here, now, at a celebration, they were unable to step across the limits and celebrate. I was angry and so I said, "Don't waste the food on us kids, feed it to the bloody pigs instead."

The old man had reached the corner. He seemed to hesi-

tate and then he turned sharply to the left and began crossing a
bridge which spanned the same river that flowed past my grandparents' cottage. I could see that river through the leaves of the
vine arbour where I was sent as punishment, to reflect in soli-
tude upon what I'd said about feeding good food to the pigs.
Two words my grandfather forbade us to use because he said
we didn't know their meanings: starve and hate. I knew my
words had cut him deeply. There were several boys playing
along the river bank trying to skip stones and I forgot about
what it was I should be thinking as I watched and wished I were
down there to show them how to do it and at the same time,
make them feel stupid. Grandfather came in and sat down
beside me. He didn't speak for a long time and then asked,
"Why are you always so angry?"

"I guess I was born that way. I can't help it. I couldn't help
being born."

"Not so, not so," he said. "God made a much brighter girl."

His way of speaking irritated me. "If you say so, then it
must be true."

He pulled at my chin in an attempt to have me look at him.
His hand smelled of sunflower seeds. His pale blue eyes were
moist with sorrow. I couldn't explain my anger. I thought I was
a freak. I didn't belong because I was totally different from every
other member of that family.

"People make me mad," I said.

"I'm sorry for you, then. Because you become their slave
when you let them make you angry. Being angry doesn't change
anything. You can never change what people say and do. The
only thing you can change in this world is your reaction to what
they say and do. You're hurting yourself by being angry. Look
here," he said. He took his penknife from his pocket. He cut a v
into a vine leaf, lightly, barely perceptible. "When you come for
German lessons on Saturday, I'll show you what anger does."

The following Saturday, the scar in the leaf had become
deep and brown and the leaf had grown, but was misshapen.
"That's what you're doing with your life," he said. "With your
anger you make marks in it that will never go away."

He left me to think on this. I thought. I thought he was
minimizing what I was feeling with cheap tricks with a penknife.
I went into the garden. I picked up the hoe. I chopped and

hacked until I had cut down all of his sunflowers.

I turned from the window, feeling morose and angry at the same time for Claudette's lack of attention to me. And for the first time I wondered, how was I going to get home?

"My mother will kill me," I said. "I think I'd better head for home."

Claudette danced over to me, stuck her fingers into my chest and pushed me backwards towards the couch without missing a beat of the music. "You can't go yet. Jimmy wants to have a dance with you."

She brought me another beer and put on a record. It was a slow song. She put her arms around Jimmy's neck, he put his hands around her waist and his leg between hers and they moved in time to the music.

I belched loudly. My stomach was swollen and felt full. I was in a haze, stupified, and so I lay down. Through half-closed eyes, I saw Jimmy place his hand on Claudette's breast, his hand, brown, against her pale blue sweater and I thought, he shouldn't do that, he's squashing the pom poms on her poodles. "Oh no," Claudette said in response to something Jimmy had whispered in her ear, "not with her here."

My stomach heaved and the room swung violently. I had heard that if you're drunk and the room moves, lie with one foot resting on the floor and the motion will stop. I tried that and closed my eyes. It didn't work. I smelled something thickly sweet, it was the Evening in Paris cologne and it made my stomach even queasier. Claudette laughed drunkenly. Jimmy manoeuvred her across the floor towards the bedroom door with his pelvis. He backed her up against the wall and kissed her, his back to me now, his head going around and around and the room turning with it. My stomach revolted.

I bolted from the couch, stumbled past them into the bathroom and retched over the toilet. My whole head was numb now. The same thing had happened when my dog Laddie got hit by a car. My mother had demanded a response of grief from me. "Cry," she said and they all stood waiting, my sisters and my mother, waiting for me to cry. "You loved that dog," she said, "why don't you cry?" And I would not cry because I knew that she did not say it out of a feeling for me, but out of the necessity to be proven right, so she could say, "I told you, the world's a dirty place." My refusal to cry had cut its mark into me. And here I was, my grandfather had died and I was a piece of wood, numb in the head, unable to express what I should be feeling for an old man who had really cared about me.

"For God's sake," Claudette said. "Vomit and get it over with."

I tried, I strained.

"Shove your finger down your throat."

I stuck my finger into my throat, gagged, but nothing happened.

"Let me help," Claudette said. She stood behind me, wrapped her arms around my stomach and squeezed suddenly and hard. The flood of vomit, everything I had eaten, drank, whooshed forth, splattering the toilet seat. Once I began, I couldn't stop. I heaved and upchucked until there was nothing to come but green bile.

Claudette brought me water to drink, slapped me on my back as though I had just achieved something great. "Way to go," she said. "You'll feel better now. Whenever I drink too much, I just stick my finger down my throat and then I can keep on going."

"I'm not keeping on going," I said. "I'm going home. My grandfather is dead."

"So?"

I put my head into Claudette's pom poms. My face began to fall apart, piece by piece. My mouth trembled and I couldn't make it stop. I began to weep. "An old man is an old man, right? It doesn't matter what nationality, they're all the same. He was old and he was mine and he died."

"Christ," Claudette said and pushed me away. "I hate sloppy drunks."

But I didn't mind. I didn't care what anyone would say.

Armin Wiebe

Practising

The year they built the TV tower I was heista kopp in love with Shaftich Shreeda's daughter, Fleeda. I was only almost sixteen and Fleeda was almost sixteen, too, and I had been in love with her all the way since we were only almost fourteen when she looked at me in her little pocket mirror from where she was sitting in the next row in school and I just went heista kopp in love. And now we were both almost sixteen and everything should have fit together real nice, only when you are almost sixteen the whole world seems to get in the way of things that you want because when you are only almost sixteen you don't have a driver's licence. That's where the puzzle doesn't fit. That's how come the weeds grow in the garden.

I mean, me and Fleeda were going pretty good. Like I walked with her home from choir practice three times, and one Sunday after dinner when I knew that her brothers weren't at home I went to visit her and we went for a walk down to the big ditch that cuts us off from the States. The new TV tower was there on the States side and we talked about how scary it would be to have to climb all the way to the top to screw in a new light bulb and we talked about some of the funny things people said when they were first building the tower. Like some said you wouldn't even have to buy a TV because the tower was so close that all you would need would be rabbit ears with a white cloth hanging over it and you would be able to see the picture. Others said that they were going to put a big ball at the top of the tower with a helicopter, and some said no, they would put big mirrors on the top because with TV you had to have mirrors because of the picture. And so some right away said that if you wanted to watch the TV you would just need to line a mirror up with the tower and you would be able to see it.

Fleeda and me laughered ourselves over these stories and I was feeling pretty good and was sneaking my hand close to Fleeda's so that I could maybe hold it a little bit because when you are heista kopp in love you should hold hands with a girl. But when my finger touched her hand just a little bit she said she would have to go back home because her mom and dad were going to visit some cousins and she wanted to go with. So we walked back to her place and I didn't try to take her hand but I was still feeling okay and I was thinking that I would come back the next Sunday in the evening because it is maybe easier to do such things in the evening. But when I did the next Sunday, Fleeda was not home and then after I found out that she had gone to the Neche show with some shluhdenz from Altbergthal and I mean I was feemaesich mad over that, but what can you do when you are only almost sixteen?

Then the next Sunday in Sunday School, Shtemm Gaufel Friesen had the nerve to say that girls mature faster than boys and the girls all sat there with their noses just a little bit higher and I thought, that's just what we need for girls to hear and they will all be going out with grandfathers like that shluhdenz from Altbergthal who is seventeen or eighteen or nineteen even. Something must be wrong with such old fortzes that they can't pick up girls their own age. Mature faster! Shtemm Gaufel must think that girls are like grain or something that he talks about maturing faster. It's just something else against you when you are only almost sixteen. Why can't the world do nothing right and let people hang around with their own age?

Well, even when you are heista kopp in love and floating in a sea of heartbreak your Muttachi still makes you stand up in the morning and go to weed beets by Yut Yut Leeven's place. And on the beetfield I make the time seem not so long by pointing my eyes all the time to Shtramel Stoezs's long legs that are sticking out from her blue jeans that are cut off quite high from the knee and are getting burned in nice and brown from the sun, and it seems like if I let myself I could fall into love with her quite easy, even if she is sixteen already. But come to me baby I'm a one-wo-man man. Still it's nice to have Shtramel weeding in front of me in the next row and if I don't look at Shtramel I can look at her sister Shups, who is fourteen only and her legs are shorter but they are so nice and smooth and have more curve than Shtramel's and if I was a cradle robber I could let myself fall into love with her, too. But I say to myself that I'm only practising looking for Fleeda, and that even if the Stoezs girls have nice legs, for sure they couldn't be so nice as Fleeda's even if I have only seen Fleeda's up to her knees when she has a dress on in church. A man needs a woman his own age and that is Fleeda Shreeda. But the Stoezs girls are nice to have on a beetfield.

So anyways on Sundays after dinner Hova Jake usually picks me up. Hova Jake is only almost sixteen, too, but he has this grandfather that's ninety years old and can't drive his own car any more, so Hova Jake drives it for him and they come to pick me up and we go looking at the crops, me in the back seat and Hova behind the steer and the grandfather sitting on the woman's side looking out the window and knacking sunflower seeds or sucking on his cigarette holder. And it sure is exciting riding around in the back seat with Hova Jake singing while he drives because the old Plymouth doesn't even have a radio and the old grandfather is singing his own song in Flat German or Russian and qwauleming smoke from his cigarette. It is a terrible thrill to ride around like that but it is better than staying home and playing catch with yourself.

Then one Sunday Hova Jake comes on Sunday evening to pick me up and his grandfather isn't with and Hova says, "C'mon Yasch, let's take some girls along." My heart starts to clapper real fast and I think maybe I should go to the beckhouse but I creep in the car and as we drive along I ask Hova, "Well, which girls do you want to take with?" and he says, "Let's see if Fleeda Shreeda is at home." And my heart clappering speeds up so much I think it will bounce right through my ribs but I say, "Well for sure." I start to wonder right away whose she will be if she comes along, and I wish I had smeared on some of Futtachi's green Rawleigh shaving lotion after I did the chores, but it's too late now because I can see Shaftich Shreeda's place already. And I am hoping Fleeda is at home and I am hoping that Fleeda isn't at home and I am terribly scared that if she is at home she will say no and I am terribly scared that she will say yes to Hova Jake and I am scared too that she will say yes to me. And I wonder if Hova Jake is scared, too, but I sure can't say what he feels because he is humming "Just as I am without one plea" and I wish there was a radio in the car because listening is easier than talking.

"Are you going to talk?" Hova asks when he slows down by Shaftich Shreeda's driveway, and before I know what I'm saying my mouth says, "Sure, okay" and then my heart clappers a hundred miles an hour. Then there is Fleeda sitting on the porch steps playing with a cat and she has her hair in rollers and she is wearing short pants with no shoes. Hova honks his horn. Fleeda looks at us but she doesn't stand up. And I wonder me a little how come she would have her hair in curlers on a Sunday evening. "Hello Fleeda," I say, almost steady. "Want to. . . ."

"Joe isn't home," she calls. "He went to Mouse Lake." Joe is her brother and I don't even like him so what the dukkat is she talking about him for? I am quiet for a minute, then I say, "Want to go for a ride?" Fleeda looks at us, then she looks to the barn. She stands up, starts to walk to the car, the cat in her arms, but she is wiggling her whole body just a little as she walks and for an eyeblink it almost seems like her legs are a bit lumpy and bowlegged and for sure far whiter than the Stoezs sisters' but that's only for an eyeblink and then she is perfect again, even with rollers in her hair, and I wish she would put the cat down so I could see everything when she walks and she is all the time looking to the barn like she is watching out for something. Then Hova Jake sticks his head past me and says, "Want to go for a ride?" Fleeda tilts her head sideways a bit and she looks us on with her eyes almost closed. She chews her gum a bit.

"Can't," she says.

"How come not?" I ask.

"Grounded."

"How come?" Hova says.

"Came home too late last night."

"Fleeda, get back in the house!"

Fleeda jerks around like a bee bit her and she runs in the house. We turn and see Shaftich Shreeda walking from the barn with two pails of milk but even then his overalls are wiggling back and forth like when a dog is wagging his tail. But it is easy to see that Shreeda isn't shaftich today. Hova starts to drive away and he says "Shit" under his breath but I am thinking in my head that maybe it's not so bad because if Fleeda is

grounded she can't go with that shluhdenz from Altbergthal
neither and I am thinking that it would have been maybe a good
time to go visiting on foot and I could have sat on the step with
Fleeda and played with the cat. But it's too late for that now and
I am wondering if Fleeda is grounded for a long time. And I am
wondering so much to myself that I don't notice that Hova has
held the car still again.

"Get in the back." Hova is opening the door for Shtramel
Stoezs. Her sister Shups is there, too, and I know that Jake wants
me to get in the back with her. Well, it's not like I'm scared of
Shups or nothing like that because we weed beets together. It's
just that I'm a one-woman man and what will Fleeda think about
this and for an eyeblink I think maybe she wouldn't give a
damn, but I wipe that away real fast. I open the door for Shups
and she slides in the back seat and I slide in after her and everybody is talking real easy and I am thinking that maybe riding
with Shups in the back seat will be good practice so I know what
to do when I get my driver's licence and I take Shaftich Shreeda's daughter Fleeda along.

The time goes quite quickly. We have so many things to
talk about because we weed beets on the same field and the
smell from the clover fields is nice and I can smell some perfume
from Shups even if she is sitting almost on the other side of the
car. It gets a little darker and we are driving slowly through a lot
of field roads because we can't go to town without a driver's
licence. Shtramel just has her learner's even if she is already
sixteen. Hova Jake sings lots of songs because the car doesn't
have a radio. Soon we are driving through some trees and there
are no farmers for some miles around and it is getting a little bit
darker and I see that Shtramel is slipping herself closer to Hova
Jake and I look at Shups and she smiles at me. The moon is
coming up and I move a little bit closer to Shups and then Hova
is driving along the road beside the ditch that cuts us off from
the States. He holds still there for a while and we can see the
lights on the TV tower blinking on and off. I think about the talk
I had with Fleeda about it and I look at Shups and she has
slipped a little bit closer to me. I carefully reach out my hand to
hers and I wish my hand wasn't so wet and I wish I had some
shaving lotion on because it seems like I can smell the barn a
little bit but Shups is holding my hand and then I only smell her

perfume and I almost forget about Fleeda Shreeda there in the moonshine in the car where we can see the TV lights blinking off and on. In the front seat Hova Jake is sitting real close to Shtramel but he doesn't do much neither. They just talk and laugh a lot and then all of a sudden Shtramel says that it's time to go home. We drive home slowly and I hold Shups's hand all the way and think this is sure good practice.

Next day on the beetfield Shups and Shtramel are real friendly, only not so friendly that the Leeven boys have anything to tease me with. Most of the time I can be quiet and look at the sisters' legs and think about Fleeda Shreeda. Then in the evening when it is almost dark and all the chores are finished I go walking down the road to Fleeda's place, just dreaming that maybe she will be walking alone, too. It would be nice to walk to the boundary ditch and stand there in the dark while the TV tower lights blink on and off and I forget that before I can get all the way to Fleeda's place I have to go past Shtramel and Shups's place, and really I am walking in my head more than on the road when all of a sudden I hear somebody say, "Who's that bum?" and I turn to look and there are Shtramel and Shups standing by their driveway. "Hallelujah, I'm a bum," I say. They laugh and come walk beside me.

We walk along the road to the States, past Fleeda's place, and I try to look at the window in the house that I think is Fleeda's without letting the girls notice it. When we are past about a quarter mile we see somebody walking toward us and soon I can see that it is Fleeda, alone. In my head I am swearing at the Stoezs girls and why did they have to come with tonight when here would have been my big chance, but I mean, two's company and three's a crowd. What can I do now except try not to let my eyes fall out while the girls stop to talk to Fleeda. Fleeda wants to know if they are walking their dog. Shtramel laughs and says "Yes" and Fleeda wants to know where they found such a mutt. Then Fleeda says she better go home and tells the Stoezs girls not to fight over who will play with the dog. We all laugh again and I am sure glad that it's night time because for sure my face must be real red.

So I walk farther with Shtramel and Shups when all of a sudden Shtramel says, "Oh, I have to ask Fleeda something," and she turns and runs back and I am left with Shups and we

---

walk alone a little while and don't say anything, but it feels real nice because it is warm and there is a little bit of wind, just enough to blow the mosquitoes away. The TV tower is blinking off and on and there is a slice of moon in the sky. I ask Shups if she ever went all the way to the tower and she says no and I can feel she has moved a little closer to me, so I tell her about the time me and Hingst Heinrichs went across the boundary all the way to the tower and there was a guy working there, just sitting in the little shack under the tower, watching a TV that was built right into a workbench and there were lots of knobs and things. We talked with him a little bit and he said we should watch out for the border patrol and we thought it was pretty funny how the States people are always so full of police stuff and every-thing, but we didn't stay long because he was finished his shift and he wanted to go home to Pembina where he lived. And while I am telling Shups all this, she is listening quietly and her hand touches mine, sometimes accidentally on purpose, and after she has done this three times I catch it in mine and we walk along the boundary ditch.

We stop walking when we're even with the tower and I almost say "Let's go all the way to the tower," but I think well maybe it's too late already and Shups is only fourteen and besides I should maybe save going to the tower for sometime when I'm with Fleeda. I mean, this walking around with Shups is just practice I figure.

"Let's sit down a little bit," I say and we do. I let the tower blink five times, then I put my arm around her and she leans her head on my shoulder and we watch the tower blink, talk about the beetfield and things that happened in school last year, and she laughs when I say a joke and she smells like clover and earth and Camay soap and I am trying to gribble out if I should kiss her or not. I mean how is a guy to know exactly how to do it, like the Danny Orlis books for sure don't say how and the Sunday School leaflets talked about fondling breasts one time, but they sure didn't say how to get from here to there and then Shups says she'll have to go home now. So I say, "Okay, but maybe next time we can go earlier so we would have time to go all the way to the tower," and Shups just giggles and says, "Maybe the border patrol will get us." I walk with my arm around her waist and it feels good and I forget to take my arm back when we walk past Fleeda Shreeda's place, but lucky nobody is looking.

When we stop by her driveway we don't want to say good night yet and I figure I should get all the practice I can so I whisper, "Shups," and she turns to me and I quickly lean over and give her a kiss on the lips. She doesn't slap me or nothing like they do on TV. She just stands there, then I say, "Good night" and Shups runs to her house.

So I feel pretty good when I walk home, thinking I got lots of good practice. I turn around a few times, looking at the tower blinking behind me, and I think next time we'll go all the way to the tower. Then I stop dead in my tracks. I am thinking that I would go next time with Shups to the tower when I should be thinking I would go next time with Fleeda. I get a funny feeling that maybe Fleeda, now that she has gone riding around in cars with all those grandfathers from Puggefeld and Prachadarp, she maybe won't want to do stuff like go walking to the tower. I mean on Sunday when me and Hova Jake tried to pick her up it was like she was talking down her nose at us. And when she said she was grounded, I don't know, she sure didn't seem like the same girl that went for a walk with me that time on a Sunday afternoon.

I have to help Futtachi get a few loads of hay the next day so I don't see Shups and Shtramel on the beetfield, and they finish the field that day so I don't see the girls till Sunday after church when the Stoezs girls and Fleeda are standing on the church steps and Shups and Shtramel have on brand new white high heels and Fleeda is wearing brown open toes with a flat heel and it seems like the real Fleeda doesn't match up with the Fleeda that I have in my head and I get all mixed up inside. Shups sees me and gives me a wink and I think, "Well, okay Fleeda if you want to go with grandfathers from those other darps well it's your own funeral." Then Fleeda holds her head a certain way and she is laughing about something and I fall heista kopp in love with her all over again.

The whole afternoon I lie on my bed listening to country songs on my red plastic radio and I'm dreaming about Fleeda Shreeda and thinking I should have won that red convertible by the Morris Stampede and how it would be driving Fleeda around all over the country with a red convertible and all the farmers with their half-tons would be jealous. I wonder if she is still grounded yet and I fall asleep and dream that I am parked with Fleeda in the red convertible under the TV tower with the red lights blinking, only the red convertible has bucket seats and I think I can't have Fleeda sitting on the gear shift with her white dress and then Shups Stoezs climbs in between us and it doesn't bother her to sit on the gear shift. Then Fortz Funk from Puggefeld honks his horn on that old half-ton truck he has and Fleeda climbs out of the red convertible in her white dress and she doesn't even open the door, she just climbs over the side and creeps into Fortz Funk's truck and I see she gets some grease on her white dress and Muttachi calls me to come and eat faspa.

Hova Jake comes to pick me up again in the evening. His grandfather isn't along and Hova says he isn't feeling so good anymore, but he doesn't seem to worry himself over it. Hova doesn't even ask where we will go. He just drives straight to Stoezs's place to pick up the girls. From the way the girls are ready, it seems like Hova must have phoned them up to say he was coming. Well, Shups doesn't wait for it to get dark to slide closer to me on the seat. Hova drives on the field roads for a while, Shtramel sitting close to him and Shups close to me, and we sing some songs because there is no radio and we laugh a lot and by the time Hova stops the car by the big ditch and the tower is blinking there a half-mile over the border, I am holding Shups's hand in my wet palm and her leg inside her stretchy slacks is pressed against mine. Hova puts his arm around Shtramel and rubs his cheek against hers and Shups is leaning against me and I am a little nervous. So I whisper in her ear, "Let's go to the tower," and she says in my ear, "Okay." We crawl out of the car and Hova and Shtramel don't even notice when we leave.

The sunset is beautiful and we walk down into the ditch through the pepper bushes that grow there and up the other side and we are in the States. There is a strip of grass, then an alfalfa field with stacks of bales all over the field and then alfalfa smell mixes with Shups's perfume as we walk together holding hands. We look at the tower with two lights blinking and two lights on steady all the time and the light second from the top is burned out. The tower gets higher and higher as we come closer and we can see the white sections and the red sections even if it is starting to get dark. Then Shups trips on a clump of dirt and I reach for her with both arms so that she doesn't fall down and she is pressed against me and I feel her breasts through my shirt and her blouse. My heart pounds real fast and I hold her like that till she says, "We're not by the tower yet," so we walk closer with our arms around each other till we have to lean our heads back to see the top.

Shups slips away from me and runs to the bottom of the tower and it's not quite dark yet and I follow her and we can see the ladder that goes up the tower that they use to put new light bulbs in. And there is a sign that I can still read in the dark: DANGER DO NOT CLIMB. I look straight up the tower and from so close I can't even see the top lights blinking. The wind is shaking the tower just a little and I step closer to Shups and reach for her to give her a kiss and she wriggles away. "Catch me if you want to kiss me!" she yells and starts to climb the ladder.

"Hey, what are you doing? You're not supposed to climb up there."

"C'mon. Catch me and give me a kiss."

Shups is already ten rungs up the ladder. Well, shit, I figure, if she can climb up I can too. So I climb after her, looking all the time at the seat of her pants, thinking that that is maybe the only place I can kiss because there is hardly any room on the ladder. She climbs higher and higher quite fast and I follow, never looking down but I can't get closer to her. She is climbing as fast as I can, not slowing down at all, and the wind shakes the tower a little. I look down for the first time and it seems like I am just as high as a hydro pole already and Shups is ten rungs still higher. The sun going under is covered with clouds and it's getting pretty dark and when I look up again I can hardly see Shups above me. I climb higher even though now I feel like I need to piss, but I have to climb just as high as she does so I call, "How high are you going to go?" She answers, "To the first light or the second!"

I look past her to where the first light is blinking and it sure seems like a hartsoft long way yet. I climb up five more rungs and I can't see Shups anymore, it's too dark, and then I can't see the ground, just dark. All I can see is the red blinking light and some yardlights back in Canada and one car going along a road. I keep climbing. My arms are starting to get tired and the tower seems to shake each time I climb another rung and when I call to Shups again she doesn't say nothing and I get scared and think that maybe she fell off only I think if she fell off she would have screamed but maybe she was so scared that she couldn't even scream. So I call for her again and still she doesn't say nothing so I keep climbing and climbing and climbing and it is getting so dark I can hardly see my hands holding on the ladder in front of me and I'm feeling along the cold iron for each rung. I call for Shups again and listen and all I can hear is the wind and the wind seems terribly strong.

"Five steps more," I say to myself. And I pull myself up one, then two, three, then four and there is something just darker than dark and something lighter and I reach up and touch rubber and it is Shups's runner.

Shups giggles. "Boy, you are sure slow. I thought you'd want a kiss more than that."

I laugh a little and say, "I thought you were going up till the first light."

"Naw, who wants to kiss with a red light on!"

"So do I get my kiss now?"

"Okay, if you want to kiss my foot."

"Climb all the way up here just to kiss a foot? No way. I want more than that."

"Well then, you'll have to wait till we get down."

"Okay." I start down one rung.

"Yasch, wait."

"Okay, what?" Shups's shoes come down past my nose and I have to lean back a little to let her legs down between me and the ladder, then the seat of her pants is in front of my face and she says, "Yasch, hug me just a little bit." So I do it the best way I can, my head leaning into the seat of her pants and my arms around her legs and the ladder and I hold on as tight as I can and it feels good and starts to feel warm. "That's good, Yasch. Now I can climb down." Then I know that she is scared, too.

So we talk all the way down and it seems to take forever and when we stop to rest I put my hand on her leg or on her ankle that's bare between her shoe and her pantleg until she says, "Okay, now I can go again."

Some clouds move away from the half moon and when I

look down I can see the tin roof of the little shack beside the tower, and it doesn't seem so terribly high any more and we climb down faster. But when our feet touch the ground our knees bend just like rubber and we fall down on the ground. I hear Shups's breathing beside me.

I raise myself up on my elbow and look at her lying there in the moonlight. Her eyes blink and they look wet. Shups sits up.

"You didn't kiss me yet," she says.

"I was just waiting for you to stop panting." I reach for her and I kiss her on the lips and squeeze her body to mine and she kisses me back and I don't think about it being practice for something else. I just do it because it is good to do right now and I think that it's good that when you are almost sixteen you don't have to climb all the way to the top of the tower. Then Shups says, "We better go back before the border patrol catches us." And I say, "Yeah, Shtramel and Hova Jake have probably smeared lipstick all over the car already." Shups gives me a poke. "Shtramel didn't have any lipstick on." So we walk back and when we can see the car already we turn and look at the tower blinking.

"How far do you think we climbed up?"

"Far enough," Shups says and she squeezes my hand.

Di Brandt

shades of sin

the temptations of men in Reinland were blatant contemptible
easily accomplished & thrown away cigarettes at Yurchaks
Sunday afternoons ancient dust curled calendar pictures of half
naked women the grey foreign monotony of tv on a tiny corner
shelf   for the women sin came much better disguised subtle
attractive creeping into every day pride for example the ever-
lurking temptation to think you were somebody hold your head
up too straight on the street or in church or forget yourself so far
as to speak your own mind   it happened to the best of
women once in a while though in my family at least they made
up for it after with extra baking & sweet talk for weeks   the
big one for Rosie & me was glamour an obviously forbidden
kind of worldliness but with peculiarly undefined edges   a
lot of our adolescent energies went into their exact location the
rules kept changing that was the confusing part   we could
understand for example that hair was an unruly item best kept
under kerchiefs & hats its dangerous tendency to shine in the
sun & spring provocative curls sometimes with prompting
we liked to cite nature as justification though the most unsophis-
ticated theologian among us could veto this claim easily with
reference to the Fall   the point was partly to protect
ourselves against the brutal demands of men whose biological
urges unlike our own could not be helped it was therefore up to
us to keep them from getting unduly aroused but mainly we
suspected to do the thing itself   beauty was altogether a
disturbing category for Mennonites no one knew quite what to
do with it even though God must have put it there for a reason if
we could only know what it was   & yet our mothers dared

to disobey their own fathers decrees so far as to cut & curl their
hair even administering the occasional home permanent to each
other & sometimes us children that was okay though looking in
the mirror longer than say thirty seconds at a time or admitting
any pleasure whatsoever in the results was strictly taboo as ever
        the hats themselves were fraught with temptation accord-
ing to the Bible women had to cover their hair for worship a
handy excuse for keeping ones Sunday headwear up to date
though one of my aunts insisted it meant 100% cotton handker-
chiefs from Gladstones tied around the chin   my mother
ordered her hats from Eatons by mail she favored a pleasant
middle of the road style neither too rakish nor too plain light
beige navy blue with a modest bit of lace   once they sent
her a thin black hat with a net veil to cover the face we loved this
hat its dangerous mystique   she wouldn't wear it until she
figured out a way to tuck the veil in so it looked only an inch
long that was what bothered me most of all the clearcut invisible
lines of propriety which could not be argued or discussed &
seemed obvious to everyone except Rosie & me   it just
didnt make sense a necklace was acceptable to God up to say
two strands if the beads were not too large or too brightly
colored but the tiniest bracelet plunged you immediately over
into heathenism   someone who could it have been gave my
mother a set of fake diamonds once she wore the necklace to
church with her embroidered blue checked cotton dress but the
earrings stayed on her dresser in a little case   we longed for
these earrings fondled them screwed them secretly in our ears
        she let us wear them sometimes for dressup but we had to
be careful not to look exuberant or glamorous a hard thing when
youre eight & wearing diamonds or my dad would threaten to
take them away to chasten our pride   she had several items
like this a pair of white satin gloves the long kind that reached
past the elbow & featured a slit at the wrist to tuck in the hand
part if you were at a ball & sitting down to dinner   a pair of
red leather shoes with open toes & three inch heels never worn
        a pair of short pink gloves with white pearls sewn at the
wrist   how did these things come to be in Reinland
when asked she would smile vaguely & murmur something
about changing her mind   when i was ten a group of
village mothers organized an educational tour to Winnipeg for

their children   we left in the morning by bus Rosie & i
wearing blue pedal pushers our mothers whipped up late the
night before on the Singer sewing machine   our first stop
was CKY i cant for the life of me imagine how such a worldly
radio station got on the agenda since we werent allowed to listen
to anything but CFAM in Reinland i dont remember anything
about the tour itself except the lady who showed us around she
was the most glamorous person we had ever laid our innocent
eyes on   we feasted on her gloriously wicked appearance
all up & down the halls of the CKY building from her dubiously
spiked grey leather heels to her blue shaded eyelids   the
best thing by far was her bracelet a silver chain hung with we
could hardly believe it dimes there must have been hundreds of
them rattling & jingling as she talked   we spent half the
trip home later discussing this fascinating item calculating its
worth its glitter its sinfulness its waste   our second stop
was the Christie cookie factory our mothers were more at home
here & more relaxed   we watched thousands of tiny rectan-
gle biscuits slipping off conveyor belts & being stuck together
with lemon yellow icing impressive but most of us agreed the
results fell far short of the baking we were used to at home
our third stop was the Museum after lunch someone decided we
should split into smaller groups to walk through it since there
was no tourguide we would be on our own   Rosie & i
stayed with our mother   we made a great mistake walking
into the Museum our group somehow made a wrong turn &
ended up in the Art Gallery on the other side   i dont know
what we would have seen in the Museum had we ever found it
but what we saw instead was mind boggling huge empty rooms
with nothing but pictures on the walls & such pictures nothing
pretty or picturesque like the calendars at home only weird
smudges which gave you a strange feeling in the belly   my
mother embarrassed & sweaty about the mistake hurried us
through them still hoping for stuffed buffaloes & red coats on
wooden mannikins somewhere but she only led us deeper into
the labyrinth of Art   the most incredible room of all was the
very last hung all around with naked women in various poses
our first glimpse of the shape our own bodies were destined to
become   i would have liked to stay in this room awhile &
sort out the strange emotions aroused by this totally new vision

of the world but for the sake of our education we rushed on &
made it out just as the last of the other groups emerged from the
Museum so easily located after all just across the big hall
my mother of course turned the whole adventure into an
episode in getting lost sorting through inch by inch the wrong
turns we had made our good fortune in getting out at all
she never mentioned the room full of naked women & neither
did we   there didnt seem to be any words for it but it
stayed in my memory as a kind of promise touching some
deeper hunger than i had known untouched by more familiar
shades of sin

Rudy Wiebe

The Well

One early summer as the November sun stood so directly overhead that it cast no shadow, Anna Friesen discovered when she
leaned over the rim she could not tell whether she was looking
into the well or out of it.

The well was Schoenbach's most valued possession. It
stood at the north end of the village, the last of Simons Colony
on the crooked trail to the rail-end. When they drew lots for the
village in 1928 the settlers did not know they had it; they had no
well whatever and to an untrained eye the arid campo gave not
the slightest hint about the passing of a stream, leave alone a
beautiful one. But wherever Mennonites had lived, whether in
Canada or as far back as story and strong memory could depend
on Russia, there had always been such village names: Gartental,
Blumenau, Rosenfeld, Friedensruh. Each word was a place; it
contained no word context for anyone; it was. So Schoenbach. If
they were going to live in Paraguay's "green-hell" Chaco, as
they were since Anna's parents and the Elder said, then one of
thirteen villages would be so named. The village was planned
and named while they were still at sea a year before any survey-
ing was done, when actually only five Mennonites, delegates of
1921, had ever seen the Chaco however briefly, and no one the
campos on which they were to settle: Schoenbach.

The well being what it was, the village name simply named
again their thoughtless faith. (Ten years later visiting German
scientists would conjecture, even agree from soil samples and
aerial surveys, that the campos actually were ancient stream
beds. But what possible practical difference could this make to
the two or three Mennonites who would hear about these

reports five years after that; fifteen years after the fact why puzzle your head about why, if that were so, what remained of the sweet stream should lie six meters under the sand at the edge of the clearing and not in the middle where digging first began?) A thoughtful man hauling his family through the cactus brush to the campo and raising his tents on his lot-assigned strip of sand and bittergrass would have cried, or laughed, at such a name. In the privacy of their work some women did cry; most men had no time for either. Wells had to be dug. If the sand did not collapse, at some level they found water in every shaft but when they hauled it up the few gaunt oxen swung their muzzles over it and bellowed. Not even adobe bricks they tramped out with their bare feet held together; it was brine. After the eleventh hole four men went to plead, with despair and no success, for another campo. The others persisted to the very rim of the bush, labouring inside the cribbing that was to prevent another such sand cave-in as had already buried one digger forever at the village center. Near a paratodo tree a moisture one evening became the next morning the sweet well. Everyone gathered bare-headed in the sun and thanked God, drinking. And after the initial adjustment no one in Schoenbach was ever again sick from the water.

Neither the entire village nor the Lengua Indians who soon heard and camped nearby in their wanderings nor the high ox-carts squealing on toward Endstation had ever dipped the well dry. (September 1932 and the Battle of Boqueron could really have proven their well but since they did not have, and very thankfully never wanted to have, or had, the faintest notion of military strategy, they never understood why that month did not discover the well's bottom, that is, the stream's end.) After Schoenbach there was nothing on the railroad trail except puddles, if that, and though Endstation was only seventy miles away, by ox-cart that meant undoubtedly six, perhaps as many as fifteen days, depending. The irony of Chaco cartage was invariable: in dry weather the road was loose and dust-choked and oxen could thirst into immobility between waterholes; if it rained hard enough to plow in the settlement so that eventually there could be some produce to sell for the staples that had to be hauled in, the level trail vanished in bottomless mudholes almost as numberless as mosquitoes, that demanded three floundering yoke of oxen on a four-hundred-kilo load to gain two, perhaps four miles in all the daylight one day provided. The Chaco day too was almost invariable: twelve hours of light and then at one stride the darkness. After the moon rose there was light again, but the oxen must graze; they did so even more deliberately than they walked.

Before the day's heat but considerably after the cattle watered and wandered away to forage what they could among the spined bush, the women and older girls of Schoenbach went to the well. They did not come like the Lengua women, one pot balanced on their head and the other in their hand, staring wherever their eye strayed; their pails hung from a wooden yoke, the weight of which sat mainly on the back of the shoulders. As a result, though Lengua women always walked about like stallions in spring, the women of Schoenbach stooped forward whether they carried water or not. Which was a becoming posture for a woman, according to Elder Wiebe the Younger. Humility is required, humility in keeping with a bowed head and eyes fixed upon the dust from which all come and to which all must again return when He comes to judge on His mighty throne. Looking everywhere with unblinking shamelessness can lead to nothing but—things like the Lengua women who in their savage dances were said to lay their hand on any man they pleased, to lead him to whatever she wanted, out of the firelight. Not that anyone, and certainly not the Elder, had ever seen an Indian dance. But they had heard, and knew. It was what must happen when women stared about and held themselves so erect, so fluidly and powerfully free.

And Anna Friesen knew it very nearly happened to her.

Not that she ever walked like that. (Twenty-five years later a visiting American scientist would conjecture that Lengua and most other Chaco Indian groups were matriarchies, but when this was explained it would merely corroborate what the ministers had read all along from the Bible concerning heathen; by denying the divine order that the husband is the head and authority of the wife, for Adam was created first and then Eve, the Lenguas simply showed themselves to be, as Elder Wiebe the Younger quoted, "given up to uncleanness through the lusts of their own hearts, to dishonor their own bodies between themselves.") Anna never knew how her body walked. No mirror is necessary to re-braid hair and there was no water or even windowpane to reflect her posture. But she knew that once she did not keep her eyes where they belonged and that one seeing was enough. She never thought it through, piece by piece; she never had or would think that way; Marie's complex, reasoned planning, which simmered long and boiled over sometimes when the three sisters were alone, merely made Tina smile but Anna very nearly physically ill. She could not, she did not in the least want to think like that. It was repulsive. It would have been equally repulsive for her to recognize, even for an instant, that she could possibly behave like one of those brown women whose rags, if any, hung shamelessly open wherever they hung and who with one casual shift slid her sleepy child from breast to hip; but there was not anything nearly as precise as that. Only something she might have recognized as a stray whiff of possible, of faintest potential perhaps, if she could have worked out her sensations so articulately. She could not, of course; she did not want to. She knew only that once she did not keep her eyes where they belonged and that suddenly she was terrified at the sound or sight of the Elder in *hauptcheuik* once a month or when he came to preach in Schoenbach, though he had always spoken softly to her as to any girl, and could not read a verse, leave alone sing from the *Kirchenbuch*. Nor so much as think her prayers to herself when she knelt with her sisters, but only mumble sounds that would have horrified even Marie had they all not been too exhausted to listen to each other at the end of each day when they fell upon their grass mattresses. And what had happened happened because of the well.

Everyone knew without any direct mention of the matter that it was particularly proper for the Kanadier women in a village like Schoenbach to keep their eyes and heads down. In mid-1930 the Russlander were settled in Fernland Colony just west of Simons; their freight carts also passed through Schoenbach on the trail to Endstation. These Russlander were Mennonites, of course, and had the same family names; indeed, some were perhaps even relatives, too distant to be precise about but when colony and village and name and great-grandfather's given names agreed, surmise was safe. They spoke the same Lowgerman as the Kanadier, though with a very different accent, with some unheard-of words. And they had emigrated only once for their faith. Not that the Kanadier were proud;

Elder Wiebe the Younger preached that pride was the most devilish of the Devil's many weapons. Besides there was no need for pride. It was simply a fact that a child in Simons Colony might know; their fathers left Russia in 1874-80 and emigrated to Canada because the Russian world was becoming impossible for their beliefs, but these Russlander found theirs adjustable enough to stay on until 1929. How they had become modern it was unnecessary to discuss; some, they heard, had attended technical schools and even universities in Petersburg or Kiev, perhaps Moscow. No wonder communists had to take their land away before they would leave.

Elder Wiebe the Older, who remembered very clearly the trek from Russia to Canada now almost sixty years ago and who had led them from Canada to Paraguay in 1928 not because the Canadian Government was taking land away from anyone but because, he affirmed again, it no longer allowed them to run their own schools in the German biblical way they wished, as it had promised them it would allow forever when they moved to Canada in 1874, held his last sermon three weeks after the Kanadier drove to Endstation to help cart the first Russlander to their land. He did not mention Russlander. Without raising his thin old voice but with his great jaw thrust forward as Anna had always seen him, he intoned that the Bible, the Catechism and the *Kirchenbuch,* the plow and the shovel were the faith of their fathers. It was enough for them, and it is enough for their children and children's children, now and for evermore. To have too much is to want more. New ideas, book learning, singing in several voices are unnecessary and dangerous. The desire for knowledge leads to pride and self-deception. To long for change is to fight one's destiny. Fighting one's destiny is rebellion against God. Man's duty is to obey, pray, work, and wait in terror for God's wrath.

So when Russlander men began driving through Schoenbach, as they must on their way to Endstation, cracking their whips above the ambling oxen and sometimes yodeling greetings in Lowgerman, Anna had no problem about where to look. Kornelius and Isaak told stories; when they met the Russlander on the trail, or perhaps camped nearby, they would hear them sing songs probably not even found in a Catholic hymnbook; of millers and soldiers riding to the hunt, and lovers. Those Russlander certainly knew nothing about *tschmaking,* as they called it, in the Chaco—they used breast-straps instead of collars on the few horses they had and almost choked them to death in the mudholes—but they could sing Highgerman and Russian in different voices that sounded like coyotes or wolves under the moon in Canada, and laugh and quarrel far into the night. And crazy to laugh! Hearing this, Anna knew without being told, as did every Kanadier girl, that despite their Mennonite names and talk, these men were too different, too wrong—and obvious—to even think about, leave alone remember where gaunt faces, glimpsed for an instant, broke into smile, their carefree greeting brushed something to an unwonted shiver. They would not get into heaven. When their slow procession stopped at the well it was best to wait on the path far down the road, or better yet, return later as they did for Paraguay officers. And remember, as Anna did, that on Saturday Abraham K. Funk would come and with her sit another long tongue-heavy evening away.

Abraham K. Funk was never much in her thoughts. Why he should be there when the Russlander drove by she did not try to understand; whenever it happened she simply felt later that he should have been. Neither did she explain to herself where he had been so lost that her thoughts had never once found him the day she looked into the well, but she felt a discomfort that morning which she sometimes experienced in early summer, a discomfort that came with Marie's hard jaw set and the North-wind rising with the sun and roaring like a furnace down the village street, grinding at grass roofs, blasting sand through cracks in curled doors and into windows pinned over tight with canvas. Under its shriek they heard the Russlander carts creak by south; they could not be seen for the blanket of sand winding about them. Once in an eddy Anna peered out of the dark house and distinguished a hunched shape high above the eight-foot wheels and the piled sacks before it was again hurled away. But for her dress pasted tight over her body and the crunch of her teeth, it might have been a Canadian blizzard. And she did not want to think of Canada; she had been too young to know.

When the last sounds were by a long time she shouldered her yoke, folded a cloth inside each pail cover and told her mother she would try now. Out the gate she went backwards, lunging back and pausing, the pails banging together before her when she could not hold them, staggering in the moving drifts of the hollowed path and lunging on again. Once the Northwind betrayed her and she fell heavily back, one palm striking down on a cactus spine swept bare by the sand. She scraped it off against a pail, pulled her yoke on again. She fought, reached the fence around Klaus Wiebe's grave marker, but that was no protection. None at all. When she gained the well at last she sank in the shelter of its high box. After a time the pain of her hand burned through her exhaustion and she began to fumble at the thorns. She leaned against the well, picking with a corner of broken fingernail, putting her teeth to her hard hand. It comforted her. She was doing something necessary and need not, for the moment, outface the wind.

That was how Joseph Hiebert found her. His left ox had gone lame overnight and before he reached his village he would be a day behind the others. He did not much care. One trek on this road taught there was no companionship in a storm; each driver must remain with his cart and a minute or a day behind made no difference to the misery. The Schoenbach well emerged briefly and he cupped his hands, bellowing to his span. Before he had his canteen and matte-horn unstrapped the lame ox was already kneeling, sinking to the hot earth, the yoke dragging the other down also. He bent forward against the weight of the wind and coming round the well's corner almost bumped head-on into the girl with the heel of her hand to her mouth.

For Anna what followed was like the whole day, tangled in impossible convolutions of sweat and heat and sand and an unwanting to remember. Bits flashed at her sharp as diamonds unbidden. He was there, long and thin in black lines, and his name too, though he had no face, and his voice suddenly laughed and his hand, barely wider than her own but with a long steel tension, clamped hers so tightly while he pricked at the thorns with a needle he pulled from a pocket case that even when she twitched involuntarily her hard hand on his hard knee moved not the slightest. And the new drink the Paraguayan soldiers, his voice said, had discovered: cold water drained over yerba leaves made terere, and it strained out scum and sand and most puddle-water taste. It felt scratchy, then smooth as cream in her throat as she sucked it up through his metal bambillia; that was really no worse than drinking from his canteen since the pail was impossible in the storm and she was thirsty. Yerba with hot water gave matte, a drink only Kanadier men drank, but yerba and unheated water gave terere, faintly musty and unknown till then, therefore outside regulation. Like the day, the black mustache, the Lowgerman voice slightly off-accented, it was new; strange. And the stories the voice told—perhaps they sat in the well's shelter for hours with the sand blasting by them down the street, removing paratodo tree and cart and oxen and Schoenbach—of the jokes he tried on Kanadier boys like telling them that one edge of the world was just beyond a few yards of brush north off the trail and how some of them always drove on the south after that—did he think she believed the world was round or how could he expect her to laugh at such blasphemy, as she did—or how he had ridden along Indian trails and found not very far west of Fernland Colony the end of the world nailed shut with boards or how he was teaching four Kanadier boys "Kommt ein Vogel geflogen" in four-part harmony so they could sing something new at the next Simons Colony engagement. There, exactly there she should have said about Abraham K. Funk; she should have thought at least. But she had done neither, neither then nor before that when for some unnecessary reason she looked over the well-rim with Joseph Hiebert at the ripples of his sunken pail drift gently across, away, and after a time the wind lulled an instant and the fierce sunlight showed them strangely side by side, looking together at themselves; and through the endless blue sky.

Once after that she saw him. He came with Isaak on the yard where her father and Kornelius were fixing a cultivator. He left alone a little later. She could just distinguish his length from where she was with her sisters on the back field; she was leaning a moment against the smooth warped handle of the grubbing hoe. From somewhere she heard his father was a Russlander preacher who usually preached from the Bible, but who never read his sermons and leaped around behind the pulpit. One day she heard young Hiebert had heaved his load of cotton bales onto the flatcar at Endstation and then climbed up too. To the men standing about his yoke of oxen, staring up at him, he yelled, "Keep them, butcher them up!" Years later it was heard in the two colonies that he was in Buenos Aires. The streets there were said to be narrower than Chaco roads, but between unbelievable buildings of stone and glass and jammed with millions of people, black, white, brown. It was said someone had seen him eating and drinking at a table with a painted woman.

There came a time when Anna Funk no longer remembered, from one year to the next, how once at the end of the village with Joseph Hiebert she bent down and looked into (or was it out of) the Schoenbach well as if to see to the end of the blue sky. Then she would think, "I last remembered, oh, it must be almost three years. I have almost forgotten." And she would smile a little at her baby of that year, a quietness she knew as joy moving within her.

Warren Kliewer

UHF

The transformation began on a Saturday afternoon when Mrs. Schultz had just finished hoeing the weeds along the fence at the back boundary of the parsonage lawn, and Mrs. Wiehens had come picking her way slowly across the clods in her garden to the fence which separated the two lots.

"Such weeds," Mrs. Schultz said.

Mrs. Wiehens solemnly nodded. One hand lay across her broad stomach, and with the other she shaded her eyes against the low sun. If she had turned her head slightly to the left, her big black babushka would have cast a shadow over her eyes. But then she would have had to look at the tower, and both women scrupulously kept their eyes turned away from it.

"Abram helps me with the weeds," Mrs. Wiehens said.

"What you say, Ma?" her forty-one year old bachelor son said. Following her across the garden, he still stood in the middle of the potato patch.

"You help me with the weeds."

"Yah, hoeing," he said in his high tenor.

"Pa never used to help me before he died," she added. "But Abram's a good boy."

"My man can't either," Mrs. Schultz said. "Preachers, they have to write sermons on Saturday. Us women have to do everything alone."

Mrs. Wiehens nodded again. "All except with Abram. He helps. Dries dishes even. I don't let him wash because he breaks them sometimes. But he dries nice."

"Just like now. A washline, that's what I need more than anything. I've needed one for weeks and weeks. And my man says that sure is right; I do need a new line. But he says he can't put one up because the poles are rotted off below the ground."

"Yah," Mrs. Wiehens agreed. "That living in town, that's no easier than it was living on the farm."

"Especially if you're a preacher's wife. I've asked for a new washline and asked for one and asked for one. And yah, he's always going to do it tomorrow. But then tomorrow there's a wedding or a funeral or something. And then it's day after tomorrow."

"But when we was on the farm," Mrs. Wiehens said, "Abram never had time to help me. Pa always had him out in the barn or the chicken house."

"Stringing up the washline isn't so much trouble, he says. It's putting up the poles." Then Mrs. Schultz added hesitantly, "Abram wouldn't have time sometime, would he?"

"Abram? I don't know. Abram, you don't have time, do you?"

"What you say, Ma?" he called across the garden.

"Mrs. Schultz wants you to help her."

"Right now?" he said. "You want me to help you now?"

"No, I'm done hoeing," Mrs. Schultz said. "It's washline poles I need."

"Holes? What kind of holes you want?"

"No, no, no," his mother said. "Washline."

"Oh. Washline. You want it right now?"

"Monday, Tuesday, maybe. You don't have time, do you?"

"I don't know. Do I have time, Ma?"

"I don't know. What do you have to do next week?"

"Hoe potatoes."

"That's all?"

"Dry dishes."

"Yah. I don't know. Maybe you'll have time. Why don't you do it for her."

"You think I'll have time?"

"Yah."

"All right." Turning to Mrs. Schultz he said, "Yah, I'll put up your washline." He repeated to himself, more quietly, "Monday. Washline."

And so on Monday morning Abram was waiting at six-thirty outside Jake's Hardware, wearing the clean black trousers and the clean blue shirt which he always took on Monday morning, and then when he found out at seven o'clock that they had no washline wires, waiting at the front door of Kroeker's Shoe Repair Shop until it opened at seven-thirty, and finding no washline rope there, walking to the John Deere Implement Company at the other end of town to see if he could find enough baling wire in the repair lot for the washline. So it was not until ten o'clock that he appeared in the door of Mrs. Schultz's basement where she was bent over the wobbling Maytag washing machine, and he announced, "It's done, your washline."

"You've got them up already?"

"Yah."

"Are you going to have time to put up the wires too?"

"The wires are up."

"The whole thing's up?"

He nodded.

"Where'd you get the poles?"

"Poles? Poles was already there."

"No, Abram. You can't use those old washline poles." She pulled the plug, and the washing machine rattled to a sudden silence. "Let me explain. Those old poles are no good. They're rotted off under the ground. That's why we had to put up new ones, a new washline."

He opened and closed his mouth a few times, shaking his head. "No, no. Not the old washline poles. Those new ones. Those big ones. That tower out there."

"Oh, Abram. You can't use that tower."

"Why not?"

"Well, because . . . I don't know, I guess. But I don't think you can."

And so by three in the afternoon everyone in town knew that Abram had made a mistake and that Mrs. Schultz's washline was strung up on the lower cross-beams of the television tower. Abram's mother was the first to know, and she came to look at ten-thirty, not saying anything, just looking. And when Reverend Schultz came home for dinner at twelve, he already knew. Somebody had told him, he couldn't remember who. He stood in the backyard, silently looking. Martin Heinrichs stopped in to look while on his way home from the railway depot, and Pete Kroeker walked into the yard at twelve-thirty to join the two silent men looking at the washline. And the women began arriving at one, Mrs. Kroeker who had left her dirty dinner dishes standing on the table and Mrs. Becker and her daughter Maria who had eaten on paper plates that day so that they would be able to come early. Schoolchildren began walking past at three-thirty—the first-graders who were so shy that they hurried, pretending not to look and yet looking out of the corners of their eyes, and fifteen minutes later the second-graders who walked past though not quite so quickly (all but one boy who was brave enough to slow down, though not to stop, and stare silently at it), and at four o'clock the rest of the grade school pupils who stood in a line in the street and looked, with ten or twelve who came into the yard and in a semi-circle stared at the tower with unblinking eyes.

When the crowd of schoolchildren dispersed, however, two boys hung back, the sixth-grade twins, Harry and Hanky Heinrichs. Lingering behind the three-foot hedge growing along the boundary of the parsonage lawn, lagging ever farther behind as the line of schoolchildren strung out and walked faster and faster, Harry and Hanky turned and crept back stealthily, though one watching could not have known for sure whether they were stalking a dangerous enemy or approaching a timid friend. And Harry, always the braver, was the first to touch the tower, patting the grey steel with his palm, while Hanky caressed the concrete foundation with his fingers. After walking back out to the street, they stood long and watched the blinking of the red light at the tower's peak.

Yet no one really talked about it. The tower was mentioned but not discussed. Nor, for that matter, had the matter been discussed when the Waldheim *News-Record* first announced that the UHF tower was to be built in town. And when the *News-Record* had announced the alarming news that the legs of the tower would stand in the backyard of the parsonage, no one talked about it. The *News-Record* editorial on the following week had been an open letter of protest to the Canadian Broadcasting Corporation. But the people of Waldheim had maintained stoical silence. One Sunday morning Reverend Schultz had preached a sermon on the things of the world—card-playing, drinking, dancing, Sunday baseball, half-naked boys playing basketball—which would be brought into Waldheim by television in general and Ultra-High-Frequency in particular. The people nodded as if in agreement but had not discussed, and Reverend Schultz, as if realizing the error of his stratagem, had not mentioned it again.

Nor had the people discussed the tower with the workmen who had moved their two trucks and three trailer houses into the vacant lot behind the cemetery one Sunday afternoon. As if by instinct and without their parents' instructions, girls had walked home from school more quickly than usual, and had walked on a side street that would not take them near the tower. As if by common consent, both the grocery store and the restaurant had refused to sell food to the men. On the second day after they had arrived, one of the men had tried to buy three apples, and the grocery clerk had told him, "I'm sorry, we're just closing up now," although it was three in the afternoon. And that evening they had waited for forty-five minutes in Sarah's Red Rose Cafe before a waitress, carrying neither water nor a menu, approached them.

"Well," she said.

"It's about time."

She had not answered.

"How about a menu?"

"Are you going to eat?" she had said.

"What've you got?"

"What do you usually get in a restaurant?"

"I'll take a ham dinner."

"We never carry that."

"Then give me a roast beef dinner."

"I just served the last one."

"All right. All right. Roast pork then."

Not answering, she had merely shaken her head.

The man had bit his lower lip before he said, "Hamburger."

"I've got enough for only one, not all of you."

Naturally they had left to find a restaurant in the next town, swearing never to come back to the Red Rose. And as one would expect, no one in Waldheim had seen the workmen until two days later when they had returned unshaven, haggard from loss of sleep, bewildered. For even natives sometimes got lost on the one-lane dirt road winding through the dense, dark growth of birch saplings between Eau Noir and Waldheim: even the county attorney who, two weeks after the tower had been started, had sent a letter to Reverend Schultz saying that the tower was supposed to be situated ten miles south of Waldheim, that it was being built in Waldheim because of a surveyor's error, that the minister should tell the men to stop work immediately, and that the attorney would drive down to Waldheim on the following day. But a week later another letter had come saying, "I've gotten lost three times driving out of Eau Noir. Please send a map immediately. Where is Waldheim?"

Of course Reverend Shultz, wiser now than when he had delivered his sermon, had not replied, nor had he spoken to the workmen. Every evening just before sundown he had come out to his backyard, looked up and down the completed portion of the tower, and then had said, "The Lord will provide. Yes." Thus, because of his not fighting, his waiting, Reverend Schultz was probably the only one who made an interpretive comment—"The Lord has provided. Yes. The Lord's humble servant"—when Abram's mistake transformed the Ultra-High-Frequency television booster tower into a washline.

And the next step in the transformation was inevitable. For although the desecrated site of the tower had been, as it were, disowned when the men were working on it, and although all had ignored the tower or averted their eyes when it was finished, and no one had cut the weeds or tended the grass; still, tidy Mrs. Schultz could not tolerate it that the thistles scratched her ankles when she hung up her wash, and even less that the tops of the milkweed brushed the hems of her sheets and left dark brown stains. And so the town awoke on Thursday morning to find the weeds raked into a neat pile at one corner of the tower and the soil hoed and raked smooth, and on Saturday morning to find the weeds reduced to a flattened mound of smoking ashes.

Cutting the weeds, however, presented a new problem that Mrs. Schultz had not anticipated; the bare concrete foundations now were visible showing their ugly grey above the grass and this was almost as intolerable as the weeds. Mrs. Schultz could not stand the sight of bare spots—window sills without flower pots, a toilet seat without a slip cover, a table without a doily. "Maybe we don't have such a fancy house," she would sometimes say, "but there's lots of women in Waldheim don't have as nice doilies. You can always have a respectable house with lots of doilies and flowers, and no dust."

Again it was an accident that carried the transformation further, solving the problem of the concrete foundations. One afternoon Mrs. Schultz hurried out her back door to the back fence, carrying in her hands a lump of dirt and a geranium plant.

"Mrs. Wiehens. Mrs. Wiehens," she called, the dirt slipping through her fingers in a thin trickle. "Quick." And when Mrs. Wiehens answered from her kitchen window, Mrs. Schultz called again, "Do you have an extra pot? I broke my last flower pot."

"Pot? I don't know. Abram, do we have another pot?"

"I don't know, Ma. Do we?"

Mrs. Schultz, moving nervously from one foot to the other, called again, "Hurry up. I'm losing all my dirt."

"What?"

"I'm losing all my dirt. Hurry."

"You want me to go get a doctor?"

"No no no. I don't want a doctor. I want a flower pot."

"Abram, you better go get Doctor Hiebert. Hurry."

"Now? You want me to go right now?"

"Yah, hurry."

"I just want a flower pot, not a doctor."

Mrs. Wiehens replied, "Does it hurt bad? You better go back in and go to bed."

"Nothing hurts me. All I want is a pot."

By now, however, Mrs. Wiehens was gone from the window and was hurrying down the sidewalk, calling, "Abram. Abram, wait. I want to go with you."

"Come back," Mrs. Schultz called, exasperated. "Pot."

The dirt still trickling through her fingers, she turned back toward her own house and set the dirt and the geranium in the nearest spot of shade, which happened to be the shadow of a concrete footing. And after Doctor Hiebert arrived and Mrs. Schultz explained the mix-up to him and explained it two more times to Mrs. Wiehens, it was time for her to begin cooking supper. Thus, she temporarily forgot the geranium.

"Abram," Mrs. Wiehens said as they were returning home through the parsonage yard, "look at that little flower there. That Preacher Schultz, why can't he even dig a hole for his wife?"

"Hole?" Abram said.

"Why don't you dig a hole for her?"

"Right now? Do I have time?"

"I don't know. Do you?"

And so when she remembered the geranium about eight that evening, Mrs. Schultz found it planted and watered beside the foundation of the tower, though to be sure the stalk had been shoved into the ground at a low angle.

The plant grew, however, and in two weeks a small bud appeared. As with the washline, the whole town knew on the day when the flower opened. All Waldheim walked past that day, the men in the morning, the women right after noon, the children after three-thirty. Harry and Hanky came too, glanced at the geranium, ran their eyes slowly up the legs of the tower, and gazed at the blinking red light until Mrs. Schultz told them to go home for supper and they forgot and she told them again. But that evening a different kind of parade began. Mrs. Becker came first carrying a small peony bush with the dirt wrapped in faded grey crash towels that had been pinned together neatly with safety pins. Mrs. Kroeker appeared with a paper bag of hollyhock seeds, and before long Mrs. Heinrichs walked into the yard with a spirea bush, her husband following her and carrying a shovel. All planted silently, looked at the tower for a moment, then left. And just before sundown the Schultzes came out with a cardboard box of ivy sprouts which they planted and tied up on sticks and strings and the legs of the tower. By the end of June the tower was covered to eye level with greenery, and by the end of July the ivy reached to a height of fifteen feet.

The name was changed too. No longer the tower, no longer even the washline (for the shade of the shrubs and ivy forced Mrs. Schultz to go back to her old washline), it blossomed into an item of luxury, The Arbor: blossomed into the shades of pink of the peonies, the red and yellow of the hollyhocks, the white of the spirea, all startling and bright against the dark green of the ivy. The Arbor: soon through the town the name spread, the soft luxurious sound slipping sensuously into the clipped German speech of the people, so that at least one woman was heard to say, "Well, I don't know about this, the preacher's wife getting so fancy that she has to have a Arbor."

But even the religious value of The Arbor soon became

apparent to the people of Waldheim, and again the cause was an accident. Mrs. Schultz, however, was learning how to capitalize quickly on the accidents of nature, which this time brought together an unseasonal and heavy rain on a Wednesday night in August and the Ladies' Aid Society meeting scheduled for the following afternoon, the women arriving and finding the sewers backed up and the basement of the church flooded with two inches of water.

"No, no," said Mrs. Becker. "Look at all that water."

"Abram," Mrs. Wiehens said. "I could get Abram and he could scoop out the water."

"Not all that water."

"Well," Mrs. Schultz said in a small voice, her mouth turning slightly upward toward a smile, "we could always go out to The Arbor. In the shade. In the flowers."

And she said the same thing three weeks later when in a wedding on a hot Sunday afternoon the older women sat near the windows and sweated and fanned themselves with hymnbooks, and when a young girl whose face because of the heat turned from bright pink to white in five minutes had to be accompanied out of the church before the wedding started; then Mrs. Schultz left too in order to find the bride in the vestibule and whisper in her ear. So that Mrs. Becker said to Mrs. Heinrichs who repeated to Mrs. Schultz, "My my, such a nice wedding. That Mrs. Schultz, she knows how to do things right. Such a nice wedding."

Thus by the middle of October Mrs. Schultz had forgotten that it had ever been anything but The Arbor, and she came out into the backyard with her husband one evening just before sundown, carrying in her hand a sheet of paper on which was a written and numbered list. "First thing we've got to do," she said, "is get some gravel. And you can get it free if you go out yourself and bring it in from the gravel pit. And Mrs. Heinrichs said her husband said we could have some of those stones in their backyard, enough to make a sidewalk from The Arbor to the house, and maybe he'd help you put it in too if you do it evenings. And next spring we've got to put in some more ivies, the kind that grow longer than these, and we've got to train them over the top so we'll have a roof. And we've got to be sure and get some tulips in right away so we'll have them first thing in the spring."

And she had also forgotten the snow. The storm came later than usual, in the second week in November. Two grey and overcast days preceded the breeze which began in the evening, whined through the night, roared in the morning. The wind toppled the spirea, crushed the peonies into low lumps, ripped the vines off, laid bare the steel girders rising from the soot-greyed snow and holding against the grey sky the blinking red light of the Ultra-High-Frequency tower.

On the next Saturday afternoon when the sun was shining and the air was clear, Harry and Hanky climbed halfway up the tower.

"I can see all the way to Eau Noir," Hanky called.

Harry who was twenty feet higher replied, "I can see Winnipeg from here. Boy, come here and look at it."

And Hanky said, "I bet you if we got all the way to the top, we could see Hollywood, don't you think?"

Elaine Driedger

White Christmas

Wishing it would snow so hard that we couldn't possibly go to Florida, I glare at the cold, dark window of Oma's sagging kitchen and see nothing but the reflection of my own face poking out from the swaying backs of my aunts.

In all my thirteen years I have never experienced a Christmas day as miserable as this one.

I grip a plate between the folds of my dishtowel, squeaking hot wetness from the glaze patterned with apple blossoms and a net of cracks. I've watched that window all afternoon. Watching for snow. Waiting for Janet. Dreaming of Larry.

Five aunts and Oma bustle around me, grabbing dishes from the dish rack or thumping up the steps to the pantry with zwieback and perishky left over from the Christmas fesper. Aunt Betty and Aunt Lizzy compare crimpolene prices, and my mother at the sink explains the details of her new Jello recipe to Aunt Frieda. I don't think Aunt Frieda could care less about a Jello recipe.

I am the only cousin in this steaming, rattling kitchen. The younger cousins are upstairs, watching "The Grinch Who Stole Christmas" on the T.V. in the spare room. I've sat here all afternoon as each new wave of relatives sprayed in more little cousins who flaunted new toys or scrambled under the battered table to bump my legs or snatch zwieback and cookies from the plates set out in the long, narrow pantry. I've been here every Christmas I can remember. This year should have been different.

Oma and Opa's house on Christmas day is always the same. The uncles and Opa sit in the front room and argue about Trudeau, farm co-ops, and Aeltester Nichol's latest sermon. The women are in the middle room near the kitchen, where they can keep their ears tuned to the racket and rustle of the kids. The older cousins have stopped coming. Even Janet hasn't shown up yet. She's only a year older than I am. Whatever she did today had to be more fun than sitting in a noisy farm kitchen overrun by little kids.

I turn from the window, pull the plate from my damp cloth, and push it onto the growing pile on the table. As I hoist a bowl, dull and heavy, from the dish rack, I scowl at my mother's back. There is no place for me here anymore. I'm in high school now. Janet hasn't come since she was in grade eight.

It should have been different this year. But my parents insisted on their way, saying that Uncle George should keep Janet more in line. I felt like screaming: How could I ever face Larry if he knew I was being treated like a kid?

I wince now remembering my father's teasing me in front of Oma and Aunt Frieda when we'd arrived this afternoon. My kid sister Karen hadn't said a thing, but I could see smirks all over her face.

"Linda is probably thinking about her boyfriend today, eh. Isn't that right? Real good-looking fellow. Drives a red convertible." My father's eye had winked like it was trying to catch me.

And it had. All day I've been caught—between the tinsel-sparkling, light-bubbling Christmas tree and the cool gleam of red fenders, between the sugary smell of perishky and the smarting wisps of cigarette smoke, between now and last Friday and tomorrow. Between myself and myself.

"For goodness sakes. The boy only gave her a ride home. Why fill her head with all kinds of notions?" This my mother had sung out only to make things infinitely worse. I'd hated the worry in her words.

I'm caught between my mother's common sense and a strange, new, trembling sense of being born from the touch of a boy's hand wrapped around my own and linking me with something wonderful, something my parents wouldn't see. Something they want to keep from me.

I watch my mother rinsing the last soap suds down the kitchen drain. Aunt Frieda says she wishes it would snow so it would seem more like Christmas. My mother nods briskly. "Yes, snow would be nice," she says, "but driving south tomorrow will be easier if the weather stays mild. Anyway, it is Christmas whether it snows or not."

Have to come to Oma's, I sneer to myself. Have to play with cousins. Have to go to Florida tomorrow. What if Larry tries to call? Ten days is so darn long.

I thump the bowl I'm carrying onto the stained tablecloth where the good dishes are being piled until Aunt Frieda takes them to the china cabinet in the middle room.

Who's Janet been with today? What did she mean when she'd whispered during "Hark the Herald Angels" at last night's carol sing—"I've gotta warn you about Larry. Talk to you tomorrow." I pick up a plate and keep rubbing it long after it's dry.

The kitchen smells like burnt candles and sugar icing, reminding me of the school basement at the party on the weekend. I want to hurl myself away from here, away and back to last Friday, to that carol-throbbing moment when the handsomest boy in the whole school had asked me, Linda, to be HIS partner for the party lunch. He'd held my hand as we'd run with the others along the wet, gritty sidewalk from the gym to the candle-lit, locker-lined school basement. He'd eaten two cheese sandwiches and one salami, and said he hated pickles. He told me that "White Christmas" was his favourite Christmas song. Afterwards he'd held my coat for me and then taken me home in his fabulous red convertible.

A red car flashes past the kitchen window into the yard. I bound to the door.

"Hi there. Any grub left?" It's Janet. Some friends have dropped her off. The car, I can see now, is not a convertible.

"Sure, lots." I watch the car back away. The headlights glare at me, and I can't see who's in it.

"Well, close the door, silly. It's freezing out there." Janet rolls her eyes. She turns from me to the aunts at the sink. "Hi everybody! Gee, I'm starved."

Janet is hailed by the aunts as though she's a returning queen. And what's she done to deserve that, I wonder. But I'm glad she's finally come. She's a sort of connection, a witness to last Friday. At least she knows that I am no longer a child.

"So how'd you like the party Friday?" Janet plops jam into the hollow cradle of a zwieback bottom. The women have finished in the kitchen and are talking in the middle room. Every once in a while their laughter bursts against the closed kitchen door, but it's muffled like the sound of the distant T.V. The dripping tap and Janet's chewing noises are the only sounds in the room.

"I thought it was a super party." I cup my chin in my hand as I lean on my elbow. This pushes my face directly towards her.

"Well, I didn't. I thought it was crummy. The grade twelves this year have no imagination at all. If you ask me it was a big flop. But then what can you expect at a Mennonite high school?" Janet peels the skin from a slice of salami. It comes off in an unbroken circle. "I know why you liked it so much. You didn't even notice anything. All you were looking at was that dreamy Larry Enns."

I can feel myself blush, but right now I don't care. I strain to puzzle out the expression on my cousin's face. Is she jealous? Is she happy for me? The muscles around Janet's pencil-thin mouth purse into a slight pucker. It's too blank, too fake. Did she see Larry today? Maybe he talked about me. Janet, say something.

But Janet doesn't.

The cold from the kitchen window lays a penetrating hand on my back. I struggle for something to say. "So what'd you do this afternoon?"

Janet picks up a lemon tart. "Just hang around."

"See anybody special?"

Silence. Then a sigh. "Look, Linda, I hate to tell you this because I don't want to spoil your trip to Florida."

"Tell me what?"

"Well, about Larry."

"What about him?"

"Well, you know he has a girlfriend that goes to Pelee High. You knew that didn't you?"

"Yeah, I know he used to go with somebody. So? He's not married to her."

"Just forget it."

"Good grief. Janet! Forget what? Come on. Tell me what's up."

Another sigh. "Okay. Don't say I didn't warn you. I heard that Larry and his girlfriend had a fight last week, and she was real upset, and so the night of the school party she was out in the parking lot waiting to talk to him. Get it?"

"So? She can sit around and wait." I toss my head back. My hair flicks against the window ledge behind me. I stare hard at the closed kitchen door.

"Gee, you really are immature. Look, Larry knew she was out there. He used you to make her jealous. Now you know." Janet clicks her tongue and scrapes lemon filling from her plate.

"So!" I whirl to face her. "How do you know that's what he was doing? How do you know he cared if she was out there or not?"

Janet clangs the fork down on her plate. "I know, dear cousin, because it obviously worked. I saw them together today, and, believe me, they weren't fighting anymore."

I turn slowly to stare down at the floor. Across the kitchen, the tap drips into the sink—plonk, plonk. It hadn't bothered me before. Plonk, plonk. I squeeze my eyes shut. Plonk, plonk.

I lunge to the sink and wrench both handles of the tap. My hands, gripping the steel knobs, are taut and white. The glow of feeling grown-up has disappeared. I just feel tired.

Voices in the middle room rise up behind the closed door as though someone's turned the volume up.

"Merry Christmas. . . need a good night's sleep. . . bright and early."

The kitchen door bursts open, spilling my sister and my mother and my father into the room. They've got their coats on. My mother smiles at me and holds up my jacket.

I'm not ready for this intrusion. But there they are—my stiffly smiling mother, my father, and my maddeningly self-satisfied sister Karen, who bounds across the kitchen and flings the door open. "Hey everybody, look. It's snowing!" Crisp air sweeps into the room. Big, fluffy flakes flutter in and settle on the front of her dress.

"Well, look at that, we're getting a white Christmas after all."

"It's beautiful."

Oma and some of the aunts crowd around the door with me and my family. I feel a hand squeeze my elbow. I turn and find Janet close to me. My cousin is staring down at her tightly curled, stockinged toes. "Hey, when you're lying on those gorgeous beaches, don't forget to write a little postcard to your cousin stuck up here in snow country." Janet looks up and wrinkles her nose. She pulls me closer and whispers, "Forget Larry. He's a jerk. You can do better than him."

I blink. The muscles in my throat fight down a tight ache. I search Janet's face for a moment and then we reach for each other and hug. Suddenly I want to hug them all, to bury my face in their coats and show them all it doesn't matter about Larry. But, yes, it does matter very much. And, then again, it doesn't either. I don't know which way I feel. I'm sad-happy to go to Florida. I love-hate Christmas day.

I keep close to my family as we walk across the field towards our house on the next sideroad. The sky is full of big, cottony fluffs that sting my face with cold kisses. I watch them cling to the sleeve of my jacket and melt. Early tomorrow I and my family will whisk past freshly-blanketed fields toward the emerald parks and white, sandy beaches of Florida. I've been there before. Once, when I was just a kid.

"Look at the snow. It'll sure seem different down there now." Karen's voice is happy as she speaks to me.

"Yeah, Florida will be different."

My arm brushes my mother's coat sleeve as we walk. Our shoulders touch. She reaches out and puts her arm around me.

"I know you don't really want to go, Linda. Soon you'll be taking trips of your own." Her sigh is soft. It gets lost in the murmur of the wind whispering secrets to the trees.

My mother's arm squeezes more tightly around me as though for a moment she is trying to push me down and make me small again. Then she lets go. Through my tears the sticky, feathery snowflakes explode into shimmering, long-spindled stars.

Armin Wiebe

Oata, Oata

Oata, Oata
Ossentoata
Pesst em Woata
Truff ein Koata
Truck sich dann dei Becksi oot
Funk doa einen brunen Kloot
Howd sich dann ne grote Frei
Docht dowt veah ein Ouster Ei
Schmeickt seh eesht ein kleenet Beet
Yowma me dowt ess blous Sheet

Penzel Panna made it up one day at recess time behind the girl's beckhouse while Oata was inside. By dinner the whole school had learned it off by heart, even Pug Peters who couldn't learn the shortest Bible verse, "Jesus wept." The grade oners on the horse swings said it as they pumped and pulled. The girls with their braided binder twine ropes said it while they were skipping. Some, that hide-and-go-seek played, said it instead of telling numbers to a hundred.

Everywhere Oata went on the school yard we called out the Flat German verse to her. At first she tried some of the smaller ones to chase but she was then already 180 pounds so it was easy to run from her away. So Oata gave up and sat herself down by the big climbing sugar tree and looked to the church over the road. Her back was to us and she made like she didn't listen but every once in a while her shoulders would hop up and down and we could see she was onioning her eyes out.

Oata's eyes were not onions now as she reaches out a two-back bun to me full with mustard pickles and *Pannash Worscht*. I take it without looking in those eyes, one brown and one blue, and lean myself back against the big wheel of the 4010. She has at least one button on her shirt closed now, not open and flying back in the wind like when she came bouncing the field over on the Ford Tractor.

But with Oata Needarp you never know what she will do. I found that out last year when I worked for her Foda, Nobah Naze. Muttachi was tired from me already lying the house around all winter and she made me to get a job at saddle-time with Nobah Naze Needarp. All the summer through Oata was after me to take her to ball games and Sunday Night Christian Endeavours so I was the laughing stockade of the ball team. At one game somebody wrote "Oata, Oata" with lipstick all over the window of my half-ton truck. So I was for sure happy this year I got a job with Ha Ha Nickel and his skinny daughter, Sadie, only yesterday she left me by the ball game in Panzenfeld and went to the "Town Without Pity" show with Pug Peters. And it sure didn't put any jam on my bread this morning when Ha Ha sent me to work by Nobah Naze Needarp's because the old man a heart attack had and that's why I'm here eating faspa with Oata in the shade from the 4010.

I try to quietly chew the sandwich so that Oata can't nerk me for chewing loud and I don't say nothing, just look over the ripples of earth to the end of the field. I don't want to look at the three-cornered patch of creamfat ripples showing where Oata's shirt hangs down from the one button she has closed by her tits. I hear Oata chewing, then the tin scrapes on the glass when she screws off the lid from the jar of Freshie.

"Oata, Oata, Ossentoata," she says and I feel the bottom of the jar press into my hand. I have to look at her to take the jar.

"Pissed in the water
Hit a catter"
I get some Freshie into my Sunday throat and start to cough.
"Pulled herself the panties down
Found a lump there nice and brown
Thought it was an Easter egg
Rolled it up and down her leg
Tasted first a tiny bit
Holy cow it is just shit"

Oata's finger touches the flesh of my thumb and she takes the jar out from my hand.

"Nobody ever made up a verse about you, eh?" she says, then she laughers herself so that her whole front bobbers up and down. I say nothing, only look at the weeds on the part of the field that isn't diskered yet. A klunk of earth digs into my narsch and I wonder why I always get into such a pit. Then Oata says, "You made up the English one, didn't you?" I don't look at her but I can feel that brown eye mixing with the blue one and boring me through. Salt water leaks down the side of my ribs. "But then you are a Reimer on your mother's side, aren't you, Yasch?"

I look at my clock and see that it is time to get on with the seeding or I won't get back to Ha Ha Nickel's in time to play catch with Sadie before fire evening.

"I phoned to Ha Ha Nickel," Oata says just before I press the starter button. My hand freezes. "I said to him that you would stay here for supper so you can me to the hospital take to visit Futtachi. Ha Ha said it was okay, and said you should stay for night already. I. . ."

I press the button to drown her out and rev the engine up so that the diesel coming from the stack is so black that it matches the words from my mouth. And they don't rhyme, neither, as I make the 4010 pull that disker through the field, make it struggle because that tractor is the only thing I can boss around. Everything else in the world bosses me around. It matters nothing what I want to do, there is always something to make me do what I don't want. The wind pushes a empty fertilizer sack over the summerfallow, shoves it from one klunk to another, waiting for a chance to chase it into a thorn bush or a barbed-wire fence.

I try to look my way around going to town with Oata but nothing for sure falls me by and when it is half seven already my stomach is hanging crooked and the fuel gauge is showing empty. So I finish the round and hook loose the disker and drive to the yard and hold still by the diesel tank. Oata hurries herself out of the house as soon as the motor stops and I almost trip myself over the gearshift.

That such things one can see here on Nobah Naze Needarp's farm would I me not have thought even if the bull had farrowed. From a white elephant I had heard but here coming the yard across is Oata in a pink dress like a tent that would hold almost the Brunk Tent Crusade. She has her yellow brown gray hair tied up with a pink scarf and when she closer comes I can see her mouth is smeared with pink, too. Her pink in between the toes shoes with high heels yet dig in the ground, but when she stops and leans herself with her hand against the back tire of the 4010 all I can see is the little plastic pink butterflies screwed on her ears.

"Yasch, Yasch, hurry yourself up! The visiting hours start already at seven o'clock and you must yet eat and wash the summerfallow from yourself. Go behind the house. I put fresh water in the washcumb."

My ears still ring from the tractor motor and the words from those pink-smeared lips fly me by and then, even through the stink of the diesel and the grease, my nose sucks in a sinus full of *Evening in Schanzenfeld* perfume and proost so hard that one gob of mucus membrane sizzles on the muffler.

Half-warm water in the white washcumb with the red stripe around the rim. And lye soap with *Evening in Schanzenfeld* spritzed on it. I can't gribble it out if Oata is nerking me or trying too hard with "limited resources" like the ag rep said at a 4H meeting one time.

Oata sticks out her head from the green screen door of the ovenside and says she has made something hartsoft special for my supper, and I mutter to my chin that I hope it's not porridge with lots of salt like she used to make last year all the time. And it isn't. My faspa almost climbs up from my panz when she says, "It is today so hot that I thought you would like some *Schmauntzup.*" I can hardly look at the big bowl of thick sour milk mixed up with green onions and cucumbers. Muttachi used to make it for Futtachi and he would just shovel it down like it was the best treat in the world but I could never make myself eat it. I mean I don't even like to eat glumms, except when they are in verenichi.

So I look at the white clock with the red numbers that hangs by the chimney and say, "It's feadel to seven already so we have to go or you'll for the visiting hours be late." I hurry the screen door out and Oata comes me after.

Nobah Naze's half-ton is still on the field with the seed so I flitz around the barn to the Ford tractor and hump spread-legged on to the seat. I push on the starter and there's only a click and when I reach for the key there's nothing in the key hole.

"Yasch, Yasch, not the tractor! We will the car take!"

The car? For sure, the car. Nobah Naze has a car. Only it is hard to remember it because he never drives it if he thinks there will be mud or dust. When I worked for him last year I saw it once just, in the ovenside of the chicken barn when we spent three hours in the middle of the best combining day of the harvest looking for the Jack-All. That was the one time I saw the dark green '51 Ford four door, with white walls and radio yet, and one scratch just, so small you wouldn't see it except if Nobah Naze showed it to you, there by the "R" in FORD on the trunk. Nobah Naze said to me that the bengels at church had scratched it the first Sunday when the car was new and so that's why he only the half-ton to church drives because the dow-nixes like the preacher's son and the deacon's nephew play hookey from the church and fool around with people's cars while the elders are preaching and praying and holding the collect for wayward children's homes like Ailsa Craig. "Dose studs of the church," he spits at me, "can see de flyshit in Ontario but dey can't see de snudder which from dere own nose leaks."

Oata is jingling the keys to the car by the ovenside door and I walk over trying to gribble out the "consequentlies" of taking Nobah Naze's pet car, knowing for sure that Nobah Naze will blame me even if it Oata's fault is. Oata has her door already open and throws me the keys over the roof before she squeezes herself into the woman's side and closes the door on her pink dress.

So sticks the fork in the handle, I think to myself, then I open the man's side and slide in behind the steer. For a moment I get a noseful of new car smell, then the *Evening in Schanzenfeld* drives out any other smells that might have been brave enough to even try to reek.

The car starts up like new and the gas gauge shows three-fourths full and I figure I'll fill some gas up from the tank when we get back. I slowly back out from the ovenside and as soon as I turn the door to the road Oata switches the radio on loud and CFAM sings into our ears but Oata cuts that out quick when she

pushes the button to bring in Portage. The western music makes me to feel good, even if I had started to listen to the rock and roll because that is what Sadie Nickel likes. Somehow the guitars and banjos, fiddles and steel guitars touch me in the heart and make me feel almost churchy in a funny way, like when I was just a *Jungchi* with a brushcut and I used to go to Sunday Night Christian Endeavours because that's where the action was, and the girls would sit on the choir loft benches and their skirts would pull up a little over the knees and a guy could feel right happy to be in the church even if the children's story was just a little bit young and the gospel message was always too long. But the best part of it all was when the people in the choir who could guitar play would put those coloured cords with the fuzzy tassels around their necks and put the picks on their thumbs or hold them between the fingers and line up behind the choir leader who had a hand plaything, and they would play old songs from the *Evangeliums* book and it would sound just like angels and the girls' fingers would scratch the picks over the strings and for days afterward I would make the sounds they made with my tongue—DUNG
DANG DANG, DUNG DANG
DANG, DUNG
    DUNG
      DUNG
        DUNG DANG DANG, DUNG DANG DANG
and sometimes Schallemboych Pete's bride from Somerfield would play her mandolin and go DWEET, DWEET, DWEET. But then they put up a wine-colored curtain fence in front of the choir loft so the girls' legs didn't show any more and the leader started to go to choir leading schools in Winkler or some place and learned such things as to have the choir people stand one behind the other and hit the person in the front with the edge of your hand on the back at choir practice. And they stopped the guitars to play and only tried to sing such high music like Contatas and so I stayed home on Sunday nights if Muttachi would let me and listened to a States station which good country music had on Sunday nights.

And so now the radio has on good country songs all the way to the hospital except for one Ray Price song that I don't like the fiddle for and I guess even Oata doesn't like it because that's when she starts to talk with me and tells me not to be so shittery and drive a little faster. That makes me mad and when we reach the highway I figure, let's see if this thing can squeal on pavement. I shift into low gear, rev up the motor and pop the clutch. The loose gravel squirts from the spinning tires and the rear end from the car swings to the side and when the rubber hits the pavement there is just a bit of a squeal and then the Ford hots up to sixty real fast. I check the mirrors for a green '58 Ford that the Mounties use, then I floor the thing and the needle shoots up to eighty-five and the wind blows in through the vents and lifts up that pink dress like a tarp in a tornado and I can't help myself I have to look at the creamfat white between the tops of the pink nylons and the pink elastic stuff that schneers into the soft skin under the garter. Oata doesn't bother herself to put the dress down and she just leans back in the seat with her elbow on the door handle that is like a little shelf. I had thought that maybe the speed would make her scared a little bit but she seems to like this going fast and she bounces one big round knee along with the guitars from an instrumental "Golden Wildwood Flower" and her big pink lips have half a smile on them and I start to feel like she is maybe laughering herself over me and I make that Ford go even faster and when we get to the CFAM towers the needle is showing almost a hundred and Oata's lips are smiling so that her teeth are showing and her tent dress is blowing up in her face. Then she leans over and closes the window and the vent and the pink stuff falls down like a parachute and I take my foot of the footfeed and let the car coast till we go just sixty and it's a good thing, too, because I am only going sixty for about half a minute when the green '58 Ford meets us on the curve that leads into town.

"The stripey gophers almost got you for showing off to a girl," she says and so I slow the car down to fifteen miles an hour and go slow like that till we to the hospital get.

Oata wobbles the hospital steps up on her spikes and I hunch myself down in the seat and hope that nobody will see me in Nobah Naze's car. Then I feel my stomach hanging crooked and so I go to the little store there beside the hospital and buy myself some Oh Henry bars and two bottles of Wynola. Just when I'm going to walk out the little bell klingers on the door and in comes Tiedig Wien's Mumchi who onetime best friends with Muttachi was and she talks me on and I have to talk her back. Tiedig Wienses used to be neighbours with us but now they live in town close to the hospital and the olden home so the Mumchi can better visit all those that are going dead. That's what she says me now, except that I know that Tiedig Wiens had his driving licence taken away and now he lives close enough to the parlour so that he can walk. Anyways, Tiedig Wiens' Mumchi tells me all about her boy Melvin who in Regina is learning to be an RCMP and that he likes it very much and it's easy for him because he's so smart, especially the taking care of the horses part. And I think about the time Melvin Wiens went to visit by Hingst Heinrich's place on a Sunday after dinner and the boys decided to ride the old shrug that Heinrich keeps for pulling the manure sled in winter. Now it took the shrug a little while to get the idea about what she was to do but by the time it was Melvin's turn she had it in her head that when something sat on her back she should run. The shrug took off as soon as Melvin climbed on and galloped him around the fence three times going faster and faster and Melvin is holding the mane on with both hands and yelling: "Help! Help!" so loud that Hingst Heinrich's sister (that Melvin really wanted to visit but didn't have the nerve for) comes running to the barn just in time to see the shrug dump Melvin into the pig pen beside the fence and it had rained an inch the night before. Melvin Wiens was wearing his Sunday pants yet, too. Anyways, Tiedig Wiens' Mumchi says me again how happy she is to have such a nice boy who doesn't smoke and drink and who even to RCMP church goes on Sundays. Just then the storeman's cuckoo clock goes off and the old lady lets me get away without saying her anything myself or Muttachi.

I go back to the car and eat my stuff while the sun glances off the hospital windows and the shadows get longer. The Wynola bottles get empty and I feel still thirsty and I gribble in my head if I should quickly drive to the hotel and pick up a six. But then Oata comes out the door where the sun isn't glancing off the glass any more and I watch her come down the big steps with her pink dress.

"Take me to the Dairy Dell for soft ice cream," says Oata when she has sat herself back in the car.

Now the Dairy Dell was where I wanted to take Sadie

Nickel after the ball game against Panzenfeld last Sunday only she left me before the game over was because that snuddernose Pug Peters was taking her to the "Town Without Pity" show in Neche. The Dairy Dell is the place where everybody goes in the summer time after anything is over and there is always somebody there that knows you and will come to talk you on, for sure if you have a woman along. I mean it's always that way on Sunday nights if you are lucky enough or brave enough when you are driving through all the darps or up and down the main street to hold still by some girls that are walking the road along and you find enough nerves to talk them on in a nice way and sometimes you get full of luck and they will get in the car and you can go driving the sunflower fields through on the middle roads but you always go to the Dairy Dell before the night is over. And at the Dairy Dell all those that didn't pick up some girls crowd the cars around where the girls are in and so I sure don't feel like going there with Oata in Nobah Naze's car.

But it is Monday evening and when we get to the Dairy Dell there just is one big truck and it doesn't look like it matters so I park the car close to the shack so that Oata can see the food list that's painted on the side. Besides, I didn't eat any supper. I ask Oata what she wants and she says, "Just soft ice cream" and so I go to the window and tell Trudy Teichroeb's mom that I want a soft ice cream and a nip and a milkshake. Then I lean myself on the shelf that they have by the window and look at the truck and see one beard, one polka dotted kerchief, and two little boys with suspenders. Just some Huttatolas eating soft ice cream.

My food is ready and I pay for it and I think I will be lucky enough to get from the Dairy Dell away before somebody sees me but no such luck. I am just passing Oata's ice cream through the window to her when Pug Peters and Hingst Heinrichs come skidding into the yard and throw dust over everything. I hurry myself into the car and shove the milkshake and nip to Oata and say "Hold this!" and I let loose the car and peel out of the yard with as much dust as those other guys brought in.

But it is already too late. Those dipsticks make a U-ball and come us after down the 14A. Oata hollers "*HOLEM DE GRUEL*" and rutches herself over the middle of the seat so that her side is leaning me against. Just what I yet need when I want to go fast as the Ford can and I have to steer with both hands and Oata is leaning me against so that my arm is clamped in between my ribs and her lard but I floor that thing anyway and Oata counts along with the red needle: 65 70 75 80 85 90 95 100 and I look in the mirror behind and I can see Hingst's car is getting closer and I step harder even if the pedal is flat on the floor already but the needle stays there just by hundred. And then I see it.

"LOOK, YASCH!"

The grey Vauxhall creeps the white line along, five 'n twenty miles an hour just like always and I know that Happy Heppner's grandfather is driving his Mumchi around again. But then I see in the other lane coming us on from the front a big yellow combine, and another one behind and another and another and another. Five new Cockshutt combines creeping us towards and I know for sure that Nobah Naze's '51 Ford better have good brakes or me and Oata will have to make a detour through the ditch.

Oata just leans herself closer to me and licks her ice cream when the rubber starts to squeal and the car wags its tail a little but I manage to make the Ford stop the Vauxhall five feet behind, just when the first combine is even with it. Happy Heppner's grandfather keeps just on driving and I don't think he noticed us or the combines. Burned rubber smell drowns out the *Evening in Schanzenfeld* perfume and at the same time there is loud honking behind and I know that Hingst and Pug have caught up.

I put the car back in gear and creep after the grey Vauxhall and those penzels behind us keep blowing their horn and Oata leans her head on my shoulder yet and bites off the side of the cone, but then I see my chance because the last combine is farther behind than the other ones so I floor that Ford and whip it around the Vauxhall and shoot away.

"Yippee Doodles!" yells Oata and she turns herself around to look out the back and she shteepas herself with her hand on my leg a little bit too close to the intersection for me right now because I have the footfeed flat on the floor again trying to get as far as I can before Pug gets by those combines. Well, I'm going 95 again when Oata pinches me on the leg and her chin is leaning on my shoulder and her hair is making my ear itchy and she yells: "They made it around!" So I jerk myself frontward to make that car go faster and then for sure her hand is in the wrong place and I see some lights coming from the front but I am going 100 now and then I think that I don't have my lights on but it is already too late—the car that is coming on is blinking a red light already. For a few seconds my foot stays flat on the floor, then I take it off the gas and shove Oata out of the way a little and shitts the lights on. I let the car coast till it's just going 50 then I hold it there but the blinking red light is already turning around behind us and I can hear the siren.

Oata doesn't say nothing while we wait for the police to come to the car. Then the police is there and I can see from his thin shnuitsboat that it is the same police that held me up one other time and he looked all through the half-ton cab with his flashlight but he couldn't find nothing and I got away with having a 24 of States beer under the hood.

"You were driving without your lights on," he says to me.

"Well, it wasn't yet altogether dark."

"You were travelling pretty fast too." I don't say nothing but I know now that he doesn't know for sure how fast I was going. Then he wants to see my driver's and the car registration. He looks at them for a minute then he leans his head in the window as far as his hat will let him and he says to Oata: "This your father's car?"

"Yeah," says Oata.

"Do you have a driver's licence?"

"Yeah, sure," she says, and she starts to stir around in her purse and she pulls out a driver's licence and I wonder me what the hund I am doing here when Oata could have driven herself to the hospital and I could have gone back to Ha Ha's and played catch with Sadie Nickel at fire evening. Just then a car drives slowly past and I hear Hingst Heinrichs yell: "PAUSS UP WITH NOBAH NAZE'S CAR!" My ears are sure hot and they get hotter yet when the police reaches Oata's driver's and the registration through the window to her and he says: "Why don't you drive your father's car home before show off here has an accident?"

"Okay," she says, and the police opens my door. What can a guy do? I get out and Oata rutches herself behind the steer. The police looks my driver's on a little bit more.

"Aren't you getting a bit old for these tricks?" He lets his eyes bore at me from under the hat, then he gives me back my driver's and stands there watching while I creep into Nobah Naze's car on the woman's side.

Oata starts up the car and grinds it into low gear. Then she gives it gas before she lets the clutch out and the tires spin in the dirt beside the pavement and she stalls the motor. I look back and see the police standing there and I can see he is laughering himself. Oata tries again and this time she gets the car going except she doesn't shift out from low gear and the car is making lots of noise so I say: "Shift gears already." Oata steps on the clutch but she keeps her foot on the throttle and the motor revs like crazy but she gets it into second and we go like that till we get to the turn off corner. This time she remembers to shift gears and then she even goes fast enough to need high gear so I tell her to shift again.

"Eat your nip already," she says. "Soon it will be cold."

The nip is cold, but I eat it. Oata doesn't say nothing else, she just drives and all of a sudden I'm thinking about the time when I was 10 years old and we had just moved to Gutenthal from Yanzeed, where my Futtachi was working out for a farmer by Chortitz. Handy as in Chortitz the people always said but it wasn't handy for us even if you could back up with the harrow. So Futtachi moved us to Gutenthal and for a whole year in school the other guys always ran from me away. Every time I came close they would run and hide and then say things to nerk me from behind the trees. It didn't feel so good to always be run away from and when Oata quietly says I shouldn't forget to drink the milkshake I don't feel so good about the things we used to do to her in school.

It is dark already when we get to Nobah Naze's place and it suddenly falls me by that Oata hasn't said nothing about her Futtachi, if he is very sick or not. So I ask her and she just says "Not so good" and she turns the radio louder because the song is about the old log cabin for sale.

The yard is very still and the moon is coming up over the willow trees by the waterhole where the frogs are having choir practice and I think about the time when it was forty degrees cold and Shacht Schulz brought his tape recording machine to school and played us some frog singing that he had taped by

Buffalo Creek and he thought it would warm us up to hear frogs on such a cold day. And while we were listening Irene Olfert was looking back to me with her little mirror and I got this tickling feeling in my bones and I thought it would be nice to sit on a waterhole hump with her and listen to real frogs in the summertime but when summertime came the Olferts had moved to Ontario to pick tomatoes.

Now Oata makes the door open to the house and I start to wonder me what I am doing following her to the house when I should be walking to my Muttachi's place for the night. It would be only a mile and a half across the field. Or I could even the tractor take and then come back in the morning to finish the seeding.

"Make the door closed. The mosquitos are coming in."

So I do it and I stand there in the kitchen and the lights aren't switched on and it falls me by that Nobah Naze hardly ever used the hydro at night in the summertime because he said too many flies come to the house when the lights are on. Now it doesn't seem such a silly idea after all, even if by Ha Ha Nickel's they have a yellow bulb outside by the porch door that is supposed to keep the bugs away. And anyway if the mosquitos get bad Ha Ha just lights on some do do coils, which is like having mosquito smoke, only it is handier, and stinks a little like perfume.

But here now in Nobah Naze's kitchen it is dark except for one slice of moonshine that through the little window over the cook oven shines on the Elephant Brand fertilizer calendar, and the *Evening in Schanzenfeld* is still strong enough so we don't need any do do coils. Oata steps into the streak of moonshine and her eyes blitz a little and the rhinestones on her butterfly earrings glance the light off like snow on a Christmas card. The pink dress fuschels as she goes to the cupboard and reaches the oil lamp and puts it on the table. Then she sticks her hand inside her dress by the shoulder and pulls a strap straight. "Light on the lamp, and I'll get us something to drink," Oata says and she turns on her high heels so that the dress swings around and she takes two steps then she bends over and lifts the ring in the floor and opens the lid to the cellar. The pink tent sinks down the steps and I take the chimney off the oil lamp and turn the little wheel so the wick comes up. Then I take a farmer match from the little tin holder on the wall by the stove and I light on the lamp. The lamplight makes the room darker because the flame chases the moonshine away and all the shadows are big from everything that is away from the table. I sit myself down on one of the chairs without thinking and feel right away that it is the chair with the crack in it and when I move my ham I get a pinch. So I take a different chair and sit there looking at the lamp and listen to a cricket that is fiddling away somewhere in the house. Everything is still. Even from the cellar I can't hear Oata, and I think a little bit that it would be nice if it was Sadie in the cellar, but then I remember that Sadie went to the "Town Without Pity" show with Pug Peters on Sunday, and it doesn't seem so nice if Sadie was in the cellar.

Some glass clinks down there and then creak the steps and I watch past the lamp as Oata rises from the hole in the floor. The flame from the oil lamp makes shadows on the pink dress and in her hands she holds a big catsup bottle but it sure isn't catsup that is in it. Oata sets the catsup bottle on the table beside the lamp and she goes over to the cupboard and gets out two glasses with handles, the kind you can buy peanut butter in, and she puts them down beside the lamp. Then she tries to pull the cork out from the catsup bottle but it won't come loose so she reaches it to me and I try to wiggle it but it is real tight so I put the bottle between my knees to get a better grip and then the cork starts to move and out it comes with a pop.

I reach the bottle back to Oata and she pours one glass half full and then the other one and it looks real pretty there with the flame from the lamp showing through. Oata pushes one glass over the table to me, then she sits down and lifts the other glass with the handle. I lift my glass, too, and she reaches over her glass so it clinks with mine. Then she pulls the glass to her pink lips and takes a sip. Some of the pink stays on the glass when she puts it back on the table beside the lamp. I take a sip, too, and the chokecherry wines taste a little shtroof on my tongue but it's good and I take another sip, too.

"Pretty good, huh, Yasch?" I wobble my head up and down and take another sip. "I made it myself."

Everything is still, except one cricket is playing the fiddle some place. And the white clock with the red numbers is ticking with that sound that always makes me think about a rocking chair. Every sip from the wine is better than the one before and mixed with the chokecherry smell the *Evening in Schanzenfeld* is quite nice and Oata's pink fingernails sparkle when they reach around the catsup bottle to pour us some more wine and the rhinestones in her butterfly earrings glitter when she laughs. I say, "It's good that your Foda buys catsup in such big bottles." Oata smiles and sips a little more wine and then she licks the spitz of her tongue around those pink lips and the lamplight funkles in her brown eye and then in her blue eye and I start to think some place in my head that it is maybe something special to have a blue eye and a brown eye and I wonder if the world looks better with a blue eye or a brown eye and then Oata says:

"Yasch, you have pink eyes!"

And I know for sure that I have a pink face because the stubble on my chin feels hot and Oata rutches her chair closer to me so she can pour the last wine from the catsup bottle into our glasses and as she holds the bottle so that the last drops of the chokecherry wine can leak into my glass she is leaning close by me and at first the *Evening in Schanzenfeld* is real strong again but then the nose starts to pick up something else, like if the wine and the perfume and Oata got mixed up together into one sweet blooming garden of strickroses, tea blooms, butterflowers, and sweet clover in a hay loft. And Oata clinks her glass to mine again and we both take just a little sip to make it last longer and a drop runs over her pink bottom lip and I think for sure that it shouldn't go to waste and I lean over and stick my tongue out to catch it and Oata rutches her chair closer and we share the last drops from the glasses and Oata says, "I forgot the lid to close" and she starts to stand up and I say "I will for you it close" and we are standing both beside the cellar lid and I bend over and make it closed. Then Oata leans on me and I have to shteepa myself against the door frame that leads into the *Grotestove* and the next thing we are in the moonshine on the wine-colored sofa with the big flowers all over it and I am driving the double dike along in a big rain with the big ditch between the dike and Nobah Naze's half section and the half-ton is schwaecksing from side to side on the slippery mud and the canal is half full with water and I am turning the steer from one side to the other as fast as I can and the truck plows through a deep mud puddle and the windshield is smattered full and I can't see nothing and the wipers only schmaus it fuller and I can say for sure that looks matter nothing and the tires feel the slippery road over a hump and I try the brakes to use but the truck is going already down and it is too late to be afraid of anything there could be to see and I just let myself feel what there is to know. Then the truck stops and the motor sputters and dies and I can hear my heart hammering away like an old John Deere two-cylinder driving along in road gear. I feel the water seepering in through the floor of the truck. But I just sit there till the water starts to leak into my boots and I turn and look out the window on the woman's side of the cab and I see the wild mustard blooming on Nobah Naze's field.

Then there is ringing in my ears like a saw blade hitting a nail in an old fence pole and Oata pushes me away and schluffs off to the phone with her pink stockings on her feet just. I hear her say "Hello," and "Yes" and "Oh" and then "Oh" again. Oata comes slowly back into the moonshine by the sofa. She steps on a pink shoe and she falls me beside on the bench. I take her around with my arms and she leans her head on my chest. I stroke her hair a little and she starts to shudder. Then the tears let go and I feel them when they run off from her cheek into the hairs on my belly. And there is nothing to say. Nothing to see. Just to feel. Nobah Naze Needarp is dead.

Patrick Friesen

The Wedding

Some relative of mine was getting married. A cousin, I think. From the other side of the river, near Morris. My father came from a large family, and everyone had numerous cousins and in-laws and so on. I never understood all the interrelationships. These people lived far from me. They were faces in old photographs kept in a trunk downstairs.

Cousin was the operative word. It could be first, second or third cousin. It might, in fact, be some other relationship altogether, but cousin covered all bases.

Most of my cousins were farmers. Whether they lived on a farm or not, to me they were farmers; rural, village people who still had one foot in the 19th century. I came from town; a town of maybe two or three thousand people; a town with modern-looking businesses, a wide main street to accommodate the automobiles we were supposedly famous for, twenty-some churches, a two-sheet skating rink, a restaurant with dim lights where you could go for hamburgers, and other features of urban decadence.

Anyone living outside such an environment was a farmer. People without style, crude people who horked on the ground and wiped slimy fingers on their pants or aprons, people who never appeared to be embarrassed by anything. And, worst of all, people who either could not speak English at all, or spoke it haltingly, and with an accent.

It was an accent most noteworthy for its violence to English vowels. *Dog* became *dug* and *dug* became *dog*. So that, when the neighbour's mongrel tore up the flower garden in front of your picture window, "the dug dog a hole." Or, your father might be the "bus of the boss lines." And, if you were well-off with a cottage at Falcon Lake, you might come upon a "dock at the end of the duck."

What I started to say was that some cousin of father's was getting married. In a small village near Morris. I don't remember, if I ever knew, whether it was the bride or groom who was our relative. I do remember very clearly how disappointed I was when I heard on a Saturday that we would be driving to Morris after church services next day.

It meant a long, boring, dusty trip. Not all roads in our province were paved. In those days you got car-sick sometimes. You stopped and puked in the ditch or, if you were in a hurry, kept driving while the unlucky one stuck his head out the window and barfed all along the side of the car. (When you got to your destination, you scraped off the hardened chunks of whatever those reddish bits were.)

My parents would not allow me to stay home because it would be impolite to not meet these relatives. My absence might be interpreted as a sign of "superior" feelings. It was settled. I was doomed to the stiffness of my Sunday white shirt beneath a blazing August sun on the other side of the river.

The church was white. No surprise. Quite small, with a short steeple, but no cross. Mennonites celebrated the resurrection, not the death of Christ, so they rarely used the cross as symbol. At least, this is what I was taught. The Catholics, of course, were the next thing to heathens and had only got as far as Christ's death.

The church stood in a field with no other buildings in sight. Cars were parked all over the field, grass up to the middle of the hubcaps. Parked in an orderly fashion. The sun glinting off dull black and blue roofs.

For some reason, probably mother's desire to escape my fidgeting, I was allowed to remain outside during the service. With the boys, my cousins; and I should leave the cars alone, not get my Sunday clothes dirty, and stay near the church. This was preferable to sitting inside the sweltering building.

Most services, outside of the regular Sunday ones, were funerals or weddings, and at weddings people smiled; at funerals, they wept. At weddings two people stood for hours at the front of the church, answering questions and listening. At funerals one figure lay prone in front of the podium.

A boy came up to me. I had seen his mother, before she entered church, whisper to him and point at me. He said his name was David. His white shirt was long-sleeved and buttoned to the throat. It was already grimy at the cuffs. Unlike most of the other boys here, he wore a tie; a blistering blue tie with a cream-coloured Palomino rearing in the middle of it. He had a bowl haircut, black pants and black shoes.

From the church windows drifted a piercing nasal whine and a bass unison of men and women singing some hymn written, undoubtedly, by Fanny J. Crosby.

The arid smell of August grain penetrated my nostrils. I felt chaff in my nose, and on my tongue. Sitting on the front bumper of father's '53 Dodge, I cautiously tapped an old cowpie with my freshly-polished brown shoes.

So, his name was David. I thought to myself, "It'll take you more than a few smooth stones to get me." After an awkward silence, I boasted that in my town they were building a swimming pool made of cement, and it was as long as from us to that blue half-ton over there. No stubble fields there, no sir. A real swimming pool, with showers and everything.

It didn't faze him at all. I wondered what else I could say. It really wasn't so much that I wanted to put him in place, but it was absolutely necessary that he know I was not part of all this; this church, this wedding, this white shirt, this singing, this German, these funereal cars, the chaff, the death you could hear in the buzzing of fat blue flies inside cars with their windows rolled up. I needed him to know I was something outside of all this, all this grain and Bible and black tires. Maybe I would tell him I was adopted.

David asked if I wanted to walk across the field to look at the horses. I looked. There, behind a fence, were two brown horses and a white one. The brown ones stood side by side, nose to tail, flicking flies from each other's faces. The white grazed a little way off.

The powerful haunches, the ripple of chest muscle, when they walked or galloped, was what caught me. The pure animal, the glory of sweating muscle; so disquieting and alien, so hypnotic. So unaware of itself. Bunching and loosening, as legs moved for no purpose beyond motion.

And horses had always frightened me. They were unpredictable, finely-nerved; quivering sometimes, or rearing with iron hooves slashing air; murderous.

David suggested we grab the halters of two horses, swing up on their backs, and ride. Before I could object, he crawled through the strands of barbed wire, grabbed the halter of the white horse and led him to me.

"Hold this," he said, and I did. He got one of the brown ones for himself. It shied from him, but he knew what he was doing. I said something about not wanting to dirty my pants, or tear them. He simply replied that it was easy to ride as long as you directed the horse with your knees and held on to the mane.

Voices droned from the church. My legs spread to hold the width of my horse. Before I had a good grip on his mane, or had thought of what I would do, he started trotting. My heels dug in desperately. He broke into a gallop, circling at mid-field, then right at the fence, vaulting, me grabbing handfuls of hair; all terror now confused with exhilaration as we thundered toward the church.

Bouncing wildly, I saw, through flying hair, that the church door was open. I thought the horse was going to ride right in, scattering everyone, church benches flying, then stop, hurtling me onto the podium where I would dangle, breathing my last.

When we reached the front steps, he didn't stop, he didn't enter the church, but ascended air and over, flying, across the steeple, the congregation, the marriage vows, and all the rectangular fields, trees growing small, the Red River flowing.

Up we flew, me hanging on by teeth and nails; the power, the awful length and fling of those muscles, head reaching forward, and the silence. The earth so small. I could see everything, the perspective of it all. Barns, haystacks and dirt roads all miniature, as if they belonged to children. The river only a string twisting through fields and bush.

Then, suddenly, as we strove upwards, I was unhorsed. Tumbling, a glimpse of white belly and wings. Tilting horizon, as if I was plunging deeper into the sky; then earth and buildings careening to one side. My shirt tore off, shoes flying, my pants fluttering for a moment before me, then gone, and me naked and sinking further into that endless blue sky.

And the local newspaper headline the following week: WEDDING MARRED BY MYSTERIOUS DEATH, and in *The Word*, MENNONITE YOUTH FAILS TO FLY.

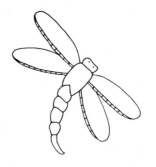

About the Authors

Sandra Birdsell, award-winning author and scriptwriter, was born to a Mennonite mother and a French Canadian/Metis father in Morris, Manitoba in 1942. A founding member and past president of the Manitoba Writers Guild, she is currently Writer in Residence at the University of Waterloo. Birdsell's stories included here are taken from *Night Travellers* (Turnstone, 1982), which won the Gerald Lampert Award, and *Ladies of the House* (Turnstone, 1984).

Di Brandt, born in 1952, grew up in Reinland, a Mennonite farming village in southern Manitoba. Winner of the 1987 Gerald H. Lampert Memorial Award from the League of Canadian Poets, she was also nominated in 1987 for the Governor General's Award for *Questions i asked my mother* (Turnstone, 1987). Brandt is a contributing editor to several literary journals and executive member of the League of Canadian Poets. She is teaching English literature at the University of Winnipeg, while completing her dissertation on "The Mother's Story as Narrative Problem" at the University of Manitoba.

Elaine Driedger was born in Leamington, Ontario in 1954 and now lives in Kitchener. Recipient of an Ontario Arts Council grant in 1986, she has written children's stories for several Mennonite publications. "White Christmas" is published here for the first time.

Patrick Friesen, poet, film-maker, playwright, critic and teacher, was born in Steinbach, Manitoba in 1946 and lives in Winnipeg. His most recent volumes of poetry include *The Shunning* (1980), which has been adapted as a stage play and produced in Winnipeg, *Unearthly Horses* (1984), and *Flicker and Hawk* (1987)—all published by Turnstone. His story "The Wedding" is published here for the first time.

Victor Carl Friesen, born on a farm near Rosthern, Saskatchewan in 1933, is a freelance writer. He has published a book on Henry Thoreau and scores of articles on prairie history. Friesen's most recent works include *The Mulberry Tree* (Queenston House, 1985), with Anna Friesen, and *The Windmill Turning* (The University of Alberta Press, 1988), a collection of Mennonite folklore. He lives in Rosthern, Saskatchewan.

Sarah Klassen was born in 1932 in Winnipeg (where she teaches high-school English). Her poems have been included in literary magazines such as *CVII, Border Crossings, The Fiddlehead* and *New Quarterly*. Turnstone published her first collection of poetry, *Journey to Yalta,* in 1988. "The Letter," published here for the first time, won first prize in the Lady Eaton Contest, sponsored by the Manitoba Chapter of the Canadian Authors' Association.

Warren Kliewer, professor, free-lance writer, director, and actor, is currently Artistic Director of The East Lynne (Theatre) Company in Secausus, New Jersey, where he lives. He was born in Mountain Lake, Minnesota in 1931. Kliewer's many publications include short stories, poetry, plays, essays, criticism, reviews and folklore studies. Included here are stories taken from *The Violators* (Marshall Jones, 1964), a collection set in the imaginary village of Waldheim, Manitoba.

Andreas Schroeder was born in Hoheneggelsen, Germany in 1946 and immigrated to Canada with his family in 1951. Currently a free-lance writer living in Mission City, British Columbia, he founded *The Journal of Contemporary Literature in Translation* (1968-80) and has been columnist, teacher, and chairman of the Writers' Union of Canada (1976-7). Schroeder is the author of several books of poetry and of *Shaking it Rough: a Prison Memoir* (Doubleday, 1976). His most recent major work is a novel, *Dustship Glory* (Doubleday, 1986). Schroeder's stories collected here are taken from *The Late Man* (Sono Nis, 1972).

Sara Stambaugh was born in New Holland, Pennsylvania in 1936 and became a Canadian citizen in 1984. A professor of Victorian literature at the University of Alberta since 1969, her publications include the novel *I Hear the Reaper's Song* (Good Books, 1984), which won a place on the short list for the *Books in Canada* First Novel Award, and *The Witch and the Goddess in the Stories of Isak Dinesen: A Feminist Reading* (UMI, 1988). Her stories are set in the Pennsylvania community where she grew up.

David Waltner-Toews was born in Winnipeg in 1948 and has since travelled throughout Europe, the Middle East, Asia, and Indonesia. A veterinary epidemiologist, he teaches at the University of Guelph. Formerly a regular contributor to *Harrowsmith* magazine, Waltner-Toews is best known for his several volumes of poetry, including *The Earth is One Body* (1979), *Good Housekeeping* (1983), and *Endangered Species* (1988)—all published by Turnstone.

Armin Wiebe was born in Altona, Manitoba in 1948 and now teaches school and writes fiction in Lac La Martre, Northwest Territories. "Practising" and "Oata, Oata" are taken from *The Salvation of Yasch Siemens* (Turnstone, 1984), which won the Stephen Leacock Medal for Humour and appeared on the short list for the *Books in Canada* First Novel Award.

Katie Funk Wiebe was born in Laird, Saskatchewan in 1924 and now lives in Hillsboro, Kansas, where she teaches at Tabor College, Her publications include *Alone: A Search for Joy (Kindred, (1976), (1987))*, *Women Among the Brethren* (Mennonite Brethren, 1979), *Who Are the Mennonite Brethren?* (Kindred, 1984) and *Bless Me Too, My Father* (Herald, 1988). Her love of story arises out of her own experiences growing up listening to tales of her parents' living through the Russian Revolution. "A Real Live Death" is published here for the first time.

Rudy Wiebe was born near Fairholme, Saskatchewan in 1934. Since 1967 he has taught Canadian literature and creative writing at the University of Alberta. Wiebe's seven novels include *Peace Shall Destroy Many* (1962), *The Blue Mountains of China* (1970) and *The Temptations of Big Bear* (1973), for which he won the Governor General's Award; all these works were published by McClelland and Stewart. Wiebe has also published three collections of short stories and a play and has edited several collections of short fiction.

Hildi Froese Tiessen teaches literature at Conrad Grebel College, the University of Waterloo, where she is also the Acting Academic Dean. The publisher of a series of art books, she is currently continuing her research and writing on Canadian ethnic literature, the subject of several articles and of lectures she has presented in Canada, the USA, France, West Germany and Belgium.

DATE DUE

9-4-89			
9.22-92			
4-12-93			
MAR 12 1998			
1-12-99			
▬▬▬▬			
▬▬▬▬			
01/14/03			
GAYLORD			PRINTED IN U.S.A.